SELECTED SHORT STORIES

DOVER THRIFT EDITIONS

Anthony Trollope

D1545561

DOVER PUBLICATIONS, INC.
MINEOLA, NEW YORK

DOVER THRIFT EDITIONS

GENERAL EDITOR: SUSAN L. RATTINER
EDITOR OF THIS VOLUME: TERRI ANN GEUS

Bibliographical Note

Selected Short Stories is a new compilation, first published by Dover Publications, Inc., in 2017. John Grafton has selected the six stories by Anthony Trollope, and has provided the introductory note and bibliographical information. The punctuation for the selections in this book has been intentionally retained as it was previously printed in an effort to preserve the consistency of the original stories.

International Standard Book Number

ISBN-13: 978-0-486-81119-2
ISBN-10: 0-486-81119-0

Manufactured in the United States by LSC Communications
81119001   2017
www.doverpublications.com

Note

Anthony Trollope's immensely productive literary career began with the novel *The Macdermots of Ballycloran*, published in 1847. This novel was not a success with the reading public, but it was a book for which the author at least retained considerable affection throughout his life. Success was not long in coming, however, beginning with *The Warden*, in 1855, the first of the six Barsetshire novels which put Trollope firmly on the Victorian literary map, a position he solidified with his finest accomplishment, the six Palliser novels beginning with *Can You Forgive Her?* in 1865 and ending with *The Duke's Children* in 1880. His forty-seven novels plus about thirty other volumes of stories and miscellaneous nonfiction works created a record of literary achievement that has seldom been equaled.

The six short stories reprinted in this volume are a minute part of that legacy, but they do show off many of the enduring features of Trollope's talent as a writer: his gift for characterization, his perceptive vision of human nature and social relationships, his genial humanity and engaging sense of humor, balanced on occasion by a surprisingly unsentimental realism. Published in the last two decades of his writing life, they are set in London and in the country, and depict the lives of older people and younger, rich and poor, well-established in Victorian society and on the perilous fringes of it. A special mention for two of them: *The Two Heroines of Plumplington* revisits Trollope's mythical Barsetshire decades after the last of the novels set there was published, and the brief sketch *Not If I Know It* is memorable, among other reasons, for being Trollope's last published work of fiction, first printed in a London periodical during the month (December 1882) in which he died.

Contents

Bibliography

The Mistletoe Bough
First published in the *Illustrated London News*, Christmas Supplement, December 21, 1861.
Reprinted in *Tales of All Countries*, Second Series, 1863.

The Parson's Daughter of Oxney Colne
First published in the *London Review*, March 2, 1861.
Reprinted in *Tales of All Countries*, Second Series, 1863.

The Spotted Dog
First published in *St. Paul's*, March–April 1870.
Reprinted in *An Editor's Tales*, 1870.

Mary Gresley
First published in *St. Paul's*, November 1869.
Reprinted in *An Editor's Tales*, 1870.

The Two Heroines of Plumplington
First published in *Good Cheer*, December 1882.

Not If I Know It
First published in *Life*, Christmas 1882.

THE MISTLETOE BOUGH

"LET THE BOYS have it if they like it," said Mrs. Garrow, pleading to her only daughter on behalf of her two sons.

"Pray don't, mamma," said Elizabeth Garrow. "It only means romping. To me all that is detestable, and I am sure it is not the sort of thing that Miss Holmes would like."

"We always had it at Christmas when we were young."

"But, mamma, the world is so changed."

The point in dispute was one very delicate in its nature, hardly to be discussed in all its bearings, even in fiction, and the very mention of which between a mother and daughter showed a great amount of close confidence between them. It was no less than this. Should that branch of mistletoe which Frank Garrow had brought home with him out of the Lowther woods be hung up on Christmas Eve in the dining-room at Thwaite Hall, according to his wishes; or should permission for such hanging be positively refused? It was clearly a thing not to be done after such a discussion, and therefore the decision given by Mrs. Garrow was against it.

I am inclined to think that Miss Garrow was right in saying that the world is changed as touching mistletoe boughs. Kissing, I fear, is less innocent now than it used to be when our grandmothers were alive, and we have become more fastidious in our amusements. Nevertheless, I think that she made herself fairly open to the raillery with which her brothers attacked her.

"Honi soit qui mal y pense," said Frank, who was eighteen.

"Nobody will want to kiss you, my lady Fineairs," said Harry, who was just a year younger.

"Because you choose to be a Puritan, there are to be no more cakes and ale in the house," said Frank.

"Still waters run deep; we all know that," said Harry.

1

The boys had not been present when the matter was decided between Mrs. Garrow and her daughter, nor had the mother been present when these little amenities had passed between the brothers and sister.

"Only that mamma has said it, and I wouldn't seem to go against her," said Frank, "I'd ask my father. He wouldn't give way to such nonsense, I know."

Elizabeth turned away without answering, and left the room. Her eyes were full of tears, but she would not let them see that they had vexed her. They were only two days home from school, and for the last week before their coming, all her thoughts had been to prepare for their Christmas pleasures. She had arranged their rooms, making everything warm and pretty. Out of her own pocket she had bought a shot-belt for one, and skates for the other. She had told the old groom that her pony was to belong exclusively to Master Harry for the holidays, and now Harry told her that still waters ran deep. She had been driven to the use of all her eloquence in inducing her father to purchase that gun for Frank, and now Frank called her a Puritan. And why? She did not choose that a mistletoe bough should be hung in her father's hall, when Godfrey Holmes was coming to visit him. She could not explain this to Frank, but Frank might have had the wit to understand it. But Frank was thinking only of Patty Coverdale, a blue-eyed little romp of sixteen, who, with her sister Kate, was coming from Penrith to spend the Christmas at Thwaite Hall. Elizabeth left the room with her slow, graceful step, hiding her tears,—hiding all emotion, as latterly she had taught herself that it was feminine to do. "There goes my lady Fineairs," said Harry, sending his shrill voice after her.

Thwaite Hall was not a place of much pretension. It was a moderate-sized house, surrounded by pretty gardens and shrubberies, close down upon the river Eamont, on the Westmoreland side of the river, looking over to a lovely wooded bank in Cumberland. All the world knows that the Eamont runs out of Ulleswater, dividing the two counties, passing under Penrith Bridge and by the old ruins of Brougham Castle, below which it joins the Eden. Thwaite Hall nestled down close upon the clear rocky stream about half way between Ulleswater and Penrith, and had been built just at a bend of the river. The windows of the dining-parlour and of the drawing-room stood at right angles to each other, and yet each commanded a reach of the stream. Immediately from a side door of the house steps were cut down through the red rock to the water's edge, and here a small boat was always moored to a chain. The chain was stretched across the river, fixed to the staples driven into the rock on either side, and the boat was pulled backwards and forwards over the stream without aid from oars or paddles. From the opposite side a path led through the woods and across the fields to Penrith, and this was the route commonly used between Thwaite Hall and the town.

Major Garrow was a retired officer of Engineers, who had seen service in all parts of the world, and who was now spending the evening of his days on a small property which had come to him from his father. He held in his own hands about twenty acres of land, and he was the owner of one small farm close by, which was let to a tenant. That, together with his half-pay, and the interest of his wife's thousand pounds, sufficed to educate his children and keep the wolf at a comfortable distance from his door. He himself was a spare thin man, with quiet, lazy, literary habits. He had done the work of life, but had so done it as to permit of his enjoying that which was left to him. His sole remaining care was the establishment of his children; and, as far as he could see, he had no ground for anticipating disappointment. They were clever, good-looking, well-disposed young people, and upon the whole it may be said that the sun shone brightly on Thwaite Hall. Of Mrs. Garrow it may suffice to say that she always deserved such sunshine.

For years past it had been the practice of the family to have some sort of gathering at Thwaite Hall during Christmas. Godfrey Holmes had been left under the guardianship of Major Garrow, and, as he had always spent his Christmas holidays with his guardian, this, perhaps, had given rise to the practice. Then the Coverdales were cousins of the Garrows, and they had usually been there as children. At the Christmas last past the custom had been broken, for young Holmes had been abroad. Previous to that, they had all been children, excepting him. But now that they were to meet again, they were no longer children. Elizabeth, at any rate, was not so, for she had already counted nineteen winters. And Isabella Holmes was coming. Now Isabella was two years older than Elizabeth, and had been educated in Brussels; moreover she was comparatively a stranger at Thwaite Hall, never having been at those early Christmas meetings.

And now I must take permission to begin my story by telling a lady's secret. Elizabeth Garrow had already been in love with Godfrey Holmes, or perhaps it might be more becoming to say that Godfrey Holmes had already been in love with her. They had already been engaged; and, alas! they had already agreed that that engagement should be broken off!

Young Holmes was now twenty-seven years of age, and was employed in a bank at Liverpool, not as a clerk, but as assistant manager, with a large salary. He was a man well to do in the world, who had money also of his own, and who might well afford to marry. Some two years since, on the eve of leaving Thwaite Hall, he had with low doubting whisper told Elizabeth that he loved her, and she had flown trembling to her mother. "Godfrey, my boy," the father said to him, as he parted with him the next morning, "Bessy is only a child, and too young to think of this yet." At the next Christmas Godfrey was in Italy, and the thing was gone by,— so at least the father and mother said to each other. But the young people had met in the summer, and one joyful letter had come from the girl home to her mother. "I have accepted him. Dearest, dearest mamma, I do love him. But don't tell papa yet, for I have not quite accepted him. I think I am sure, but I am not quite sure. I am not quite sure about him."

And then, two days after that, there had come a letter that was not at all joyful. "Dearest Mamma,—It is not to be. It is not written in the book. We have both agreed that it will not do. I am so glad that you have not told dear papa, for I could never make him understand. You will understand, for I shall tell you everything, down to his very words. But we have agreed that there shall be no quarrel. It shall be exactly as it was, and he will come at Christmas all the same. It would never do that he and papa should be separated, nor could we now put off Isabella. It is better so in every way, for there is and need be no quarrel. We still like each other. I am sure I like him, but I know that I should not make him happy as his wife. He says it is my fault. I, at any rate, have never told him that I thought it his." From all which it will be seen that the confidence between the mother and daughter was very close.

Elizabeth Garrow was a very good girl, but it might almost be a question whether she was not too good. She had learned, or thought that she had learned, that most girls are vapid, silly, and useless,—given chiefly to pleasure-seeking and a hankering after lovers; and she had resolved that she would not be such a one. Industry, self-denial, and a religious purpose in life, were the tasks which she set herself; and she went about the performance of them with much courage. But such tasks, though they are excellently well adapted to fit a young lady for the work of living, may also be carried too far, and thus have the effect of unfitting her for that work. When Elizabeth Garrow made up her mind that the finding of a husband was not the only purpose of life, she did very well. It is very well that a young lady should feel herself capable of going through the world happily without one. But in teaching herself this she also taught herself to think that there was a certain merit in refusing herself the natural delight of a lover, even though the possession of the lover were compatible with all her duties to herself, her father and mother, and the world at large. It was not that she had determined to have no lover. She made no such resolve, and when the proper lover came he was admitted to her heart. But she declared to herself unconsciously that she must put a guard upon herself, lest she should be betrayed into weakness by her own happiness. She had resolved that in loving her lord she would not worship him, and that in giving her heart she would only so give it as it should be given to a human creature like herself. She had acted on these high resolves, and hence it had come to pass,—not unnaturally,—that Mr. Godfrey Holmes had told her that it was "her fault."

She was a pretty, fair girl, with soft dark-brown hair, and soft long dark eyelashes. Her grey eyes, though quiet in their tone, were tender and lustrous. Her face was oval, and the lines of her cheek and chin perfect in their symmetry. She was generally quiet in her demeanour, but when moved she could rouse herself to great energy, and speak with feeling and almost with fire. Her fault was a reverence for martyrdom in general, and a feeling, of which she was unconscious, that it became a young woman to be unhappy in secret;—that it became a young woman I might rather say, to have a source of unhappiness hidden from the world in general, and endured without any detriment to her outward cheerfulness. We know the story of the Spartan boy who held the fox under his tunic. The fox was biting into him,—into the very entrails; but the young hero spake never a word. Now Bessy Garrow was inclined to think that it was a good thing to have a fox always biting, so that the torment caused no ruffling to her outward smiles. Now at this moment the fox within her bosom was biting her sore enough, but she bore it without flinching.

"If you would rather that he should not come I will have it arranged," her mother had said to her.

"Not for worlds," she had answered. "I should never think well of myself again."

Her mother had changed her own mind more than once as to the conduct in this matter which might be best for her to follow, thinking solely of her daughter's welfare. "If he comes they will be reconciled, and she will be happy," had been her first idea. But then there was a stern fixedness of purpose in Bessy's words when she spoke of Mr. Holmes, which had expelled this hope, and Mrs. Garrow had for a while thought it better that the young man should not come. But Bessy would not permit this. It would vex her father, put out of course the arrangements of other people, and display weakness on her own part. He should come, and she would endure without flinching while the fox gnawed at her.

That battle of the mistletoe had been fought on the morning before Christmas-day, and the Holmes's came on Christmas-eve. Isabella was comparatively a stranger, and therefore received at first the greater share of attention. She and Elizabeth had once seen each other, and for the last year or two had corresponded, but personally they had never been intimate. Unfortunately for the latter, that story of Godfrey's offer and acceptance had been communicated to Isabella, as had of course the immediately subsequent story of their separation. But now it would be almost impossible to avoid the subject in conversation. "Dearest Isabella, let it be as though it had never been," she had said in one of her letters. But sometimes it is very difficult to let things be as though they had never been.

The first evening passed over very well. The two Coverdale girls were there, and there had been much talking and merry laughter, rather juvenile in its nature, but on the whole none the worse for that. Isabella Holmes was a fine, tall, handsome girl; good-humoured, and well disposed to be pleased; rather Frenchified in her manners, and quite able to take care of herself. But she was not above round games, and did not turn up her nose at the boys. Godfrey behaved himself excellently, talking much to the Major, but by no means avoiding Miss Garrow. Mrs. Garrow, though she had known him since he was a boy, had taken an aversion to him since he had quarrelled with her daughter; but there was no room on this first night for showing such aversion, and everything went off well.

"Godfrey is very much improved," the Major said to his wife that night.

"Do you think so?"

"Indeed I do. He has filled out and become a fine man."

"In personal appearance, you mean. Yes, he is well-looking enough."

"And in his manner too. He is doing uncommonly well in Liverpool, I can tell you; and if he should think of Bessy—"

"There is nothing of that sort," said Mrs. Garrow.

"He did speak to me, you know,—two years ago. Bessy was too young then, and so indeed was he. But if she likes him—"

"I don't think she does."

"Then there's an end of it." And so they went to bed.

"Frank," said the sister to her elder brother, knocking at his door when they had all gone up stairs, "may I come in,—if you are not in bed?"

"In bed," said he, looking up with some little pride from his Greek book; "I've one hundred and fifty lines to do before I can get to bed. It'll be two, I suppose. I've got to mug uncommon hard these holidays. I have only one more half, you know, and then—"

"Don't overdo it, Frank."

"No; I won't overdo it. I mean to take one day a week, and work eight hours a day on the other five. That will be forty hours a week, and will give me just two hundred hours for the holidays. I have got it all down here on a table. That will be a hundred and five for Greek play, forty for Algebra—" and so he explained to her the exact destiny of all his long hours of proposed labour. He had as yet been home a day and a half, and had succeeded in drawing out with red lines and blue figures the table which he showed her. "If I can do that, it will be pretty well; won't it?"

"But, Frank, you have come home for your holidays,—to enjoy yourself?"

"But a fellow must work now-a-days."

"Don't overdo it, dear; that's all. But, Frank, I could not rest if I went to bed without speaking to you. You made me unhappy to-day."

"Did I, Bessy?"

"You called me a Puritan, and then you quoted that ill-natured French proverb at me. Do you really believe your sister thinks evil, Frank?" and as she spoke she put her arm caressingly round his neck.

"Of course I don't."

"Then why say so? Harry is so much younger and so thoughtless that I can bear what he says without so much suffering. But if you and I are not friends I shall be very wretched. If you knew how I have looked forward to your coming home!"

"I did not mean to vex you, and I won't say such things again."

"That's my own Frank. What I said to mamma, I said because I thought it right; but you must not say that I am a Puritan. I would do anything in my power to make your holidays bright and pleasant. I know that boys require so much more to amuse them than girls do. Good night, dearest; pray don't overdo yourself with work, and do take care of your eyes." So saying she kissed him and went her way. In twenty minutes after that, he had gone to sleep over his book; and when he woke up to find the candle guttering down, he resolved that he would not begin his measured hours till Christmas-day was fairly over.

The morning of Christmas-day passed very quietly. They all went to church, and then sat round the fire chatting until the four-o'clock dinner was ready. The Coverdale girls thought it was rather more dull than former Thwaite Hall festivities, and Frank was seen to yawn. But then everybody knows that the real fun of Christmas never begins till the day itself be passed. The beef and pudding are ponderous, and unless there be absolute children in the party, there is a difficulty in grafting any special afternoon amusements on the Sunday pursuits of the morning. In the evening they were to have a dance;—that had been distinctly promised to Patty Coverdale; but the dance would not commence till eight. The beef and pudding were ponderous, but with due efforts they were overcome and disappeared. The glass of port was sipped, the almonds and raisins were nibbled, and then the ladies left the room. Ten minutes after that Elizabeth found herself seated with Isabella Holmes over the fire in her father's little book-room. It was not by her that this meeting was arranged, for she dreaded such a constrained confidence; but of course it could not be avoided, and perhaps it might be as well now as hereafter.

"Bessy," said the elder girl, "I am dying to be alone with you for a moment."

"Well, you shall not die; that is, if being alone with me will save you."

"I have so much to say to you. And if you have any true friendship in you, you also will have so much to say to me." Miss Garrow perhaps had no true friendship in her at that moment, for she would gladly have avoided saying anything, had that been possible. But, in order to prove that she was not deficient in friendship, she gave her friend her hand.

"And now tell me everything about Godfrey," said Isabella.

"Dear Bella, I have nothing to tell;—literally nothing."

"That is nonsense. Stop a moment, dear, and understand that I do not mean to offend you. It cannot be that you have nothing to tell, if you choose to tell it. You are not the girl to have accepted Godfrey without loving him, nor is he the man to have asked you without loving you. When you write me word that you have changed your mind, as you might about a dress, of course I know you have not told me all. Now I insist upon knowing it,—that is, if we are to be friends. I would not speak a word to Godfrey till I had seen you, in order that I might hear your story first."

"Indeed, Bella, there is no story to tell."

"Then I must ask him."

"If you wish to play the part of a true friend to me, you will let the matter pass by and say nothing. You must understand that, circumstanced as we are, your brother's visit here,—what I mean is, that it is very difficult for me to act and speak exactly as I should do, and a few unfortunate words spoken may make my position unendurable."

"Will you answer me one question?"

"I cannot tell. I think I will."

"Do you love him?" For a moment or two Bessy remained silent, striving to arrange her words so that they should contain no falsehood, and yet betray no truth. "Ah, I see you do," continued Miss Holmes. "But of course you do. Why else did you accept him?"

"I fancied that I did, as young ladies do sometimes fancy."

"And will you say that you do not, now?" Again Bessy was silent, and then her friend rose from her seat. "I see it all," she said.

"What a pity it was that you both had not some friend like me by you at the time! But perhaps it may not be too late."

I need not repeat at length all the protestations which upon this were poured forth with hot energy by poor Bessy. She endeavoured to explain how great had been the difficulty of her position. This Christmas visit had been arranged before that unhappy affair at Liverpool had occurred. Isabella's visit had been partly one of business, it being necessary that certain money affairs should be arranged between her, her brother, and the Major. "I determined," said Bessy, "not to let my feelings stand in the way; and hoped that things might settle down to their former friendly footing. I already fear that I have been wrong, but it will be ungenerous in you to punish me." Then she went on to say that if anybody attempted to interfere with her, she should at once go away to her mother's sister, who lived at Hexham, in Northumberland.

Then came the dance, and the hearts of Kate and Patty Coverdale were at last happy. But here again poor Bessy was made to understand how terribly difficult was this experiment of entertaining on a footing of friendship a lover with whom she had quarrelled only a month or two before. That she must as a necessity become the partner of Godfrey Holmes she had already calculated, and so much she was prepared to endure. Her brothers would of course dance with the Coverdale girls, and her father would of course stand up with Isabella. There was no other possible arrangement, at any rate as a beginning. She had schooled herself too as to the way in which she would speak to him on the occasion, and how she would remain mistress of herself and of her thoughts. But when the time came the difficulty was almost too much for her.

"You do not care much for dancing, if I remember?" said he.

"Oh yes, I do. Not as Patty Coverdale does. It's a passion with her. But then I am older than Patty Coverdale." After that he was silent for a minute or two.

"It seems so odd to me to be here again," he said. It was odd;— she felt that it was odd. But he ought not to have said so.

"Two years make a great difference. The boys have grown so much."

"Yes, and there are other things," said he.

"Bella was never here before; at least not with you."

"No. But I did not exactly mean that. All that would not make the place so strange. But your mother seems altered to me. She used to be almost like my own mother."

"I suppose she finds that you are a more formidable person as you grow older. It was all very well scolding you when you were a clerk in the bank, but it does not do to scold the manager. These are the penalties men pay for becoming great."

"It is not my greatness that stands in my way, but—"

"Then I'm sure I cannot say what it is. But Patty will scold you if you do not mind the figure, though you were the whole Board of Directors packed into one. She won't respect you if you neglect your present work."

When Bessy went to bed that night she began to feel that she had attempted too much. "Mamma," she said, "could I not make some excuse and go away to Aunt Mary?"

"What, now?"

"Yes, mamma; now; to-morrow. I need not say that it will make me very unhappy to be away at such a time, but I begin to think that it will be better."

"What will papa say?"

"You must tell him all."

"And Aunt Mary must be told also. You would not like that. Has he said anything?"

"No, nothing;—very little, that is. But Bella has spoken to me. Oh, mamma, I think we have been very wrong in this. That is, I have been wrong. I feel as though I should disgrace myself, and turn the whole party here into a misfortune."

It would be dreadful, that telling of the story to her father and to her aunt, and such a necessity must, if possible, be avoided. Should such a necessity actually come, the former task would, no doubt, be done by her mother, but that would not lighten the load materially. After a fortnight she would again meet her father, and would be forced to discuss it. "I will remain if it be possible," she said; "but, mamma, if I wish to go, you will not stop me?" Her mother promised that she would not stop her, but strongly advised her to stand her ground.

On the following morning, when she came down stairs before breakfast, she found Frank standing in the hall with his gun of which he was trying the lock. "It is not loaded, is it, Frank?" said she.

"Oh dear, no; no one thinks of loading now-a-days till he has got out of the house. Directly after breakfast I am going across with Godfrey to the back of Greystock, to see after some moor-fowl. He asked me to go, and I couldn't well refuse."

"Of course not. Why should you?"

"It will be deuced hard work to make up the time. I was to have been up at four this morning, but that alarum went off and never woke me. However, I shall be able to do something to-night."

"Don't make a slavery of your holidays, Frank. What's the good of having a new gun if you're not to use it?"

"It's not the new gun. I'm not such a child as that comes to. But, you see, Godfrey is here, and one ought to be civil to him. I'll tell you what I want you girls to do, Bessy. You must come and meet us on our way home. Come over in the boat and along the path to the Patterdale road. We'll be there under the hill at about five."

"And if you are not, we are to wait in the snow?"

"Don't make difficulties, Bessy. I tell you we will be there. We are to go in the cart, and so shall have plenty of time."

"And how do you know the other girls will go?"

"Why, to tell you the truth, Patty Coverdale has promised. As for Miss Holmes, if she won't, why you must leave her at home with mamma. But Kate and Patty can't come without you."

"Your discretion has found that out, has it?"

"They say so. But you will come; won't you Bessy? As for waiting, it's all nonsense. Of course you can walk on. But we'll be at the stile by five. I've got my watch, you know." And then Bessy promised him. What would she not have done for him that was in her power to do?

"Go! Of course I'll go," said Miss Holmes. "I'm up to anything. I'd have gone with them this morning, and have taken a gun if they'd asked me. But, by the bye, I'd better not."

"Why not?" said Patty, who was hardly yet without fear lest something should mar the expedition.

"What will three gentlemen do with four ladies?"

"Oh, I forgot," said Patty innocently.

"I'm sure I don't care," said Kate; "you may have Harry if you like."

"Thank you for nothing," said Miss Holmes. "I want one for myself. It's all very well for you to make the offer, but what should I do if Harry wouldn't have me? There are two sides, you know, to every bargain."

"I'm sure he isn't anything to me," said Kate. "Why, he's not quite seventeen years old yet!"

"Poor boy! What a shame to dispose of him so soon. We'll let him off for a year or two; won't we, Miss Coverdale? But as there seems by acknowledgment to be one beau with unappropriated services—"

"I'm sure I have appropriated nobody," said Patty, "and didn't intend."

"Godfrey, then, is the only knight whose services are claimed," said Miss Holmes, looking at Bessy. Bessy made no immediate answer with either her eyes or tongue; but when the Coverdales were gone, she took her new friend to task.

"How can you fill those young girls' heads with such nonsense?"

"Nature has done that, my dear."

"But nature should be trained; should it not? You will make them think that those foolish boys are in love with them."

"The foolish boys, as you call them, will look after that themselves. It seems to me that the foolish boys know what they are about better than some of their elders." And then, after a moment's pause, she added, "As for my brother, I have no patience with him."

"Pray do not discuss your brother," said Bessy. "And, Bella, unless you wish to drive me away, pray do not speak of him and me together as you did just now."

"Are you so bad as that,—that the slightest commonplace joke upsets you? Would not his services be due to you as a matter of course? If you are so sore about it, you will betray your own secret."

"I have no secret,—none at least from you, or from mamma; and, indeed, none from him. We were both very foolish, thinking that we knew each other and our own hearts, when we knew neither."

"I hate to hear people talk of knowing their hearts. My idea is, that if you like a young man, and he asks you to marry him, you ought to have him. That is, if there is enough to live on. I don't know what more is wanted. But girls are getting to talk and think as though they were to send their hearts through some fiery furnace of trial before they may give them up to a husband's keeping. I'm not at all sure that the French fashion is not the best, and that these things shouldn't be managed by the fathers and mothers, or perhaps by the family lawyers. Girls who are so intent upon knowing their own hearts generally end by knowing nobody's heart but their own; and then they die old maids."

"Better that than give themselves to the keeping of those they don't know and cannot esteem."

"That's a matter of taste. I mean to take the first that comes, so long as he looks like a gentleman, and has not less than eight hundred a year. Now Godfrey does look like a gentleman, and has double that. If I had such a chance I shouldn't think twice about it."

"But I have no such chance. And if you have not, you would not think of it at all."

"That's the way the wind blows; is it?"

"No, no. Oh, Bella, pray, pray leave me alone. Pray do not interfere. There is no wind blowing in any way. All that I want is your silence and your sympathy."

"Very well. I will be silent and sympathetic as the grave. Only don't imagine that I am cold as the grave also. I don't exactly appreciate your ideas; but if I can do no good, I will at any rate endeavour to do no harm."

After lunch, at about three, they started on their walk, and managed to ferry themselves over the river. "Oh, do let me, Bessy," said Kate Coverdale. "I understand all about it. Look here, Miss Holmes. You pull the chain through your hands—"

"And inevitably tear your gloves to pieces," said Miss Holmes. Kate certainly had done so, and did not seem to be particularly well pleased with the accident. "There's a nasty nail in the chain," she said. "I wonder those stupid boys did not tell us."

Of course they reached the trysting-place much too soon, and were very tired of walking up and down to keep their feet warm, before the sportsmen came up. But this was their own fault, seeing that they had reached the stile half an hour before the time fixed.

"I never will go anywhere to meet gentlemen again," said Miss Holmes. "It is most preposterous that ladies should be left in the snow for an hour. Well, young men, what sport have you had?"

"I shot the big black cock," said Harry.

"Did you indeed?" said Kate Coverdale.

"And here are the feathers out of his tail for you. He dropped them in the water, and I had to go in after them up to my middle. But I told you that I would, so I was determined to get them."

"Oh you silly, silly boy," said Kate. "But I'll keep them for ever. I will indeed." This was said a little apart, for Harry had managed to draw the young lady aside before he presented the feathers.

Frank had also his trophies for Patty, and the tale to tell of his own prowess. In that he was a year older than his brother, he was by a year's growth less ready to tender his present to his lady-love, openly in the presence of them all. But he found his opportunity, and then he and Patty went on a little in advance. Kate also was deep in her consolations to Harry for his ducking; and therefore the four disposed of themselves in the manner previously suggested by Miss Holmes. Miss Holmes, therefore, and her brother, and Bessy Garrow, were left together in the path, and discussed the performances of the day in a manner that elicited no very ecstatic interest. So they walked for a mile, and by degrees the conversation between them dwindled down almost to nothing.

"There is nothing I dislike so much as coming out with people younger than myself," said Miss Holmes. "One always feels so old and dull. Listen to those children there; they make me feel as though I were an old maiden aunt, brought out with them to do propriety."

"Patty won't at all approve if she hears you call her a child."

"Nor shall I approve, if she treats me like an old woman," and then she stepped on and joined the children. "I wouldn't spoil even their sport if I could help it," she said to herself. "But with them I shall only be a temporary nuisance; if I remain behind I shall become a permanent evil." And thus Bessy and her old lover were left by themselves.

"I hope you will get on well with Bella," said Godfrey, when they had remained silent for a minute or two.

"Oh, yes. She is so good-natured and light-spirited that everybody must like her. She has been used to so much amusement and active life, that I know she must find it very dull here."

"She is never dull anywhere,—even at Liverpool, which, for a young lady, I sometimes think the dullest place on earth. I know it is for a man."

"A man who has work to do can never be dull; can he?"

"Indeed he can; as dull as death. I am so often enough. I have never been very bright there, Bessy, since you left us." There was nothing in his calling her Bessy, for it had become a habit with him since they were children; and they had formerly agreed that everything between them should be as it had been before that foolish whisper of love had been spoken and received. Indeed, provision had been made by them specially on this point, so that there need be no awkwardness in this mode of addressing each other. Such provision had seemed to be very prudent, but it hardly had the desired effect on the present occasion.

"I hardly know what you mean by brightness," she said, after a pause. "Perhaps it is not intended that people's lives should be what you call bright."

"Life ought to be as bright as we can make it."

"It all depends on the meaning of the word. I suppose we are not very bright here at Thwaite Hall, but yet we think ourselves very happy."

"I am sure you are," said Godfrey. "I very often think of you here."

"We always think of places where we have been when we were young," said Bessy; and then again they walked on for some way in silence, and Bessy began to increase her pace with the view of catching the children. The present walk to her was anything but bright, and she bethought herself with dismay that there were still two miles before she reached the Ferry.

"Bessy," Godfrey said at last. And then he stopped as though he were doubtful how to proceed. She, however, did not say a word, but walked on quickly, as though her only hope was in catching the party before her. But they also were walking quickly, for Bella had determined that she would not be caught.

"Bessy, I must speak to you once of what passed between us at Liverpool."

"Must you?" said she.

"Unless you positively forbid it."

"Stop, Godfrey," she said. And they did stop in the path, for now she no longer thought of putting an end to her embarrassment by overtaking her companions. "If any such words are necessary for your comfort, it would hardly become me to forbid them. Were I to speak so harshly you would accuse me afterwards in your own heart. It must be for you to judge whether it is well to re-open a wound that is nearly healed."

"But with me it is not nearly healed. The wound is open always."

"There are some hurts," she said, "which do not admit of an absolute and perfect cure, unless after long years." As she said so, she could not but think how much better was his chance of such perfect cure than her own. With her,—so she said to herself,—such curing was all but impossible; whereas with him, it was as impossible that the injury should last.

"Bessy," he said, and he again stopped her on the narrow path, standing immediately before her on the way, "you remember all the circumstances that made us part?"

"Yes; I think I remember them."

"And you still think that we were right to part?"

She paused for a moment before she answered him; but it was only for a moment, and then she spoke quite firmly. "Yes, Godfrey, I do; I have thought about it much since then. I have thought, I fear, to no good purpose about aught else. But I have never thought that we had been unwise in that."

"And yet I think you loved me."

"I am bound to confess I did so, as otherwise I must confess myself a liar. I told you at the time that I loved you, and I told you so truly. But it is better, ten times better, that those who love should part, even though they still should love, than that two should be joined together who are incapable of making each other happy. Remember what you told me."

"I do remember."

"You found yourself unhappy in your engagement, and you said it was my fault."

"Bessy, there is my hand. If you have ceased to love me, there is an end of it. But if you love me still, let all that be forgotten."

"Forgotten, Godfrey! How can it be forgotten? You were unhappy, and it was my fault. My fault, as it would be if I tried to solace a sick child with arithmetic, or feed a dog with grass. I had no right to love you, knowing you as I did; and knowing also that my ways would not be your ways. My punishment I understand, and it is not more than I can bear; but I had hoped that your punishment would have been soon over."

"You are too proud, Bessy."

"That is very likely. Frank says that I am a Puritan, and pride was the worst of their sins."

"Too proud and unbending. In marriage should not the man and woman adapt themselves to each other?"

"When they are married, yes. And every girl who thinks of marrying should know that in very much she must adapt herself to her husband. But I do not think that a woman should be the ivy, to take the direction of every branch of the tree to which she clings. If she does so, what can be her own character? But we must go on, or we shall be too late."

"And you will give me no other answer?"

"None other, Godfrey. Have you not just now, at this very moment, told me that I was too proud? Can it be possible that you should wish to tie yourself for life to female pride? And if you tell me that now, at such a moment as this, what would you tell me in the close intimacy of married life, when the trifles of every day would have worn away the courtesies of guest and lover?"

There was a sharpness of rebuke in this which Godfrey Holmes could not at the moment overcome. Nevertheless he knew the girl, and understood the workings of her heart and mind. Now, in her present state, she could be unbending, proud, and almost rough. In that she had much to lose in declining the renewed offer which he made her, she would, as it were, continually prompt herself to be harsh and inflexible. Had he been poor, had she not loved him, had not all good things seemed to have attended the promise of such a marriage, she would have been less suspicious of herself in receiving the offer, and more gracious in replying to it. Had he lost all his money before he came back to her, she would have taken him at once; or had he been deprived of an eye, or become crippled in his legs, she would have done so. But, circumstanced as he was, she had no motive to tenderness. There was an organic defect in her character, which no doubt was plainly marked by its own bump in her cranium,—the bump of philomartyrdom, it might properly be called. She had shipwrecked her own happiness in rejecting Godfrey Holmes; but it seemed to her to be the proper thing that a well-behaved young lady should shipwreck her own happiness. For the last month or two she had been tossed about by the waters and was nearly drowned. Now there was beautiful land again close to her, and a strong pleasant hand stretched out to save her. But though she had suffered terribly among the waves, she still thought it wrong to be saved. It would be so pleasant to take that hand, so sweet, so joyous, that it surely must be wrong. That was her doctrine; and Godfrey Holmes, though he hardly analyzed the matter, partly understood that it was so. And yet, if once she were landed on that green island, she would be so happy. She spoke with scorn of a woman clinging to a tree like ivy; and yet, were she once married, no woman would cling to her husband with sweeter feminine tenacity than Bessy Garrow. He spoke no further word to her as he walked home, but in handing her down to the ferry-boat he pressed her hand. For a second it seemed as though she had returned this pressure. If so, the action was involuntary, and her hand instantly resumed its stiffness to his touch.

It was late that night when Major Garrow went to his bed-room, but his wife was still up, waiting for him. "Well," said she, "what has he said to you? He has been with you above an hour."

"Such stories are not very quickly told; and in this case it was necessary to understand him very accurately. At length I think I do understand him."

It is not necessary to repeat at length all that was said on that night between Major and Mrs. Garrow, as to the offer which had now for a third time been made to their daughter. On that evening after the ladies had gone, and when the two boys had taken themselves off, Godfrey Holmes told his tale to his host, and had honestly explained to him what he believed to be the state of his daughter's feelings. "Now you know all," said he. "I do believe that she loves me, and if she does, perhaps she may still listen to you." Major Garrow did not feel sure that he "knew it all." But when he had fully discussed the matter that night with his wife, then he thought that perhaps he had arrived at that knowledge.

On the following morning Bessy learned from the maid, at an early hour, that Godfrey Holmes had left Thwaite Hall and gone back to Liverpool. To the girl she said nothing on the subject, but she felt obliged to say a word or two to Bella. "It is his coming that I regret," she said;—"that he should have had the trouble and annoyance for nothing. I acknowledge that it was my fault, and I am very sorry."

"It cannot be helped," said Miss Holmes, somewhat gravely. "As to his misfortunes, I presume that his journeys between here and Liverpool are not the worst of them."

After breakfast on that day Bessy was summoned into her father's book-room, and found him there, and her mother also. "Bessy," said he, "sit down, my dear. You know why Godfrey has left us this morning?"

Bessy walked round the room, so that in sitting she might be close to her mother and take her mother's hand in her own. "I suppose I do, papa," she said.

"He was with me late last night, Bessy; and when he told me what had passed between you I agreed with him that he had better go."

"It was better that he should go, papa."

"But he has left a message for you."

"A message, papa?"

"Yes, Bessy. And your mother agrees with me that it had better be given to you. It is this,—that if you will send him word to come again, he will be here by Twelfth-night. He came before on my invitation, but if he returns it must be on yours."

"Oh, papa, I cannot."

"I do not say that you can, but think of it calmly before you altogether refuse. You shall give me your answer on New Year's morning."

"Mamma knows that it would be impossible," said Bessy.

"Not impossible, dearest.

"In such a matter you should do what you believe to be right," said her father.

"If I were to ask him here again, it would be telling him that I would—"

"Exactly, Bessy. It would be telling him that you would be his wife. He would understand it so, and so would your mother and I. It must be so understood altogether."

"But, papa, when we were at Liverpool—"

"I have told him everything, dearest," said Mrs. Garrow.

"I think I understand the whole," said the Major; "and in such a matter as this I will not give you counsel on either side. But you must remember that in making up your mind, you must think of him as well as of yourself. If you do not love him;—if you feel that as his wife you should not love him, there is not another word to be said. I need not explain to my daughter that under such circumstances she would be wrong to encourage the visits of a suitor. But your mother says you do love him."

"Oh, mamma!"

"I will not ask you. But if you do;—if you have so told him, and allowed him to build up an idea of his life-happiness on such telling, you will, I think, sin greatly against him by allowing a false feminine pride to mar his happiness. When once a girl has confessed to a man that she loves him, the confession and the love together put upon her the burden of a duty towards him, which she cannot with impunity throw aside." Then he kissed her, and bidding her give him a reply on the morning of the new year, left her with her mother.

She had four days for consideration, and they went past her by no means easily. Could she have been alone with her mother, the struggle would not have been so painful; but there was the necessity that she should talk to Isabella Holmes, and the necessity also that she should not neglect the Coverdales. Nothing could have been kinder than Bella. She did not speak on the subject till the morning of the last day, and then only in a very few words. "Bessy," she said, "as you are great, be merciful."

"But I am not great, and it would not be mercy."

"As to that," said Bella, "he has surely a right to his own opinion."

On that evening she was sitting alone in her room when her mother came to her, and her eyes were red with weeping. Pen and paper were before her, as though she were resolved to write, but hitherto no word had been written.

"Well, Bessy," said her mother, sitting down close beside her; "is the deed done?"

"What deed, mamma? Who says that I am to do it?"

"The deed is not the writing, but the resolution to write. Five words will be sufficient,—if only those five words may be written."

"It is for one's whole life, mamma. For his life, as well as my own."

"True, Bessy;—that is quite true. But equally true whether you bid him come or allow him to remain away. That task of making up one's mind for life, must at last be done in some special moment of that life."

"Mamma, mamma; tell me what I should do."

But this Mrs. Garrow would not do. "I will write the words for you if you like," she said, "but it is you who must resolve that they shall be written. I cannot bid my darling go away and leave me for another home;—I can only say that in my heart I do believe that home would be a happy one."

It was morning before the note was written, but when the morning came Bessy had written it and brought it to her mother. "You must take it to papa," she said. Then she went and hid herself from all eyes till the noon had passed. "Dear Godfrey," the letter ran, "Papa says that you will return on Wednesday if I write to ask you. Do come back to us,—if you wish it. Yours always, BESSY."

"It is as good as though she had filled the sheet," said the Major. But in sending it to Godfrey Holmes, he did not omit a few accompanying remarks of his own.

An answer came from Godfrey by return of post; and on the afternoon of the sixth of January, Frank Garrow drove over to the station at Penrith to meet him. On their way back to Thwaite Hall there grew up a very close confidence between the two future brothers-in-law, and Frank explained with great perspicuity a little plan which he had arranged himself. "As soon as it is dark, so that she won't see it, Harry will hang it up in the dining-room," he said, "and mind you go in there before you go anywhere else."

"I am very glad you have come back, Godfrey," said the Major, meeting him in the hall.

"God bless you, dear Godfrey," said Mrs. Garrow, "you will find Bessy in the dining-room," she whispered; but in so whispering she was quite unconscious of the mistletoe bough.

And so also was Bessy, nor do I think that she was much more conscious when that introduction was over. Godfrey had made all manner of promises to Frank, but when the moment arrived, he had found the moment too important for any special reference to the little bough above his head. Not so, however, Patty Coverdale. "It's a shame," she said, bursting out of the room, "and if I'd known what you had done, nothing on earth should have induced me to go in. I won't enter the room till I know that you have taken it out." Nevertheless her sister Kate was bold enough to solve the mystery before the evening was over.

THE PARSON'S DAUGHTER OF OXNEY COLNE

THE PRETTIEST SCENERY in all England—and if I am contradicted in that assertion, I will say in all Europe—is in Devonshire, on the southern and south-eastern skirts of Dartmoor, where the rivers Dart, and Avon, and Teign form themselves, and where the broken moor is half cultivated, and the wild-looking upland fields are half moor. In making this assertion I am often met with much doubt, but it is by persons who do not really know the locality. Men and women talk to me on the matter, who have travelled down the line of railway from Exeter to Plymouth, who have spent a fortnight at Torquay, and perhaps made an excursion from Tavistock to the convict prison on Dartmoor. But who knows the glories of Chagford? Who has walked through the parish of Manaton? Who is conversant with Lustleigh Cleeves and Withycombe in the moor? Who has explored Holne Chase? Gentle reader, believe me that you will be rash in contradicting me, unless you have done these things.

There or thereabouts—I will not say by the waters of which little river it is washed—is the parish of Oxney Colne. And for those who would wish to see all the beauties of this lovely country, a sojourn in Oxney Colne would be most desirable, seeing that the sojourner would then be brought nearer to all that he would wish to visit, than at any other spot in the country. But there is an objection to any such arrangement. There are only two decent houses in the whole parish, and these are—or were when I knew the locality—small and fully occupied by their possessors. The larger and better is the parsonage, in which lived the parson and his daughter; and the smaller is the freehold residence of a certain Miss Le

Smyrger, who owned a farm of a hundred acres, which was rented by one Farmer Cloysey, and who also possessed some thirty acres round her own house, which she managed herself, regarding herself to be quite as great in cream as Mr. Cloysey, and altogether superior to him in the article of cider. "But yeu has to pay no rent, Miss," Farmer Cloysey would say, when Miss Le Smyrger expressed this opinion of her art in a manner too defiant. "Yeu pays no rent, or yeu couldn't do it." Miss Le Smyrger was an old maid, with a pedigree and blood of her own, a hundred and thirty acres of fee-simple land on the borders of Dartmoor, fifty years of age, a constitution of iron, and an opinion of her own on every subject under the sun.

And now for the parson and his daughter. The parson's name was Woolsworthy—or Woolathy as it was pronounced by all those who lived around him—the Rev. Saul Woolsworthy; and his daughter was Patience Woolsworthy, or Miss Patty, as she was known to the Devonshire world of those parts. That name of Patience had not been well chosen for her, for she was a hot-tempered damsel, warm in her convictions, and inclined to express them freely. She had but two closely intimate friends in the world, and by both of them this freedom of expression had now been fully permitted to her since she was a child. Miss Le Smyrger and her father were well accustomed to her ways, and on the whole well satisfied with them. The former was equally free and equally warm-tempered as herself, and as Mr. Woolsworthy was allowed by his daughter to be quite paramount on his own subject—for he had a subject—he did not object to his daughter being paramount on all others. A pretty girl was Patience Woolsworthy at the time of which I am writing, and one who possessed much that was worthy of remark and admiration, had she lived where beauty meets with admiration, or where force of character is remarked. But at Oxney Colne, on the borders of Dartmoor, there were few to appreciate her, and it seemed as though she herself had but little idea of carrying her talent further afield, so that it might not remain for ever wrapped in a blanket.

She was a pretty girl, tall and slender, with dark eyes and black hair. Her eyes were perhaps too round for regular beauty, and her hair was perhaps too crisp; her mouth was large and expressive; her nose was finely formed, though a critic in female form might have declared it to be somewhat broad. But her countenance altogether was wonderfully attractive—if only it might be seen without that resolution for dominion which occasionally marred it, though sometimes it even added to her attractions.

It must be confessed on behalf of Patience Woolsworthy, that the circumstances of her life had peremptorily called upon her to exercise dominion. She had lost her mother when she was sixteen, and had had neither brother nor sister. She had no neighbours near her fit either from education or rank to interfere in the conduct of her life, excepting always Miss Le Smyrger. Miss Le Smyrger would have done anything for her, including the whole management of her morals and of the parsonage household, had Patience been content with such an arrangement. But much as Patience had ever loved Miss Le Smyrger, she was not content with this, and therefore she had been called on to put forth a strong hand of her own. She had put forth this strong hand early, and hence had come the character which I am attempting to describe. But I must say on behalf of this girl, that it was not only over others that she thus exercised dominion. In acquiring that power she had also acquired the much greater power of exercising rule over herself.

But why should her father have been ignored in these family arrangements? Perhaps it may almost suffice to say, that of all living men her father was the man best conversant with the antiquities of the county in which he lived. He was the Jonathan Oldbuck of Devonshire, and especially of Dartmoor, without that decision of character which enabled Oldbuck to keep his womenkind in some kind of subjection, and probably enabled him also to see that his weekly bills did not pass their proper limits. Our Mr. Oldbuck, of Oxney Colne, was sadly deficient in these. As a parish pastor with but a small cure, he did his duty with sufficient energy to keep him, at any rate, from reproach. He was kind and charitable to the poor, punctual in his services, forbearing with the farmers around him, mild with his brother clergymen, and indifferent to aught that bishop or archdeacon might think or say of him. I do not name this latter attribute as a virtue, but as a fact. But all these points were as nothing in the known character of Mr. Woolsworthy, of Oxney Colne. He was the antiquarian of Dartmoor. That was his line of life. It was in that capacity that he was known to the Devonshire world; it was as such that he journeyed about with his humble carpet-bag, staying away from his parsonage a night or two at a time; it was in that character that he received now and again stray visitors in the single spare bedroom—not friends asked to see him and his girl because of their friendship—but men who knew something as to this buried stone, or that old land-mark. In all these things his daughter let him have his own way, assisting and encouraging him. That was his line of life, and therefore she respected it. But in all other matters she chose to be paramount at the parsonage.

Mr. Woolsworthy was a little man, who always wore, except on Sundays, grey clothes—clothes of so light a grey that they would hardly have been regarded as clerical in a district less remote. He had now reached a goodly age, being full seventy years old; but still he was wiry and active, and shewed but few symptoms of decay. His head was bald, and the few remaining locks that surrounded it were nearly white. But there was a look of energy about his mouth, and a humour in his light grey eye, which forbade those who knew him to regard him altogether as an old man. As it was, he could walk from Oxney Colne to Priestown, fifteen long Devonshire miles across the moor; and he who could do that could hardly be regarded as too old for work.

But our present story will have more to do with his daughter than with him. A pretty girl, I have said, was Patience Woolsworthy; and one, too, in many ways remarkable. She had taken her outlook into life, weighing the things which she had and those which she had not, in a manner very unusual, and, as a rule, not always desirable for a young lady. The things which she had not were very many. She had not society; she had not a fortune; she had not any assurance of future means of livelihood; she had not high hope of procuring for herself a position in life by marriage; she had not that excitement and pleasure in life which she read of in such books as found their way down to Oxney Colne Parsonage. It would be easy to add to the list of the things which she had not; and this list against herself she made out with the utmost vigour. The things which she had, or those rather which she assured herself of having, were much more easily counted. She had the birth and education of a lady, the strength of a healthy woman, and a will of her own. Such was the list as she made it out for herself, and I protest that I assert no more than the truth in saying that she never added to it either beauty, wit, or talent.

I began these descriptions by saying that Oxney Colne would, of all places, be the best spot from which a tourist could visit those parts of Devonshire, but for the fact that he could obtain there none of the accommodation which tourists require. A brother antiquarian might, perhaps, in those days have done so, seeing that there was, as I have said, a spare bedroom at the parsonage. Any intimate friend of Miss Le Smyrger's might be as fortunate, for she was equally well provided at Oxney Combe, by which name her house was known. But Miss Le Smyrger was not given to extensive hospitality, and it was only to those who were bound to her, either by ties of blood or of very old friendship, that she delighted to open her doors. As her old friends were very few in number, as those few lived at a distance, and as her nearest relations were higher in the world than she was, and were said by herself to look down upon her, the visits made to Oxney Combe were few and far between.

But now, at the period of which I am writing, such a visit was about to be made. Miss Le Smyrger had a younger sister, who had inherited a property in the parish of Oxney Colne equal to that of the lady who now lived there; but this the younger sister had inherited beauty also, and she therefore, in early life, had found sundry lovers, one of whom became her husband. She had married a man even then well to do in the world, but now rich and almost mighty; a Member of Parliament, a Lord of this and that board, a man who had a house in Eaton-square, and a park in the north of England; and in this way her course of life had been very much divided from that of our Miss Le Smyrger. But the Lord of the Government board had been blessed with various children; and perhaps it was now thought expedient to look after Aunt Penelope's Devonshire acres. Aunt Penelope was empowered to leave them to whom she pleased; and though it was thought in Eaton-square that she must, as a matter of course, leave them to one of the family, nevertheless a little cousinly intercourse might make the thing more certain. I will not say that this was the sole cause for such a visit, but in these days a visit was to be made by Captain Broughton to his aunt. Now Captain John Broughton was the second son of Alfonso Broughton, of Clapham Park and Eaton-square, Member of Parliament, and Lord of the aforesaid Government Board.

"And what do you mean to do with him?" Patience Woolsworthy asked of Miss Le Smyrger when that lady walked over from the Combe to say that her nephew John was to arrive on the following morning.

"Do with him? Why, I shall bring him over here to talk to your father."

"He'll be too fashionable for that, and papa won't trouble his head about him if he finds that he doesn't care for Dartmoor."

"Then he may fall in love with you, my dear."

"Well, yes; there's that resource at any rate, and for your sake I dare say I should be more civil to him than papa. But he'll soon get tired of making love, and what you'll do then I cannot imagine."

That Miss Woolsworthy felt no interest in the coming of the Captain I will not pretend to say. The advent to any stranger with whom she would be called on to associate must be matter of interest to her in that secluded place; and she was not so absolutely unlike other young ladies that the arrival of an unmarried young man would be the same to her as the advent of some patriarchal pater-familias. In taking that outlook into life of which I have spoken she had never said to herself that she despised those things from which other girls received the excitement, the joys, and the disappointment of their lives. She had simply given herself to understand that very little of such things would come her way, and that it behoved her to live—to live happily if such might be possible—without experiencing the need of them. She had heard, when there was no thought of any such visit to Oxney Colne, that John Broughton was a handsome, clever man—one who thought much of himself, and was thought much of by others—that there had been some talk of his marrying a great heiress, which marriage, however, had not taken place through unwillingness on his part, and that he was on the whole a man of more mark in the world than the ordinary captain of ordinary regiments.

Captain Broughton came to Oxney Combe, stayed there a fort-night,—the intended period for his projected visit having been fixed at three or four days—and then went his way. He went his way back to his London haunts, the time of the year then being the close of the Easter holydays; but as he did so he told his aunt that he should assuredly return to her in the autumn.

"And assuredly I shall be happy to see you, John—if you come with a certain purpose. If you have no such purpose, you had better remain away."

"I shall assuredly come," the Captain had replied, and then he had gone on his journey.

The summer passed rapidly by, and very little was said between Miss Le Smyrger and Miss Woolsworthy about Captain Broughton. In many respects—nay, I may say, as to all ordinary matters, no two women could well be more intimate with each other than they were,—and more than that, they had the courage each to talk to the other with absolute truth as to things concerning themselves— a courage in which dear friends often fail. But, nevertheless, very little was said between them about Captain John Broughton. All that was said may be here repeated.

"John says that he shall return here in August," Miss Le Smyrger said, as Patience was sitting with her in the parlour at Oxney Combe, on the morning after that gentleman's departure.

"He told me so himself," said Patience; and as she spoke her round dark eyes assumed a look of more than ordinary self-will. If Miss Le Smyrger had intended to carry the conversation any further, she changed her mind as she looked at her companion. Then, as I said, the summer ran by, and towards the close of the warm days of July, Miss Le Smyrger, sitting in the same chair in the same room, again took up the conversation.

"I got a letter from John this morning. He says that he shall be here on the third."

"Does he?"

"He is very punctual to the time he named."

"Yes; I fancy that he is a punctual man," said Patience.

"I hope that you will be glad to see him," said Miss Le Smyrger.

"Very glad to see him," said Patience, with a bold clear voice; and then the conversation was again dropped, and nothing further was said till after Captain Broughton's second arrival in the parish.

Four months had then passed since his departure, and during that time Miss Woolsworthy had performed all her usual daily duties in their accustomed course. No one could discover that she had been less careful in her household matters than had been her wont, less willing to go among her poor neighbours, or less assiduous in her attentions to her father. But not the less was there a feeling in the minds of those around her that some great change had come upon her. She would sit during the long summer evenings on a certain spot outside the parsonage orchard, at the top of a small sloping field in which their solitary cow was always pastured, with a book on her knees before her, but rarely reading. There she would sit, with the beautiful view down to the winding river below her, watching the setting sun, and thinking, thinking, thinking—thinking of something of which she had never spoken. Often would Miss Le Smyrger come upon her there, and sometimes would pass by her even without a word; but never—never once did she dare to ask her of the matter of her thoughts. But she knew the matter well enough. No confession was necessary to inform her that Patience Woolsworthy was in love with John Broughton—ay, in love, to the full and entire loss of her whole heart.

On one evening she was so sitting till the July sun had fallen and hidden himself for the night, when her father came upon her as he returned from one of his rambles on the moor. "Patty," he said, "you are always sitting there now. Is it not late? Will you not be cold?"

"No, papa," she said, "I shall not be cold."

"But won't you come to the house? I miss you when you come in so late that there's no time to say a word before we go to bed."

She got up and followed him into the parsonage, and when they were in the sitting-room together, and the door was closed, she came up to him and kissed him. "Papa," she said, "would it make you very unhappy if I were to leave you?"

"Leave me!" he said, startled by the serious and almost solemn tone of her voice. "Do you mean for always?"

"If I were to marry, papa?"

"Oh, marry! No; that would not make me unhappy. It would make me very happy, Patty, to see you married to a man you would love—very, very happy; though my days would be desolate without you."

"That is it, papa. What would you do if I went from you?"

"What would it matter, Patty? I should be free, at any rate, from a load which often presses heavy on me now. What will you do when I shall leave you? A few more years and all will be over with me. But who is it, love? Has anybody said anything to you?"

"It was only an idea, papa. I don't often think of such a thing; but I did think of it then." And so the subject was allowed to pass by. This had happened before the day of the second arrival had been absolutely fixed and made known to Miss Woolsworthy.

And then that second arrival took place. The reader may have understood from the words with which Miss Le Smyrger authorised her nephew to make his second visit to Oxney Combe that Miss Woolsworthy's passion was not altogether unauthorised. Captain Broughton had been told that he was not to come unless he came with a certain purpose; and having been so told, he still persisted in coming. There can be no doubt but that he well understood the purport to which his aunt alluded. "I shall assuredly come," he had said. And true to his word, he was now there.

Patience knew exactly the hour at which he must arrive at the station at Newton Abbot, and the time also which it would take to travel over those twelve uphill miles from the station to Oxney. It need hardly be said that she paid no visit to Miss Le Smyrger's house on that afternoon; but she might have known something of Captain Broughton's approach without going thither. His road to the Combe passed by the parsonage-gate, and had Patience sat even at her bedroom window she must have seen him. But on such a morning she would not sit at her bedroom window—she would do nothing which would force her to accuse herself of a restless longing for her lover's coming. It was for him to seek her. If he chose to do so, he knew the way to the parsonage.

Miss Le Smyrger—good, dear, honest, hearty Miss Le Smyrger, was in a fever of anxiety on behalf of her friend. It was not that she wished her nephew to marry Patience—or rather that she had entertained any such wish when he first came among them. She was not given to match-making, and moreover thought, or had thought within herself, that they of Oxney Colne could do very well without any admixture from Eaton-square. Her plan of life had been that, when old Mr. Woolsworthy was taken away from Dartmoor, Patience should live with her; and that when she also shuffled off her coil, then Patience Woolsworthy should be the maiden mistress of Oxney Combe—of Oxney Combe and Mr. Cloysey's farm—to the utter detriment of all the Broughtons. Such had been her plan before nephew John had come among them—a plan not to be spoken of till the coming of that dark day which should make Patience an orphan. But now her nephew had been there, and all was to be altered. Miss Le Smyrger's plan would have provided a companion for her old age; but that had not been her chief object. She had thought more of Patience than of herself, and now it seemed that a prospect of a higher happiness was opening for her friend.

"John," she said, as soon as the first greetings were over, "do you remember the last words that I said to you before you went away?" Now, for myself, I much admire Miss Le Smyrger's heartiness, but I do not think much of her discretion. It would have been better, perhaps, had she allowed things to take their course.

"I can't say that I do," said the Captain. At the same time the Captain did remember very well what those last words had been.

"I am so glad to see you, so delighted to see you, if—if—if—," and then she paused, for with all her courage she hardly dared to ask her nephew whether he had come there with the express purpose of asking Miss Woolsworthy to marry him.

To tell the truth—for there is no room for mystery within the limits of this short story,—to tell, I say, at a word the plain and simple truth, Captain Broughton had already asked that question. On the day before he left Oxney Colne, he had in set terms proposed to the parson's daughter, and indeed the words, the hot and frequent words, which previously to that had fallen like sweetest honey into the ears of Patience Woolsworthy, had made it imperative on him to do so. When a man in such a place as that has talked to a girl of love day after day, must not he talk of it to some definite purpose on the day on which he leaves her? Or if he do not, must he not submit to be regarded as false, selfish, and almost fraudulent? Captain Broughton, however, had asked the question honestly and truly. He had done so honestly and truly, but in words, or, perhaps, simply with a tone, that had hardly sufficed to satisfy the proud spirit of the girl he loved. She by that time had confessed to herself that she loved him with all her heart; but she had made no such confession to him. To him she had spoken no word, granted no favour, that any lover might rightfully regard as a token of love returned. She had listened to him as he spoke, and bade him keep such sayings for the drawing-rooms of his "fashionable friends." Then he had spoken out and had asked for that hand,—not, perhaps, as a suitor tremulous with hope,—but as a rich man who knows that he can command that which he desires to purchase.

"You should think more of this," she had said to him at last. "If you would really have me for your wife, it will not be much to you to return here again when time for thinking of it shall have passed by." With these words she had dismissed him, and now he had again come back to Oxney Colne. But still she would not place herself at the window to look for him, nor dress herself in other than her simple morning country dress, nor omit one item of her daily work. If he wished to take her at all, he should wish to take her as she really was, in her plain country life, but he should take her also with full observance of all those privileges which maidens are allowed to claim from their lovers. He should contract no ceremonious observance because she was the daughter of a poor country parson who would come to him without a shilling, whereas he stood high in the world's books. He had asked her to give him all that she had, and that all she was ready to give, without stint. But the gift must be valued before it could be given or received. He also was to give her as much, and she would accept it as being beyond all price. But she would not allow that that which was offered to her was in any degree the more precious because of his outward worldly standing.

She would not pretend to herself that she thought he would come to her that day, and therefore she busied herself in the kitchen and about the house, giving directions to her two maids as though the afternoon would pass as all other days did pass in that household. They usually dined at four, and she rarely, in these summer months, went far from the house before that hour. At four precisely she sat down with her father, and then said that she was going up as far as Helpholme after dinner. Helpholme was a solitary farmhouse in another parish, on the border of the moor, and Mr. Woolsworthy asked her whether he should accompany her.

"Do, papa," she said, "if you are not too tired." And yet she had thought how probable it might be that she should meet John Broughton on her walk. And so it was arranged; but, just as dinner was over, Mr. Woolsworthy remembered himself.

"Gracious me," he said, "how my memory is going. Gribbles, from Ivybridge, and old John Poulter, from Bovey, are coming to meet here by appointment. You can't put Helpholme off till tomorrow?"

Patience, however, never put off anything, and therefore at six o'clock, when her father had finished his slender modicum of toddy, she tied on her hat and went on her walk. She started forth with a quick step, and left no word to say by which route she would go. As she passed up along the little lane which led towards Oxney Combe, she would not even look to see if he was coming towards her; and when she left the road, passing over a stone stile into a little path which ran first through the upland fields, and then across the moor ground towards Helpholme, she did not look back once, or listen for his coming step.

She paid her visit, remaining upwards of an hour with the old bedridden mother of the tenant of Helpholme. "God bless you, my darling!" said the old woman as she left her; "and send you some

one to make your own path bright and happy through the world."
These words were still ringing in her ears with all their significance
as she saw John Broughton waiting for her at the first stile which
she had to pass after leaving the farmer's haggard.

"Patty," he said, as he took her hand, and held it close within
both his own, "what a chase I have had after you!"

"And who asked you, Captain Broughton?" she answered, smiling. "If the journey was too much for your poor London strength,
could you not have waited till to-morrow morning, when you
would have found me at the parsonage?" But she did not draw her
hand away from him, or in any way pretend that he had not a right
to accost her as a lover.

"No, I could not wait. I am more eager to see those I love than
you seem to be."

"How do you know whom I love, or how eager I might be to
see them? There is an old woman there whom I love, and I have
thought nothing of this walk with the object of seeing her." And
now, slowly drawing her hand away from him, she pointed to the
farmhouse which she had left.

"Patty," he said, after a minute's pause, during which she had
looked full into his face with all the force of her bright eyes; "I have
come from London to-day, straight down here to Oxney, and from
my aunt's house close upon your footsteps after you, to ask you that
one question. Do you love me?"

"What a Hercules!" she said, again laughing. "Do you really
mean that you left London only this morning? Why, you must have
been five hours in a railway carriage and two in a postchaise, not to
talk of the walk afterwards. You ought to take more care of yourself, Captain Broughton!"

He would have been angry with her—for he did not like to be
quizzed—had she not put her hand on his arm as she spoke, and
the softness of her touch had redeemed the offence of her words.

"All that have I done," said he, "that I may hear one word from
you."

"That any word of mine should have such potency! But let us
walk on, or my father will take us for some of the standing stones
of the moor. How have you found your aunt? If you only knew
the cares that have sat on her dear shoulders for the last week past,
in order that your high mightiness might have a sufficiency to eat
and drink in these desolate half-starved regions."

"She might have saved herself such anxiety. No one can care less for such things than I do."

"And yet I think I have heard you boast of the cook of your club." And then again there was silence for a minute or two.

"Patty," said he, stopping again in the path; "answer my question. I have a right to demand an answer. Do you love me?"

"And what if I do? What if I have been so silly as to allow your perfections to be too many for my weak heart? What then, Captain Broughton?"

"It cannot be that you love me, or you would not joke now."

"Perhaps not, indeed," she said. It seemed as though she were resolved not to yield an inch in her own humour. And then again they walked on.

"Patty," he said once more, "I shall get an answer from you to-night,—this evening; now, during this walk, or I shall return to-morrow, and never revisit this spot again."

"Oh, Captain Broughton, how should we ever manage to live without you?"

"Very well," he said; "up to the end of this walk I can bear it all;—and one word spoken then will mend it all."

During the whole of this time she felt that she was ill-using him. She knew that she loved him with all her heart; that it would nearly kill her to part with him; that she had heard his renewed offer with an ecstacy of joy. She acknowledged to herself that he was giving proof of his devotion as strong as any which a girl could receive from her lover. And yet she could hardly bring herself to say the word he longed to hear. That word once said, and then she knew that she must succumb to her love for ever! That word once said, and there would be nothing for her but to spoil him with her idolatry! That word once said, and she must continue to repeat it into his ears, till perhaps he might be tired of hearing it! And now he had threatened her, and how could she speak it after that? She certainly would not speak it unless he asked her again without such threat. And so they walked on again in silence.

"Patty," he said at last. "By the heavens above us you shall answer me. Do you love me?"

She now stood still, and almost trembled as she looked up into his face. She stood opposite to him for a moment, and then placing her two hands on his shoulders, she answered him. "I do, I do, I do," she said, "with all my heart; with all my heart—with all my heart and strength." And then her head fell upon his breast.

Captain Broughton was almost as much surprised as delighted by the warmth of the acknowledgment made by the eager-hearted passionate girl whom he now held within his arms. She had said it now; the words had been spoken; and there was nothing for her but to swear to him over and over again with her sweetest oaths, that those words were true—true as her soul. And very sweet was the walk down from thence to the parsonage gate. He spoke no more of the distance of the ground, or the length of his day's journey. But he stopped her at every turn that he might press her arm the closer to his own, that he might look into the brightness of her eyes, and prolong his hour of delight. There were no more gibes now on her tongue, no raillery at his London finery, no laughing comments on his coming and going. With downright honesty she told him everything: how she had loved him before her heart was warranted in such a passion; how, with much thinking, she had resolved that it would be unwise to take him at his first word, and had thought it better that he should return to London, and then think over it; how she had almost repented of her courage when she had feared, during those long summer days, that he would forget her; and how her heart had leapt for joy when her old friend had told her that he was coming.

"And yet," said he, "you were not glad to see me!"

"Oh, was I not glad? You cannot understand the feelings of a girl who has lived secluded as I have done. Glad is no word for the joy I felt. But it was not seeing you that I cared for so much. It was the knowledge that you were near me once again. I almost wish now that I had not seen you till to-morrow." But as she spoke she pressed his arm, and this caress gave the lie to her last words.

"No, do not come in to-night," she said, when she reached the little wicket that led up to the parsonage. "Indeed, you shall not. I could not behave myself properly if you did."

"But I don't want you to behave properly."

"Oh! I am to keep that for London, am I? But, nevertheless, Captain Broughton, I will not invite you either to tea or to supper to-night."

"Surely I may shake hands with your father."

"Not to-night—not till—. John, I may tell him, may I not? I must tell him at once."

"Certainly," said he.

"And then you shall see him to-morrow. Let me see—at what hour shall I bid you come?"

"To breakfast."

"No, indeed. What on earth would your aunt do with her broiled turkey and the cold pie? I have got no cold pie for you."

"I hate cold pie."

"What a pity! But, John, I should be forced to have you directly after breakfast. Come down—come down at two, or three; and then I will go back with you to Aunt Penelope. I must see her to-morrow;" and so at last the matter was settled, and the happy Captain, as he left her, was hardly resisted in his attempt to press her lips to his own.

When she entered the parlour in which her father was sitting, there still were Gribbles and Poulter discussing some knotty point of Devon lore. So Patience took off her hat, and sat herself down, waiting till they should go. For full an hour she had to wait, and then Gribbles and Poulter did go. But it was not in such matters as this that Patience Woolsworthy was impatient. She could wait, and wait, and wait, curbing herself for weeks and months, while the thing waited for was in her eyes good; but she could not curb her hot thoughts or her hot words when things came to be discussed which she did not think to be good.

"Papa," she said, when Gribbles' long-drawn last word had been spoken at the door. "Do you remember how I asked you the other day what you would say if I were to leave you?"

"Yes, surely," he replied, looking up at her in astonishment.

"I am going to leave you now," she said. "Dear, dearest father, how am I to go from you?"

"Going to leave me," said he, thinking of her visit to Helpholme, and thinking of nothing else.

Now, there had been a story about Helpholme. That bed-ridden old lady there had a stalwart son, who was now the owner of the Helpholme pastures. But though owner in fee of all those wild acres, and of the cattle which they supported, he was not much above the farmers around him, either in manners or education. He had his merits, however; for he was honest, well-to-do in the world, and modest withal. How strong love had grown up, springing from neighbourly kindness, between our Patience and his mother, it needs not here to tell; but rising from it had come another love—or an ambition which might have grown to love. The young man, after much thought, had not dared to speak to Miss Woolsworthy, but he had sent a message by Miss Le Smyrger. If there could be any hope for him, he would present himself as a suitor—on trial. He did not owe a shilling in the world, and had money by him—saved. He wouldn't ask the parson for a shilling of fortune. Such had been the tenor of his message, and Miss Le Smyrger had delivered it faithfully. "He does not mean it," Patience had said with her stern voice. "Indeed he does, my dear. You may be sure he is in earnest," Miss Le Smyrger had replied; "and there is not an honester man in these parts."

"Tell him," said Patience, not attending to the latter portion of her friend's last speech, "that it cannot be—make him understand, you know—and tell him also that the matter shall be thought of no more." The matter had, at any rate, been spoken of no more, but the young farmer still remained a bachelor, and Helpholme still wanted a mistress. But all this came back upon the parson's mind when his daughter told him that she was about to leave him.

"Yes, dearest," she said; and as she spoke she now knelt at his knees. "I have been asked in marriage, and I have given myself away."

"Well, my love, if you will be happy——"

"I hope I shall; I think I shall. But you, papa?"

"You will not be far from us."

"Oh, yes; in London."

"In London?"

"Captain Broughton lives in London generally."

"And has Captain Broughton asked you to marry him?"

"Yes, papa—who else? Is he not good? Will you not love him? Oh, papa, do not say that I am wrong to love him?"

He never told her his mistake, or explained to her that he had not thought it possible that the high-placed son of the London great man should have fallen in love with his undowered daughter; but he embraced her, and told her, with all his enthusiasm, that he rejoiced in her joy, and would be happy in her happiness. "My own Patty," he said, "I have ever known that you were too good for this life of ours here." And then the evening wore away into the night, with many tears, but still with much happiness.

Captain Broughton, as he walked back to Oxney Combe, made up his mind that he would say nothing on the matter to his aunt till the next morning. He wanted to think over it all, and to think it

over, if possible, by himself. He had taken a step in life, the most
important that a man is ever called on to take, and he had to reflect
whether or no he had taken it with wisdom.

"Have you seen her?" said Miss Le Smyrger, very anxiously,
when he came into the drawing-room.

"Miss Woolsworthy you mean," said he. "Yes, I've seen her. As
I found her out, I took a long walk, and happened to meet her. Do
you know, aunt, I think I'll go to bed; I was up at five this morning,
and have been on the move ever since."

Miss Le Smyrger perceived that she was to hear nothing that
evening, so she handed him his candlestick and allowed him to go
to his room.

But Captain Broughton did not immediately retire to bed, nor
when he did so was he able to sleep at once. Had this step that he
had taken been a wise one? He was not a man who, in worldly
matters, had allowed things to arrange themselves for him, as is the
case with so many men. He had formed views for himself, and had
a theory of life. Money for money's sake he had declared to himself
to be bad. Money, as a concomitant to things which were in themselves good, he had declared to himself to be good also. That concomitant in this affair of his marriage, he had now missed. Well; he
had made up his mind to that, and would put up with the loss. He
had means of living of his own, the means not so extensive as might
have been desirable. That it would be well for him to become a
married man, looking merely to that state of life as opposed to his
present state, he had fully resolved. On that point, therefore, there
was nothing to repent. That Patty Woolsworthy was good, affectionate, clever, and beautiful he was sufficiently satisfied. It would
be odd indeed if he were not so satisfied now, seeing that for the
last four months he had so declared to himself daily with many
inward asseverations. And yet though, he repeated, now again that
he was satisfied, I do not think that he was so fully satisfied of it as
he had been throughout the whole of those four months. It is sad
to say so, but I fear—I fear that such was the case. When you have
your plaything, how much of the anticipated pleasure vanishes,
especially if it be won easily.

He had told none of his family what were his intentions in this
second visit to Devonshire, and now he had to bethink himself
whether they would be satisfied. What would his sister say, she who
had married the Honourable Augustus Gumbleton, gold-stick-in-

waiting to Her Majesty's Privy Council? Would she receive Patience with open arms, and make much of her about London? And then how far would London suit Patience, or would Patience suit London? There would be much for him to do in teaching her, and it would be well for him to set about the lesson without loss of time. So far he got that night, but when the morning came he went a step further, and began mentally to criticise her manner to himself. It had been very sweet, that warm, that full, that ready declaration of love. Yes; it had been very sweet; but—but—; when, after her little jokes, she did confess her love, had she not been a little too free for feminine excellence? A man likes to be told that he is loved, but he hardly wishes that the girl he is to marry should fling herself at his head!

Ah me! yes; it was thus he argued to himself as on that morning he went through the arrangements of his toilet. "Then he was a brute," you say, my pretty reader. I have never said that he was not a brute. But this I remark, that many such brutes are to be met with in the beaten paths of the world's high highway. When Patience Woolsworthy had answered him coldly, bidding him go back to London and think over his love; while it seemed from her manner that at any rate as yet she did not care for him; while he was absent from her, and, therefore, longing for her, the possession of her charms, her talent and bright honesty of purpose had seemed to him a thing most desirable. Now they were his own. They had, in fact, been his own from the first. The heart of this country-bred girl had fallen at the first word from his mouth. Had she not so confessed to him? She was very nice—very nice indeed. He loved her dearly. But had he not sold himself too cheaply?

I by no means say that he was not a brute. But whether brute or no he was an honest man, and had no remotest dream, either then, on that morning, or during the following days on which such thoughts pressed more thickly on his mind—of breaking away from his pledged word. At breakfast on that morning he told all to Miss Le Smyrger, and that lady, with warm and gracious intentions, confided to him her purpose regarding her property. "I have always regarded Patience as my heir," she said, "and shall do so still."

"Oh, indeed," said Captain Broughton.

"But it is a great, great pleasure to me to think that she will give back the little property to my sister's child. You will have your mother's, and thus it will all come together again."

"Ah!" said Captain Broughton. He had his own ideas about property, and did not, even under existing circumstances, like to hear that his aunt considered herself at liberty to leave the acres away to one who was by blood quite a stranger to the family.

"Does Patience know of this?" he asked.

"Not a word," said Miss Le Smyrger. And then nothing more was said upon the subject.

On that afternoon he went down and received the parson's benediction and congratulations with a good grace. Patience said very little on the occasion, and, indeed was absent during the greater part of the interview. The two lovers then walked up to Oxney Combe, and there were more benedictions and more congratulations. "All went merry as a marriage bell," at any rate as far as Patience was concerned. Not a word had yet fallen from that dear mouth, not a look had yet come over that handsome face, which tended in any way to mar her bliss. Her first day of acknowledged love was a day altogether happy, and when she prayed for him as she knelt beside her bed there was no feeling in her mind that any fear need disturb her joy.

I will pass over the next three or four days very quickly, merely saying that Patience did not find them so pleasant as that first day after her engagement. There was something in her lover's manner—something which at first she could not define—which by degrees seemed to grate against her feelings. He was sufficiently affectionate, that being a matter on which she did not require much demonstration; but joined to his affection there seemed to be——; she hardly liked to suggest to herself a harsh word, but could it be possible that he was beginning to think that she was not good enough for him? And then she asked herself the question—was she good enough for him? If there were doubt about that, the match should be broken off, though she tore her own heart out in the struggle. The truth, however, was this—that he had begun that teaching which he had already found to be so necessary. Now, had any one essayed to teach Patience German or mathematics, with that young lady's free consent, I believe that she would have been found a meek scholar. But it was not probable that she would be meek when she found a self-appointed tutor teaching her manners and conduct without her consent.

So matters went on for four or five days, and on the evening of the fifth day, Captain Broughton and his aunt drank tea at the

parsonage. Nothing very especial occurred; but as the parson and
Miss Le Smyrger insisted on playing backgammon with devoted
perseverance during the whole evening, Broughton had a good
opportunity of saying a word or two about those changes in his
lady-love which a life in London would require—and some word
he said also—some single slight word as to the higher station in
life to which he would exalt his bride. Patience bore it—for her
father and Miss Le Smyrger were in the room—she bore it well,
speaking no syllable of anger, and enduring, for the moment, the
implied scorn of the old parsonage. Then the evening broke up,
and Captain Broughton walked back to Oxney Combe with his
aunt. "Patty," her father said to her before they went to bed, "he
seems to me to be a most excellent young man." "Dear papa," she
answered, kissing him. "And terribly deep in love," said Mr.
Woolsworthy. "Oh, I don't know about that," she answered, as
she left him with her sweetest smile. But though she could thus
smile at her father's joke, she had already made up her mind that
there was still something to be learned as to her promised husband
before she could place herself altogether in his hands. She would
ask him whether he thought himself liable to injury from this
proposed marriage; and though he should deny any such thought,
she would know from the manner of his denial what his true feelings were.

And he, too, on that night, during his silent walk with Miss Le
Smyrger, had entertained some similar thoughts. "I fear she is obstinate," he had said to himself, and then he had half accused her of
being sullen also. "If that be her temper, what a life of misery I have
before me!"

"Have you fixed a day yet?" his aunt asked him as they came
near to her house.

"No, not yet: I don't know whether it will suit me to fix it before I leave."

"Why, it was but the other day you were in such a hurry."

"Ah—yes—I have thought more about it since then."

"I should have imagined that this would depend on what Patty
thinks," said Miss Le Smyrger, standing up for the privileges of her
sex. "It is presumed that the gentleman is always ready as soon the
lady will consent."

"Yes, in ordinary cases it is so; but when a girl is taken out of her
own sphere—"

"Her own sphere! Let me caution you, Master John, not to talk to Patty about her own sphere."

"Aunt Penelope, as Patience is to be my wife and not yours, I must claim permission to speak to her on such subjects as may seem suitable to me." And then they parted—not in the best humour with each other.

On the following day Captain Broughton and Miss Woolsworthy did not meet till the evening. She had said, before those few ill-omened words had passed her lover's lips, that she would probably be at Miss Le Smyrger's house on the following morning. Those ill-omened words did pass her lover's lips, and then she remained at home. This did not come from sullenness, nor even from anger, but from a conviction that it would be well that she should think much before she met him again. Nor was he anxious to hurry a meeting. His thought—his base thought—was this; that she would be sure to come up to the Combe after him; but she did not come, and therefore in the evening he went down to her, and asked her to walk with him.

They went away by the path that led to Helpholme, and little was said between them till they had walked some miles together. Patience, as she went along the path, remembered almost to the letter the sweet words which had greeted her ears as she came down that way with him on the night of his arrival; but he remembered nothing of that sweetness then. Had he not made an ass of himself during these last six months? That was the thought which very much had possession of his mind.

"Patience," he said at last, having hitherto spoken only an indifferent word now and again since they had left the parsonage, "Patience, I hope you realise the importance of the step which you and I are about to take?"

"Of course I do," she answered: "what an odd question that is for you to ask!"

"Because," said he, "sometimes I almost doubt it. It seems to me as though you thought you could remove yourself from here to your new home with no more trouble than when you go from home up to the Combe."

"Is that meant for a reproach, John?"

"No, not for a reproach, but for advice. Certainly not for a reproach."

"I am glad of that."

"But I should wish to make you think how great is the leap in the world which you are about to take." Then again they walked on for many steps before she answered him.

"Tell me then, John," she said, when she had sufficiently considered what words she would speak; and as she spoke a bright colour suffused her face, and her eyes flashed almost with anger. "What leap do you mean? Do you mean a leap upwards?"

"Well, yes; I hope it will be so."

"In one sense, certainly, it would be a leap upwards. To be the wife of the man I loved; to have the privilege of holding his happiness in my hand; to know that I was his own—the companion whom he had chosen out of all the world—that would, indeed, be a leap upwards; a leap almost to heaven, if all that were so. But if you mean upwards in any other sense——"

"I was thinking of the social scale."

"Then, Captain Broughton, your thoughts were doing me dishonour."

"Doing you dishonour!"

"Yes, doing me dishonour. That your father is, in the world's esteem, a greater man than mine is doubtless true enough. That you, as a man, are richer than I am as a woman, is doubtless also true. But you dishonour me, and yourself also, if these things can weigh with you now."

"Patience,—I think you can hardly know what words you are saying to me."

"Pardon me, but I think I do. Nothing that you can give me—no gifts of that description—can weigh aught against that which I am giving you. If you had all the wealth and rank of the greatest lord in the land, it would count as nothing in such a scale. If—as I have not doubted—if in return for my heart you have given me yours, then—then—then you have paid me fully. But when gifts such as those are going, nothing else can count even as a make-weight."

"I do not quite understand you," he answered, after a pause. "I fear you are a little high-flown." And then, while the evening was still early, they walked back to the parsonage almost without another word.

Captain Broughton at this time had only one full day more to remain at Oxney Colne. On the afternoon following that he was to go as far as Exeter, and thence return to London. Of course, it was to be expected that the wedding day would be fixed before he went, and much had been said about it during the first day or two of his engagement. Then he had pressed for an early time, and Patience, with a girl's usual diffidence, had asked for some little delay. But now nothing was said on the subject; and how was it probable that such a matter could be settled after such a conversation as that which I have related? That evening, Miss Le Smyrger asked whether the day had been fixed. "No," said Captain Broughton harshly; "nothing has been fixed." "But it will be arranged before you go." "Probably not," he said; and then he subject was dropped for the time.

"John," she said, just before she went to bed, "if there be anything wrong between you and Patience, I conjure you to tell me."

"You had better ask her," he replied. "I can tell you nothing."

On the following morning he was much surprised by seeing Patience on the gravel path before Miss Le Smyrger's gate immediately after breakfast. He went to the door to open it for her, and she, as she gave him her hand, told him that she came up to speak to him. There was no hesitation in her manner, nor any look of anger in her face. But there was in her gait and form, in her voice and countenance, a fixedness of purpose which he had never seen before, or at any rate had never acknowledged.

"Certainly," said he. "Shall I come out with you, or will you come up stairs?"

"We can sit down in the summer-house," she said; and thither they both went.

"Captain Broughton," she said—and she began her task the moment that they were both seated—"You and I have engaged ourselves as man and wife, but perhaps we have been over rash."

"How so?" said he.

"It may be—and indeed I will say more—it is the case that we have made this engagement without knowing enough of each other's character."

"I have not thought so."

"The time will perhaps come when you will so think, but for the sake of all that we most value, let it come before it is too late. What would be our fate—how terrible would be our misery—if such a thought should come to either of us after we have linked our lots together."

There was a solemnity about her as she thus spoke which almost repressed him,—which for a time did prevent him from taking that tone of authority which on such a subject he would choose to adopt. But he recovered himself. "I hardly think that this comes well from you," he said.

"From whom else should it come? Who else can fight my battle for me; and, John, who else can fight that same battle on your behalf? I tell you this, that with your mind standing towards me as it does stand at present, you could not give me your hand at the altar with true words and a happy conscience. Am I not true? You have half repented of your bargain already. Is it not so?"

He did not answer her; but getting up from his seat walked to the front of the summer-house, and stood there with his back turned upon her. It was not that he meant to be ungracious, but in truth he did not know how to answer her. He had half repented of his bargain.

"John," she said, getting up and following him, so that she could put her hand upon his arm, "I have been very angry with you."

"Angry with me!" he said, turning sharp upon her.

"Yes, angry with you. You would have treated me like a child. But that feeling has gone now. I am not angry now. There is my hand;—the hand of a friend. Let the words that have been spoken between us be as though they had not been spoken. Let us both be free."

"Do you mean it?" he asked.

"Certainly I mean it." As she spoke these words her eyes were filled with tears, in spite of all the efforts she could make; but he was not looking at her, and her efforts had sufficed to prevent any sob from being audible.

"With all my heart," he said; and it was manifest from his tone that he had no thought of her happiness as he spoke. It was true that she had been angry with him—angry, as she had herself declared; but nevertheless, in what she had said and what she had done, she had thought more of his happiness than of her own. Now she was angry once again.

"With all your heart, Captain Broughton! Well, so be it. If with all your heart, then is the necessity so much the greater. You go tomorrow. Shall we say farewell now?"

"Patience, I am not going to be lectured."

"Certainly not by me. Shall we say farewell now?"

"Yes, if you are determined."

"I am determined. Farewell, Captain Broughton. You have all my wishes for your happiness." And she held out her hand to him.

"Patience!" he said. And he looked at her with a dark frown, as though he would strive to frighten her into submission. If so, he might have saved himself any such attempt.

"Farewell, Captain Broughton. Give me your hand, for I cannot stay." He gave her his hand, hardly knowing why he did so. She lifted it to her lips and kissed it, and then, leaving him, passed from the summer-house down through the wicket-gate, and straight home to the parsonage.

During the whole of that day she said no word to anyone of what had occurred. When she was once more at home she went about her household affairs as she had done on that day of his arrival. When she sat down to dinner with her father he observed nothing to make him think that she was unhappy; nor during the evening was there any expression in her face, or any tone in her voice, which excited his attention. On the following morning Captain Broughton called at the parsonage, and the servant-girl brought word to her mistress that he was in the parlour. But she would not see him. "Laws, miss, you ain't a quarrelled with your beau?" the poor girl said. "No, not quarrelled," she said; "but give him that." It was a scrap of paper, containing a word or two in pencil. "It is better that we should not meet again. God bless you." And from that day to this, now more than ten years, they never have met.

"Papa," she said to her father that afternoon, "dear papa, do not be angry with me. It is all over between me and John Broughton. Dearest, you and I will not be separated."

It would be useless here to tell how great was the old man's surprise and how true his sorrow. As the tale was told to him no cause was given for anger with anyone. Not a word was spoken against the suitor who had on that day returned to London with a full conviction that now at least he was relieved from his engagement. "Patty, my darling child," he said, "may God grant that it be for the best!"

"It is for the best," she answered stoutly. "For this place I am fit; and I much doubt whether I am fit for any other."

On that day she did not see Miss Le Smyrger, but on the following morning, knowing that Captain Broughton had gone off, having heard the wheels of the carriage as they passed by the parsonage gate on his way to the station,—she walked up to the Combe.

"He has told you, I suppose?" said she.

"Yes," said Miss Le Smyrger. "And I will never see him again unless he asks your pardon on his knees. I have told him so. I would not even give him my hand as he went."

"But why so, thou kindest one? The fault was mine more than his."

"I understand. I have eyes in my head," said the old maid. "I have watched him for the last four or five days. If you could have kept the truth to yourself and bade him keep off from you, he would have been at your feet now, licking the dust from your shoes."

"But, dear friend, I do not want a man to lick dust from my shoes."

"Ah, you are a fool. You do not know the value of your own wealth."

"True; I have been a fool. I was a fool to think that one coming from such a life as he has led could be happy with such as I am. I know the truth now. I have bought the lesson dearly,—but perhaps not too dearly, seeing that it will never be forgotten."

There was but little more said about the matter between our three friends at Oxney Colne. What, indeed, could be said? Miss Le Smyrger for a year or two still expected that her nephew would return and claim his bride; but he has never done so, nor has there been any correspondence between them. Patience Woolsworthy had learned her lesson dearly. She had given her whole heart to the man; and, though she so bore herself that no one was aware of the violence of the struggle, nevertheless the struggle within her bosom was very violent. She never told herself that she had done wrong; she never regretted her loss; but yet—yet!—the loss was very hard to bear. He also had loved her, but he was not capable of a love which could much injure his daily peace. Her daily peace was gone for many a day to come.

Her father is still living; but there is a curate now in the parish. In conjunction with him and with Miss Le Smyrger she spends her time in the concerns of the parish. In her own eyes she is a confirmed old maid; and such is my opinion also. The romance of her life was played out in that summer. She never sits now lonely on the hill-side thinking how much she might do for one whom she really loved. But with a large heart she loves many, and, with no romance, she works hard to lighten the burdens of those she loves.

As for Captain Broughton, all the world knows that he did marry that great heiress with whom his name was once before connected, and that he is now a useful member of Parliament, working on committees three or four days a week with a zeal that is indefatigable. Sometimes, not often, as he thinks of Patience Woolsworthy, a gratified smile comes across his face.

THE SPOTTED DOG

PART I. THE ATTEMPT

SOME FEW YEARS since we received the following letter;—

"DEAR SIR,

"I write to you for literary employment, and I implore you to provide me with it if it be within your power to do so. My capacity for such work is not small, and my acquirements are considerable. My need is very great, and my views in regard to remuneration are modest. I was educated at——, and was afterwards a scholar of——College, Cambridge. I left the university without a degree, in consequence of a quarrel with the college tutor. I was rusticated, and not allowed to return. After that I became for awhile a student for the Chancery Bar. I then lived for some years in Paris, and I understand and speak French as though it were my own language. For all purposes of literature I am equally conversant with German. I read Italian. I am, of course, familiar with Latin. In regard to Greek I will only say that I am less ignorant of it than nineteen-twentieths of our national scholars. I am well read in modern and ancient history. I have especially studied political economy. I have not neglected other matters necessary to the education of an enlightened man,—unless it be natural philosophy. I can write English, and can write it with rapidity. I am a poet;—at least, I so esteem myself. I am not a believer. My character will not bear investigation;—in saying which, I mean you to understand, not that I steal or cheat, but that I live in a dirty lodging, spend many of my hours in a public-house, and cannot pay tradesmen's bills where tradesmen have been found to trust me. I have a wife and four children,—which burden forbids me to free myself from all care by a bare bodkin. I am just past forty, and since I quarrelled with my family because I could not understand The Trinity, I have never been the owner of a ten-pound note. My wife was not a lady. I married her because I was determined to take refuge from the conventional thraldom of so-called "gentlemen" amidst the liberty of the lower orders. My life, of course, has been a mistake. Indeed, to live at all,—is it not a folly?

"I am at present employed on the staff of two or three of the "Penny Dreadfuls." Your august highness in literature has perhaps never heard of a "Penny Dreadful." I write for them matter, which we among ourselves call "blood and nastiness,"—and which is copied from one to another. For this I am paid forty-five shillings a week. For thirty shillings a week I will do any work that you may impose upon me for the term of six months. I write this letter as a last effort to rescue myself from the filth of my present position, but I entertain no hope of any success. If you ask it I will come and see you; but do not send for me unless you mean to employ me, as I am ashamed of myself. I live at No. 3, Cucumber Court, Gray's Inn Lane;—but if you write, address to the care of Mr. Grimes, the Spotted Dog, Liquorpond Street. Now I have told you my whole life, and you may help me if you will. I do not expect an answer.

"Yours truly,
"JULIUS MACKENZIE."

Indeed he had told us his whole life, and what a picture of a life he had drawn! There was something in the letter which compelled attention. It was impossible to throw it, half read, into the waste-paper basket, and to think of it not at all. We did read it, probably twice, and then put ourselves to work to consider how much of it might be true and how much false. Had the man been a boy at——, and then a scholar of his college? We concluded that, so far, the narrative was true. Had he abandoned his dependence on wealthy friends from conscientious scruples, as he pretended; or had other and less creditable reasons caused the severance? On that point we did not quite believe him. And then, as to those assertions made by himself in regard to his own capabilities,—how far did they gain credence with us? We think that we believed them all, making some small discount,—with the exception of that one in which he proclaimed himself to be a poet. A man may know whether he understands French, and be quite ignorant whether the rhymed lines which he produces are or are not poetry. When he told us that he was an infidel, and that his character would not bear investigation, we went with him altogether. His allusion to suicide we regarded as a foolish boast. We gave him credit for the four children, but were not certain about the wife. We quite believed the general assertion of his impecuniosity. That stuff about "conventional thraldom" we hope we took at its worth. When he told us that his life had been a mistake he spoke to us Gospel truth.

Of the "Penny Dreadfuls," and of "blood and nastiness," so called, we had never before heard, but we did not think it remarkable that a man so gifted as our correspondent should earn forty-five shillings a week by writing for the cheaper periodicals. It did not, however, appear to us probable that any one so remunerated would be willing to leave that engagement for another which should give him only thirty shillings. When he spoke of the "filth of his present position," our heart began to bleed for him. We know what it is so well, and can fathom so accurately the degradation of the educated man who, having been ambitious in the career of literature, falls into that slough of despond by which the profession of literature is almost surrounded. There we were with him, as brothers together. When we came to Mr. Grimes and the Spotted Dog, in Liquorpond Street, we thought that we had better refrain from answering the letter,—by which decision on our part he would not, according to his own statement, be much disappointed. Mr. Julius Mackenzie! Perhaps at this very time rich uncles and aunts were buttoning up their pockets against the sinner because of his devotion to the Spotted Dog. There are well-to-do people among the Mackenzies. It might be the case that that heterodox want of comprehension in regard to The Trinity was the cause of it; but we have observed that in most families, grievous as are doubts upon such sacred subjects, they are not held to be cause of hostility so invincible as is a thorough-going devotion to a Spotted Dog. If the Spotted Dog had brought about these troubles, any interposition from ourselves would be useless.

For twenty-four hours we had given up all idea of answering the letter; but it then occurred to us that men who have become disreputable as drunkards do not put forth their own abominations when making appeals for aid. If this man were really given to drink he would hardly have told us of his association with the public-house. Probably he was much at the Spotted Dog, and hated himself for being there. The more we thought of it the more we fancied that the gist of his letter might be true. It seemed that the man had desired to tell the truth as he himself believed it.

It so happened that at that time we had been asked to provide an index to a certain learned manuscript in three volumes. The intended publisher of the work had already procured an index from a professional compiler of such matters; but the thing had been so badly done that it could not be used. Some knowledge of the classics was required, though it was not much more than a familiarity with the names of Latin and Greek authors, to which perhaps should be added some acquaintance, with the names also, of the better-known editors and commentators. The gentleman who had had the task in hand had failed conspicuously, and I had been told by my enterprising friend Mr. X——, the publisher, that £25 would be freely paid on the proper accomplishment of the undertaking. The work, apparently so trifling in its nature, de-manded a scholar's acquirements, and could hardly be completed in less than two months. We had snubbed the offer, saying that we should be ashamed to ask an educated man to give his time and labour for so small a remuneration;—but to Mr. Julius Mackenzie £25 for two months' work would manifestly be a godsend. If Mr. Julius Mackenzie did in truth possess the knowledge for which he gave himself credit; if he was, as he said, "familiar with Latin," and was "less ignorant of Greek than nineteen-twentieths of our na-tional scholars," he might perhaps be able to earn this £25. We certainly knew no one else who could and who would do the work properly for that money. We therefore wrote to Mr. Julius Mackenzie, and requested his presence. Our note was short, cau-tious, and also courteous. We regretted that a man so gifted should be driven by stress of circumstances to such need. We could undertake nothing, but if it would not put him to too much trouble to call upon us, we might perhaps be able to suggest something to him. Precisely at the hour named Mr. Julius Mackenzie came to us.

We well remember his appearance, which was one unutterably painful to behold. He was a tall man, very thin,—thin we might say as a whipping-post, were it not that one's idea of a whipping-post conveys erectness and rigidity, whereas this man, as he stood before us, was full of bends, and curves, and crookedness. His big head seemed to lean forward over his miserably narrow chest. His back was bowed, and his legs were crooked and tottering. He had told us that he was over forty, but we doubted, and doubt now, whether he had not added something to his years, in order partially to excuse the wan, worn weariness of his countenance. He carried an infinity of thick, ragged, wild, dirty hair, dark in colour, though not black, which age had not yet begun to grizzle. He wore a miserable attempt at a beard, stubbly, uneven, and half shorn,—as though it had been cut down within an inch of his chin with blunt scissors. He had two ugly projecting teeth, and his cheeks were hollow. His eyes were deep-set, but very bright, illuminating his whole face; so that it was impossible to look at him and to think him to be one wholly insignificant. His eyebrows were large and shaggy, but well formed, not meeting across the brow, with single, stiffly-projecting hairs,—a pair of eyebrows which added much strength to his countenance. His nose was long and well shaped,—but red as a huge carbuncle. The moment we saw him we connected that nose with the Spotted Dog. It was not a blotched nose, not a nose covered with many carbuncles, but a brightly red, smooth, well-formed nose, one glowing carbuncle in itself. He was dressed in a long brown great-coat, which was buttoned up round his throat, and which came nearly to his feet. The binding of the coat was frayed, the buttons were half uncovered, the button-holes were tattered, the velvet collar had become party-coloured with dirt and usage. It was in the month of December, and a great-coat was needed; but this great-coat looked as though it were worn because other garments were not at his command. Not an inch of linen or even of flannel shirt was visible. Below his coat we could only see his broken boots and the soiled legs of his trousers, which had reached that age which in trousers defies description. When we looked at him we could not but ask ourselves whether this man had been born a gentleman and was still a scholar. And yet there was that in his face which prompted us to believe the account he had given of himself. As we looked at him we felt sure that he possessed keen intellect, and that he was too much of a man to boast of acquirements which he did not believe himself to possess. We shook hands with him, asked him to sit down, and murmured something of our sorrow that he should be in distress.

"I am pretty well used to it," said he. There was nothing mean in his voice;—there was indeed a touch of humour in it, and in his manner there was nothing of the abjectness of supplication. We had his letter in our hands, and we read a portion of it again as he sat opposite to us. We then remarked that we did not understand how he, having a wife and family dependent on him, could offer to give up a third of his income with the mere object of changing the nature of his work. "You don't know what it is," said he, "to write for the 'Penny Dreadfuls.' I'm at it seven hours a day, and hate the very words that I write. I cursed myself afterwards for sending that letter. I know that to hope is to be an ass. But I did send it, and here I am."

We looked at his nose and felt that we must be careful before we suggested to our learned friend Dr.——to put his manuscript into the hands of Mr. Julius Mackenzie. If it had been a printed book the attempt might have been made without much hazard, but our friend's work, which was elaborate, and very learned, had not yet reached the honours of the printing-house. We had had our own doubts whether it might ever assume the form of a real book; but our friend, who was a wealthy as well as a learned man, was, as yet, very determined. He desired, at any rate, that the thing should be perfected, and his publisher had therefore come to us offering £25 for the codification and index. Were anything other than good to befall his manuscript, his lamentations would be loud, not on his own score,—but on behalf of learning in general. It behoved us therefore to be cautious. We pretended to read the letter again, in order that we might gain time for a decision, for we were greatly frightened by that gleaming nose.

Let the reader understand that the nose was by no means Bardolphian. If we have read Shakespeare aright Bardolph's nose was a thing of terror from its size as well as its hue. It was a mighty vat, into which had ascended all the divinest particles distilled from the cellars of the hostelrie in Eastcheap. Such at least is the idea which stage representations have left upon all our minds. But the nose now before us was a well-formed nose, would have been a commanding nose,—for the power of command shows itself much in the nasal organ,—had it not been for its colour. While we were thinking of this, and doubting much as to our friend's manuscript, Mr. Mackenzie interrupted us. "You think I am a drunkard," said he. The man's mother-wit had enabled him to read our inmost thoughts.

As we looked up the man had risen from his chair, and was standing over us. He loomed upon us very tall, although his legs were crooked, and his back bent. Those piercing eyes, and that nose which almost assumed an air of authority as he carried it, were a great way above us. There seemed to be an infinity of that old brown great-coat. He had divined our thoughts, and we did not dare to contradict him. We felt that a weak, vapid, unmanly smile was creeping over our face. We were smiling as a man smiles who intends to imply some contemptuous assent with the self-depreciating comment of his companion. Such a mode of expression is in our estimation most cowardly, and most odious. We had not intended it, but we knew that the smile had pervaded us. "Of course you do," said he. "I was a drunkard, but I am not one now. It doesn't matter;—only I wish you hadn't sent for me. I'll go away at once."

So saying, he was about to depart, but we stopped him. We assured him with much energy that we did not mean to offend him. He protested that there was no offence. He was too well used to that kind of thing to be made "more than wretched by it." Such was his heart breaking phrase. "As for anger, I've lost all that long ago. Of course you take me for a drunkard, and I should still be a drunkard, only——"

"Only what?" I asked.

"It don't matter," said he. "I need not trouble you with more than I have said already. You haven't got anything for me to do, I suppose?" Then I explained to him that I had something he might do, if I could venture to entrust him with the work. With some trouble I got him to sit down again, and to listen while I explained to him the circumstances. I had been grievously afflicted when he alluded to his former habit of drinking,—a former habit as he himself now stated,—but I entertained no hesitation in raising questions as to his erudition. I felt almost assured that his answers would be satisfactory, and that no discomfiture would arise from such questioning. We were quickly able to perceive that we at any rate could not examine him in classical literature. As soon as we mentioned the name and nature of the work he went off at score, and satisfied us amply that he was familiar at least with the title-pages of editions. We began, indeed, to fear whether he might not be too caustic a critic on our own friend's performance. "Dr.——is only an amateur himself," said we, deprecating in advance any such exercise of the red-nosed man's too severe erudition. "We never get much beyond dilettanteism here," said he, "as far as Greek and Latin are concerned." What a terrible man he would have been could he have got upon the staff of the *Saturday Review*, instead of going to the Spotted Dog!

We endeavoured to bring the interview to an end by telling him that we would consult the learned Doctor from whom the manuscript had emanated; and we hinted that a reference would be of course acceptable. His impudence,—or perhaps we should rather call it his straightforward sincere audacity,—was unbounded. "Mr. Grimes of the Spotted Dog knows me better than any one else," said he. We blew the breath out of our mouth with astonishment. "I'm not asking you to go to him to find out whether I know Latin and Greek," said Mr. Mackenzie. "You must find that out for yourself." We assured him that we thought we had found that out. "But he can tell you that I won't pawn your manuscript." The man was so grim and brave that he almost frightened us. We hinted, however, that literary reference should be given. The gentleman who paid him forty-five shillings a week,—the manager, in short, of the "Penny Dreadful,"—might tell us something of him. Then he wrote for us a name on a scrap of paper, and added to it an address in the close vicinity of Fleet Street, at which we remembered to have seen the title of a periodical which we now knew to be a "Penny Dreadful."

Before he took his leave he made us a speech, again standing up over us, though we also were on our legs. It was that bend in his neck, combined with his natural height, which gave him such an air of superiority in conversation. He seemed to overshadow us, and to have his own way with us, because he was enabled to look down upon us. There was a footstool on our hearth-rug, and we remember to have attempted to stand upon that, in order that we might escape this supervision; but we stumbled, and had to kick it from us, and something was added to our sense of inferiority by this little failure. "I don't expect much from this," he said. "I never do expect much. And I have misfortunes independent of my poverty which make it impossible that I should be other than a miserable wretch."

"Bad health?" we asked.

"No;—nothing absolutely personal;—but never mind. I must not trouble you with more of my history. But if you can do this thing for me, it may be the means of redeeming me from utter degradation." We then assured him that we would do our best, and he left us with a promise that he would call again on that day week.

The first step which we took on his behalf was one the very idea of which had at first almost moved us to ridicule. We made inquiry respecting Mr. Julius Mackenzie, of Mr. Grimes, the landlord of the Spotted Dog. Though Mr. Grimes did keep the Spotted Dog, he might be a man of sense and, possibly, of conscience. At any rate he would tell us something, or confirm our doubts by refusing to tell us anything. We found Mr. Grimes seated in a very neat little back parlour, and were peculiarly taken by the appearance of a lady in a little cap and black silk gown, whom we soon found to be Mrs. Grimes. Had we ventured to employ our intellect in personifying for ourselves an imaginary Mrs. Grimes as the landlady of a Spotted Dog public-house in Liquorpond Street, the figure we should have built up for ourselves would have been the very opposite of that which this lady presented to us. She was slim, and young, and pretty, and had pleasant little tricks of words, in spite of occasional slips in her grammar, which made us almost think that it might be our duty to come very often to the Spotted Dog to inquire about Mr. Julius Mackenzie. Mr. Grimes was a man about forty,—fully ten years the senior of his wife,—with a clear grey eye, and a mouth and chin from which we surmised that he would be competent to clear the Spotted Dog of unruly visitors after twelve o'clock, whenever it might be his wish to do so. We soon made known our request. Mr. Mackenzie had come to us for literary employment. Could they tell us anything about Mr. Mackenzie?

"He's as clever an author, in the way of writing and that kind of thing, as there is in all London," said Mrs. Grimes with energy. Perhaps her opinion ought not to have been taken for much, but it had its weight. We explained, however, that at the present moment we were specially anxious to know something of the gentleman's character and mode of life. Mr. Grimes, whose manner to us was quite courteous, sat silent, thinking how to answer us. His more impulsive and friendly wife was again ready with her assurance. "There ain't an honester gentleman breathing;—and I say he is a gentleman, though he's that poor he hasn't sometimes a shirt to his back."

"I don't think he's ever very well off for shirts," said Mr. Grimes.

"I wouldn't be slow to give him one of yours, John, only, I know he wouldn't take it," said Mrs. Grimes. "Well now, look here, sir;—we've that feeling for him that our young woman there would draw anything for him he'd ask,—money or no money.

She'd never venture to name money to him if he wanted a glass of anything,—hot or cold, beer or spirits. Isn't that so, John?"

"She's fool enough for anything as far as I know," said Mr. Grimes.

"She ain't no fool at all; and I'd do the same if I was there;—and so'd you, John. There is nothing Mackenzie'd ask as he wouldn't give him," said Mrs. Grimes, pointing with her thumb over her shoulder to her husband, who was standing on the hearth-rug;—"that is, in the way of drawing liquor, and refreshments, and such like. But he never raised a glass to his lips in this house as he didn't pay for, nor yet took a biscuit out of that basket. He's a gentleman all over, is Mackenzie."

It was strong testimony; but still we had not quite got at the bottom of the matter. "Doesn't he raise a great many glasses to his lips?" we asked.

"No he don't," said Mrs. Grimes,—"only in reason."

"He's had misfortunes," said Mr. Grimes.

"Indeed he has," said the lady,—"what I call the very troublesomest of troubles. If you was troubled like him, John, where'd you be?"

"I know where you'd be," said John.

"He's got a bad wife, sir; the worst as ever was," continued Mrs. Grimes. "Talk of drink;—there is nothing that woman wouldn't do for it. She'd pawn the very clothes off her children's back in midwinter to get it. She'd rob the food out of her husband's mouth for a drop of gin. As for herself,—she ain't no woman's notions left of keeping herself any way. She'd as soon be picked out of the gutter as not;—and as for words out of her mouth or clothes on her back, she hasn't got, sir, not an item of a female's feelings left about her."

Mrs. Grimes had been very eloquent, and had painted the "troublesomest of all troubles" with glowing words. This was what the wretched man had come to by marrying a woman who was not a lady in order that he might escape the "conventional thraldom" of gentility! But still the drunken wife was not all. There was the evidence of his own nose against himself, and the additional fact that he had acknowledged himself to have been formerly a drunkard. "I suppose he has drunk, himself?" we said.

"He has drunk, in course," said Mrs. Grimes.

"The world has been pretty rough with him, sir," said Mr. Grimes.

"But he don't drink now," continued the lady. "At least if he do, we don't see it. As for her, she wouldn't show herself inside our door."

"It ain't often that man and wife draws their milk from the same cow," said Mr. Grimes.

"But Mackenzie is here every day of his life," said Mrs. Grimes. "When he's got a sixpence to pay for it, he'll come in here and have a glass of beer and a bit of something to eat. We does make him a little extra welcome, and that's the truth of it. We knows what he is, and we knows what he was. As for book learning, sir;— it don't matter what language it is, it's all as one to him. He knows 'em all round just as I know my catechism."

"Can't you say fairer than that for him, Polly?" asked Mr. Grimes.

"Don't you talk of catechisms, John; nor yet of nothing else as a man ought to set his mind to;—unless it is keeping the Spotted Dog. But as for Mackenzie;—he knows off by heart whole books full of learning. There was some furreners here as come from,—I don't know where it was they come from, only it wasn't France, nor yet Germany, and he talked to them just as though he hadn't been born in England at all. I don't think there ever was such a man for knowing things. He'll go on with poetry out of his own head till you think it comes from him like web from a spider." We could not help thinking of the wonderful companionship which there must have been in that parlour while the reduced man was spinning his web and Mrs. Grimes, with her needlework lying idle in her lap, was sitting by, listening with rapt admiration. In passing by the Spotted Dog one would not imagine such a scene to have its existence within. But then so many things do have existence of which we imagine nothing!

Mr. Grimes ended the interview. "The fact is, sir, if you can give him employment better than what he has now, you'll be helping a man who has seen better days, and who only wants help to see 'em again. He's got it all there," and Mr. Grimes put his finger up to his head.

"He's got it all here too," said Mrs. Grimes, laying her hand upon her heart. Hereupon we took our leave, suggesting to these excellent friends that if it should come to pass that we had further dealings with Mr. Mackenzie we might perhaps trouble them again. They assured us that we should always be welcome, and Mr.

Grimes himself saw us to the door, having made profuse offers of such good cheer as the house afforded. We were upon the whole much taken with the Spotted Dog.

From thence we went to the office of the "Penny Dreadful," in the vicinity of Fleet Street. As we walked thither we could not but think of Mrs. Grimes' words. The troublesomest of troubles! We acknowledged to ourselves that they were true words. Can there be any trouble more troublesome than that of suffering from the shame inflicted by a degraded wife? We had just parted from Mr. Grimes,—not, indeed, having seen very much of him in the course of our interview;—but little as we had seen, we were sure that he was assisted in his position by a buoyant pride in that he called himself the master, and owner, and husband of Mrs. Grimes. In the very step with which he passed in and out of his own door you could see that there was nothing that he was ashamed of about his household. When abroad he could talk of his "missus" with a conviction that the picture which the word would convey to all who heard him would redound to his honour. But what must have been the reflections of Julius Mackenzie when his mind dwelt upon his wife? We remembered the words of his letter. "I have a wife and four children, which burden forbids me to free myself from all care with a bare bodkin." As we thought of them, and of the story which had been told to us at the Spotted Dog, they lost that tone of rhodomontade with which they had invested themselves when we first read them. A wife who is indifferent to being picked out of the gutter, and who will pawn her children's clothes for gin, must be a trouble than which none can be more troublesome.

We did not find that we ingratiated ourselves with the people at the office of the periodical for which Mr. Mackenzie worked; and yet we endeavoured to do so, assuming in our manner and tone something of the familiarity of a common pursuit. After much delay we came upon a gentleman sitting in a dark cupboard, who twisted round his stool to face us while he spoke to us. We believe that he was the editor of more than one "Penny Dreadful," and that as many as a dozen serial novels were being issued to the world at the same time under his supervision. "Oh!" said he, "so you're at that game, are you?" We assured him that we were at no game at all, but were simply influenced by a desire to assist a distressed scholar. "That be blowed," said our brother. "Mackenzie's doing as well here as he'll do anywhere. He's a drunken blackguard, when all's said and done. So you're going to buy him up, are you? You won't keep him long,—and then he'll have to starve." We assured the gentleman that we had no desire to buy up Mr. Mackenzie; we explained our ideas as to the freedom of the literary profession, in accordance with which Mr. Mackenzie could not be wrong in applying to us for work; and we especially deprecated any severity on our brother's part towards the man, more especially begging that nothing might be decided, as we were far from thinking it certain that we could provide Mr. Mackenzie with any literary employment. "That's all right," said our brother, twisting back his stool. "He can't work for both of us;—that's all. He has his bread here regular, week after week; and I don't suppose you'll do as much as that for him." Then we went away, shaking the dust off our feet, and wondering much at the great development of literature which latter years have produced. We had not even known of the existence of these papers;—and yet there they were, going forth into the hands of hundreds of thousands of readers, all of whom were being, more or less, instructed in their modes of life and manner of thinking by the stories which were thus brought before them.

But there might be truth in what our brother had said to us. Should Mr. Mackenzie abandon his present engagement for the sake of the job which we proposed to put in his hands, might he not thereby injure rather than improve his prospects? We were acquainted with only one learned doctor desirous of having his manuscripts codified and indexed at his own expense. As for writing for the periodical with which we were connected, we knew enough of the business to be aware that Mr. Mackenzie's gifts of erudition would very probably not so much assist him in attempting such work as would his late training act against him. A man might be able to read and even talk a dozen languages,—"just as though he hadn't been born in England at all,"—and yet not write the language with which we dealt after the fashion which suited our readers. It might be that he would fly much above our heads, and do work infinitely too big for us. We did not regard our own heads as being very high. But, for such altitude as they held, a certain class of writing was adapted. The gentleman whom we had just left would require, no doubt, altogether another style. It was probable that Mr. Mackenzie had already fitted himself to his present audience. And, even were it not so, we could not promise him forty-five shillings a week, or even that thirty shillings for which he asked. There is nothing more dangerous than the attempt to be-friend a man in middle life by transplanting him from one soil to another.

When Mr. Mackenzie came to us again we endeavoured to explain all this to him. We had in the meantime seen our friend the Doctor, whose beneficence of spirit in regard to the unfortunate man of letters was extreme. He was charmed with our account of the man, and saw with his mind's eye the work, for the performance of which he was pining, perfected in a manner that would be a blessing to the scholars of all future ages. He was at first anxious to ask Julius Mackenzie down to his rectory, and, even after we had explained to him that this would not at present be expedient, was full of a dream of future friendship with a man who would be able to discuss the digamma with him, who would have studied Greek metres, and have an opinion of his own as to Porson's canon. We were in possession of the manuscript, and had our friend's authority for handing it over to Mr. Mackenzie.

He came to us according to appointment, and his nose seemed to be redder than ever. We thought that we discovered a discouraging flavour of spirits in his breath. Mrs. Grimes had declared that he drank,—only in reason; but the ideas of the wife of a publican,—even though that wife were Mrs. Grimes,—might be very different from our own as to what was reasonable in that matter. And as we looked at him he seemed to be more rough, more ragged, almost more wretched than before. It might be that, in taking his part with my brother of the "Penny Dreadful," with the Doctor, and even with myself in thinking over his claims, I had endowed him with higher qualities than I had been justified in giving to him. As I considered him and his appearance I certainly could not assure myself that he looked like a man worthy to be trusted. A policeman, seeing him at a street corner, would have had an eye upon him in a moment. He rubbed himself together within his old coat, as men do when they come out of gin-shops. His eye was as bright as before, but we thought that his mouth was meaner, and his nose redder. We were almost disenchanted with him. We said nothing to him at first about the Spotted Dog, but suggested to him our fears that if he undertook work at our hands he would lose the much more permanent employment which he got from the gentleman whom we had seen in the cupboard. We then explained to him that we could promise to him no continuation of employment.

The violence with which he cursed the gentleman who had sat in the cupboard appalled us, and had, we think, some effect in bringing back to us that feeling of respect for him which we had almost lost. It may be difficult to explain why we respected him because he cursed and swore horribly. We do not like cursing and swearing, and were any of our younger contributors to indulge themselves after that fashion in our presence we should, at the very least,—frown upon them. We did not frown upon Julius Mackenzie, but stood up, gazing into his face above us, again feeling that the man was powerful. Perhaps we respected him because he was not in the least afraid of us. He went on to assert that he cared not,—not a straw, we will say,—for the gentleman in the cupboard. He knew the gentleman in the cupboard very well; and the gentleman in the cupboard knew him. As long as he took his work to the gentleman in the cupboard, the gentleman in the cupboard would be only too happy to purchase that work at the rate of sixpence for a page of manuscript containing two hundred and fifty words. That was his rate of payment for prose fiction, and at that rate he could earn forty-five shillings a week. He wasn't afraid of the gentleman in the cupboard. He had had some words with the gentleman in the cupboard before now, and they two understood each other very well. He hinted, moreover, that there were other gentlemen in other cupboards; but with none of them could he advance beyond forty-five shillings a week. For this he had to sit, with his pen in his hand, seven hours seven days a week, and the very paper, pens, and ink came to fifteenpence out of the money. He had struck for wages once, and for a halcyon month or two had carried his point of sevenpence halfpenny a page; but the gentlemen in the cupboards had told him that it could not be. They, too, must live. His matter was no doubt attractive; but any price above sixpence a page unfitted it for their market. All this Mr. Julius Mackenzie explained to us with much violence of expression. When I named Mrs. Grimes to him the tone of his voice was altered. "Yes;" said he,—"I thought they'd say a word for me. They're the best friends I've got now. I don't know that you ought quite to believe her, for I think she'd perhaps tell a lie to do me a service." We assured him that we did believe every word Mrs. Grimes had said to us.

After much pausing over the matter we told him that we were empowered to trust him with our friend's work, and the manuscript was produced upon the table. If he would undertake the work and perform it, he should be paid £8 6s. 8d. for each of the three volumes as they were completed. And we undertook, moreover, on our own responsibility, to advance him money in small amounts through the hands of Mrs. Grimes, if he really settled himself to the task. At first he was in ecstasies, and, as we explained to him the way in which the index should be brought out and the codification performed, he turned over the pages rapidly, and showed us that he understood at any rate the nature of the work to be done. But when we came to details he was less happy. In what workshop was this new work to be performed? There was a moment in which we almost thought of telling him to do the work in our own room; but we hesitated, luckily, remembering that his continual presence with us for two or three months would probably destroy us altogether. It appeared that his present work was done sometimes at the Spotted Dog, and sometimes at home in his lodgings. He said not a word to us about his wife, but we could understand that there would be periods in which to work at home would be impossible to him. He did not pretend to deny that there might be danger on that score, nor did he ask permission to take the entire manuscript at once away to his abode. We knew that if he took part he must take the whole, as the work could not be done in parts. Counter references would be needed. "My circumstances are bad;—very bad indeed," he said. We expressed the great trouble to which we should be subjected if any evil should happen to the manuscript. "I will give it up," he said, towering over us again, and shaking his head. "I cannot expect that I should be trusted." But we were determined that it should not be given up. Sooner than give the matter up we would make some arrangement by hiring a place in which he might work. Even though we were to pay ten shillings a week for a room for him out of the money, the bargain would be a good one for him. At last we determined that we would pay a second visit to the Spotted Dog, and consult Mrs. Grimes. We felt that we should have a pleasure in arranging together with Mrs. Grimes any scheme of benevolence on behalf of this unfortunate and remarkable man. So we told him that we would think over the matter, and send a letter to his address at the Spotted Dog, which he should receive on the following morning. He then gathered himself up, rubbed himself together again inside his coat, and took his departure.

As soon as he was gone we sat looking at the learned Doctor's manuscript, and thinking of what we had done. There lay the work of years, by which our dear and venerable old friend expected that he would take rank among the great commentators of modern times. We, in truth, did not anticipate for him all the glory to which he looked forward. We feared that there might be disappointment. Hot discussion on verbal accuracies or on rules of metre are perhaps not so much in vogue now as they were a hundred years ago. There might be disappointment and great sorrow; but we could not with equanimity anticipate the prevention of this sorrow by the possible loss or destruction of the manuscript which had been entrusted to us. The Doctor himself had seemed to anticipate no such danger. When we told him of Mackenzie's learning and misfortunes, he was eager at once that the thing should be done, merely stipulating that he should have an interview with Mr. Mackenzie before he returned to his rectory.

That same day we went to the Spotted Dog, and found Mrs. Grimes alone. Mackenzie had been there immediately after leaving our room, and had told her what had taken place. She was full of the subject and anxious to give every possible assistance. She confessed at once that the papers would not be safe in the rooms inhabited by Mackenzie and his wife. "He pays five shillings a week," she said, "for a wretched place round in Cucumber Court. They are all huddled together, any way; and how he manages to do a thing at all there,—in the way of author-work,—is a wonder to everybody. Sometimes he can't, and then he'll sit for hours together at the little table in our tap-room." We went into the tap-room and saw the little table. It was a wonder indeed that any one should be able to compose and write tales of imagination in a place so dreary, dark, and ill-omened. The little table was hardly more than a long slab or plank, perhaps eighteen inches wide. When we visited the place there were two brewers' draymen seated there, and three draggled, wretched-looking women. The carters were eating enormous hunches of bread and bacon, which they cut and put into their mouths slowly, solemnly, and in silence. The three women were seated on a bench, and when I saw them had no signs of festivity before them. It must be presumed that they had paid for something, or they would hardly have been allowed to sit there. "It's empty now," said Mrs. Grimes, taking no immediate notice of the men or of the women; "but sometimes he'll sit writing in that corner, when there's such a jabber of voices as you wouldn't hear a cannon go off over at Reid's, and that thick with smoke you'd a'most cut it with a knife. Don't he, Peter?" The man whom she addressed endeavoured to prepare himself for answer by swallowing at the moment three square inches of bread and bacon, which he had just put into his mouth. He made an awful effort, but failed; and, failing, nodded his head three times. "They all know him here, sir," continued Mrs. Grimes. "He'll go on writing, writing, writing, for hours together; and nobody'll say nothing to him. Will they, Peter?" Peter, who was now half-way through the work he had laid out for himself, muttered some inarticulate grunt of assent.

We then went back to the snug little room inside the bar. It was quite clear to me that the man could not manipulate the Doctor's manuscript, of which he would have to spread a dozen sheets before him at the same time, in the place I had just visited. Even could he have occupied the chamber alone, the accommodation would not have been sufficient for the purpose. It was equally clear that he could not be allowed to use Mrs. Grimes' snuggery. "How are we to get a place for him?" said I, appealing to the lady. "He shall have a place," she said, "I'll go bail; he shan't lose the job for want of a workshop." Then she sat down and began to think it over. I was just about to propose the hiring of some decent room in the neighbourhood, when she made a suggestion, which I acknowledge startled me. "I'll have a big table put into my own bed-room," said she, "and he shall do it there. There ain't another hole or corner about the place as' d suit; and he can lay the gentleman's papers all about on the bed, square and clean and orderly. Can't he now? And I can see after 'em, as he don't lose 'em. Can't I now?"

By this time there had sprung up an intimacy between ourselves and Mrs. Grimes which seemed to justify an expression of the doubt which I then threw on the propriety of such a disarrangement of her most private domestic affairs. "Mr. Grimes will hardly approve of that," we said.

"Oh, John won't mind. What'll it matter to John as long as Mackenzie is out in time for him to go to bed? We ain't early birds, morning or night,—that's true. In our line folks can't be early. But from ten to six there's the room, and he shall have it. Come up and see, sir." So we followed Mrs. Grimes up the narrow staircase to the marital bower. "It ain't large, but there'll be room for the table, and for him to sit at it;—won't there now?"

It was a dark little room, with one small window looking out under the low roof, and facing the heavy high dead wall of the brewery opposite. But it was clean and sweet, and the furniture in it was all solid and good, old-fashioned, and made of mahogany. Two or three of Mrs. Grimes' gowns were laid upon the bed, and other portions of her dress were hung on pegs behind the doors. The only untidy article in the room was a pair of "John's" trousers, which he had failed to put out of sight. She was not a bit abashed, but took them up and folded them and patted them, and laid them in the capacious wardrobe. "We'll have all these things away," she said, "and then he can have all his papers out upon the bed just as he pleases."

We own that there was something in the proposed arrangement which dismayed us. We also were married, and what would our wife have said had we proposed that a contributor,—even a contributor not red-nosed and seething with gin,—that any best-disciplined contributor should be invited to write an article within the precincts of our sanctum? We could not bring ourselves to believe that Mr. Grimes would authorise the proposition. There is something holy about the bed-room of a married couple; and there would be a special desecration in the continued presence of Mr. Julius Mackenzie. We thought it better that we should explain something of all this to her. "Do you know," we said, "this seems to be hardly prudent?"

"Why not prudent?" she asked.

"Up in your bed-room, you know! Mr. Grimes will be sure to dislike it."

"What,—John! Not he. I know what you're a-thinking of, Mr.——," she said. "But we're different in our ways than what you are. Things to us are only just what they are. We haven't time, nor yet money, nor perhaps edication, for seemings and thinkings as you have. If you was travelling out amongst the wild Injeans, you'd ask any one to have a bit in your bed-room as soon as look at 'em, if you'd got a bit for 'em to eat. We're travelling among wild Injeans all our lives, and a bed-room ain't no more to us than any other room. Mackenzie shall come up here, and I'll have the table fixed for him, just there by the window." I hadn't another word to say to her, and I could not keep myself from thinking for many an hour afterwards, whether it may not be a good thing for men, and for women also, to believe that they are always travelling among wild Indians.

When we went down Mr. Grimes himself was in the little parlour. He did not seem at all surprised at seeing his wife enter the
room from above accompanied by a stranger. She at once began her
story, and told the arrangement which she proposed,—which she
did, as I observed, without any actual request for his sanction.
Looking at Mr. Grimes' face, I thought that he did not quite like
it; but he accepted it, almost without a word, scratching his head
and raising his eyebrows. "You know, John, he could no more do
it at home than he could fly," said Mrs. Grimes.

"Who said he could do it at home?"

"And he couldn't do it in the tap-room;—could he? If so, there
ain't no other place, and so that's settled." John Grimes again
scratched his head, and the matter was settled. Before we left the
house Mackenzie himself came in, and was told in our presence of
the accommodation which was to be prepared for him. "It's just
like you, Mrs. Grimes," was all he said in the way of thanks. Then
Mrs. Grimes made her bargain with him somewhat sternly. He
should have the room for five hours a day,—ten till three, or twelve
till five; but he must settle which, and then stick to his hours. "And
I won't have nothing up there in the way of drink," said John
Grimes.

"Who's asking to have drink there?" said Mackenzie.

"You're not asking now, but maybe you will. I won't have it,
that's all."

"That shall be all right, John," said Mrs. Grimes, nodding her
head.

"Women are that soft,—in the way of judgment,—that they'll
go and do a'most anything, good or bad, when they've got their
feelings up." Such was the only rebuke which in our hearing Mr.
Grimes administered to his pretty wife. Mackenzie whispered
something to the publican, but Grimes only shook his head. We
understood it all thoroughly. He did not like the scheme, but he
would not contradict his wife in an act of real kindness. We then
made an appointment with the scholar for meeting our friend and
his future patron at our rooms, and took our leave of the Spotted
Dog. Before we went, however, Mrs. Grimes insisted on producing some cherry-bounce, as she called it, which, after sundry refus-
als on our part, was brought in on a small round shining tray, in a
little bottle covered all over with gold sprigs, with four tiny glasses
similarly ornamented. Mrs. Grimes poured out the liquor, using a
very sparing hand when she came to the glass which was intended

for herself. We find it, as a rule, easier to talk with the Grimeses of the world than to eat with them or to drink with them. When the glass was handed to us we did not know whether or no we were expected to say something. We waited, however, till Mr. Grimes and Mackenzie had been provided with their glasses. "Proud to see you at the Spotted Dog, Mr.——," said Grimes. "That we are," said Mrs. Grimes, smiling at us over her almost imperceptible drop of drink. Julius Mackenzie just bobbed his head, and swallowed the cordial at a gulp,—as a dog does a lump of meat, leaving the impression on his friends around him that he has not got from it half the enjoyment which it might have given him had he been a little more patient in the process. I could not but think that had Mackenzie allowed the cherry-bounce to trickle a little in his palate, as I did myself, it would have gratified him more than it did in being chucked down his throat with all the impetus which his elbow could give to the glass. "That's tidy tipple," said Mr. Grimes, winking his eye. We acknowledged that it was tidy. "My mother made it, as used to keep the Pig and Magpie, at Colchester," said Mrs. Grimes. In this way we learned a good deal of Mrs. Grimes' history. Her very earliest years had been passed among wild Indians.

Then came the interview between the Doctor and Mr. Mackenzie. We must confess that we greatly feared the impression which our younger friend might make on the elder. We had of course told the Doctor of the red nose, and he had accepted the information with a smile. But he was a man who would feel the contamination of contact with a drunkard, and who would shrink from an unpleasant association. There are vices of which we habitually take altogether different views in accordance with the manner in which they are brought under our notice. This vice of drunkenness is often a joke in the mouths of those to whom the thing itself is a horror. Even before our boys we talk of it as being rather funny, though to see one of them funny himself would almost break our hearts. The learned commentator had accepted our account of the red nose as though it were simply a part of the undeserved misery of the wretched man; but should he find the wretched man to be actually redolent of gin his feelings might be changed. The Doctor was with us first, and the volumes of the MS. were displayed upon the table. The compiler of them, as he lifted here a page and there a page, handled them with the gentleness of a lover. They had been exquisitely arranged, and were very fair.

The pagings, and the margins, and the chapterings, and all the complementary paraphernalia of authorship, were perfect. "A lifetime, my friend; just a lifetime!" the Doctor had said to us, speaking of his own work while we were waiting for the man to whose hands was to be entrusted the result of so much labour and scholarship. We wished at that moment that we had never been called on to interfere in the matter.

Mackenzie came, and the introduction was made. The Doctor was a gentleman of the old school, very neat in his attire,—dressed in perfect black, with knee-breeches and black gaiters, with a closely-shorn chin, and an exquisitely white cravat. Though he was in truth simply the rector of his parish, his parish was one which entitled him to call himself a dean, and he wore a clerical rosette on his hat. He was a well-made, tall, portly gentleman, with whom to take the slightest liberty would have been impossible. His well-formed full face was singularly expressive of benevolence, but there was in it too an air of command which created an involuntary respect. He was a man whose means were ample, and who could afford to keep two curates, so that the appanages of a Church dignitary did in some sort belong to him. We doubt whether he really understood what work meant,—even when he spoke with so much pathos of the labour of his life; but he was a man not at all exacting in regard to the work of others, and who was anxious to make the world as smooth and rosy to those around him as it had been to himself. He came forward, paused a moment, and then shook hands with Mackenzie. Our work had been done, and we remained in the background during the interview. It was now for the Doctor to satisfy himself with the scholarship,—and, if he chose to take cognizance of the matter, with the morals of his proposed assistant.

Mackenzie himself was more subdued in his manner than he had been when talking with ourselves. The Doctor made a little speech, standing at the table with one hand on one volume and the other on another. He told of all his work, with a mixture of modesty as to the thing done, and self-assertion as to his interest in doing it, which was charming. He acknowledged that the sum proposed for the aid which he required was inconsiderable;—but it had been fixed by the proposed publisher. Should Mr. Mackenzie find that the labour was long he would willingly increase it. Then he commenced a conversation respecting the Greek dramatists, which had none of the air or tone of an examination, but which still served the purpose of enabling Mackenzie to show his scholarship. In that respect there was no doubt that the ragged, red-nosed, disreputable man, who stood there longing for his job, was the greater proficient of the two. We never discovered that he had had access to books in later years; but his memory of the old things seemed to be perfect. When it was suggested that references would be required, it seemed that he did know his way into the library of the British Museum. "When I wasn't quite so shabby," he said boldly, "I used to be there." The Doctor instantly produced a ten-pound note, and insisted that it should be taken in advance. Mackenzie hesitated, and we suggested that it was premature; but the Doctor was firm. "If an old scholar mayn't assist one younger than himself," he said, "I don't know when one man may aid another. And this is no alms. It is simply a pledge for work to be done." Mackenzie took the money, muttering something of an assurance that as far as his ability went, the work should be done well. "It should certainly," he said, "be done diligently."

When money had passed, of course the thing was settled; but in truth the bank-note had been given, not from judgment in settling the matter, but from the generous impulse of the moment. There was, however, no receding. The Doctor expressed by no hint a doubt as to the safety of his manuscript. He was by far too fine a gentleman to give the man whom he employed pain in that direction. If there were risk, he would now run the risk. And so the thing was settled.

We did not, however, give the manuscript on that occasion into Mackenzie's hands, but took it down afterwards, locked in an old despatch box of our own, to the Spotted Dog, and left the box with the key of it in the hands of Mrs. Grimes. Again we went up into that lady's bedroom, and saw that the big table had been placed by the window for Mackenzie's accommodation. It so nearly filled the room, that, as we observed, John Grimes could not get round at all to his side of the bed. It was arranged that Mackenzie was to begin on the morrow.

PART II. THE RESULT

During the next month we saw a good deal of Mr. Julius Mackenzie, and made ourselves quite at home in Mrs. Grimes' bed-room. We went in and out of the Spotted Dog as if we had known that establishment all our lives, and spent many a quarter of an hour with the hostess in her little parlour, discussing the prospects of Mr. Mackenzie and his family. He had procured for himself decent, if not exactly new, garments out of the money so liberally provided by my learned friend the Doctor, and spent much of his time in the library of the British Museum. He certainly worked very hard, for he did not altogether abandon his old engagement. Before the end of the first month the index of the first volume, nearly completed, had been sent down for the inspection of the Doctor, and had been returned with ample eulogium and some little criticism. The criticisms Mackenzie answered by letter, with true scholarly spirit, and the Doctor was delighted. Nothing could be more pleasant to him than a correspondence, prolonged almost indefinitely, as to the respective merits of a τò or a τõυ, or on the demand for a spondee or an iamb. When he found that the work was really in industrious hands, he ceased to be clamorous for early publication, and gave us to understand privately that Mr. Mackenzie was not to be limited to the sum named. The matter of remuneration was, indeed, left very much to ourselves, and Mackenzie had certainly found a most efficient friend in the author whose works had been confided to his hands.

All this was very pleasant, and Mackenzie throughout that month worked very hard. According to the statements made to me by Mrs. Grimes he took no more gin than what was necessary for a hard-working man. As to the exact quantity of that cordial which she imagined to be beneficial and needful, we made no close inquiry. He certainly kept himself in a condition for work, and so far all went on happily. Nevertheless, there was a terrible skeleton in the cupboard,—or rather out of the cupboard, for the skeleton could not be got to hide itself. A certain portion of his prosperity reached the hands of his wife, and she was behaving herself worse than ever. The four children had been covered with decent garments under Mrs. Grimes' care, and then Mrs. Mackenzie had appeared at the Spotted Dog, loudly demanding a new outfit for herself. She came not only once, but often, and Mr. Grimes was beginning to protest that he saw too much of the family. We had become very intimate with Mrs. Grimes, and she did not hesitate to confide to us her fears lest "John should cut up rough" before the thing was completed. "You see," she said, "it is against the house, no doubt, that woman coming nigh it." But still she was firm, and Mackenzie was not disturbed in the possession of the bed-room. At last Mrs. Mackenzie was provided with some articles of female attire;—and then, on the very next day, she and the four children were again stripped almost naked. The wretched creature must have steeped herself in gin to the shoulders, for in one day she made a sweep of everything. She then came in a state of furious intoxication to the Spotted Dog, and was removed by the police under the express order of the landlord.

We can hardly say which was the most surprising to us, the loyalty of Mrs. Grimes or the patience of John. During that night, as we were told two days afterwards by his wife, he stormed with passion. The papers she had locked up in order that he should not get at them and destroy them. He swore that everything should be cleared out on the following morning. But when the morning came he did not even say a word to Mackenzie, as the wretched, downcast, broken-hearted creature passed up-stairs to his work. "You see I knows him, and how to deal with him," said Mrs. Grimes, speaking of her husband. There ain't another like himself nowheres;—he's that good. A softer-hearteder man there ain't in the public line. He can speak dreadful when his dander is up, and can look——; oh, laws, he just can look at you! But he could no more put his hands upon a woman, in the way of hurting,—no more than be an archbishop." Where could be the man, thought we to ourselves as this was said to us, who could have put a hand,—in the way of hurting,—upon Mrs. Grimes?

On that occasion, to the best of our belief, the policeman contented himself with depositing Mrs. Mackenzie at her own lodgings. On the next day she was picked up drunk in the street, and carried away to the lock-up house. At the very moment in which the story was being told to us by Mrs. Grimes, Mackenzie had gone to the police office to pay the fine, and to bring his wife home. We asked with dismay and surprise why he should interfere to rescue her,—why he did not leave her in custody as long as the police would keep her? "Who'd there be to look after the children?" asked Mrs. Grimes, as though she were offended at our suggestion. Then she went on to explain that in such a household as that of poor Mackenzie the wife is absolutely a necessity, even though she be an habitual drunkard. Intolerable as she was, her services were necessary to him. "A husband as drinks is bad," said Mrs. Grimes,—with something, we thought, of an apologetic tone for the vice upon which her own prosperity was partly built,—"but when a woman takes to it, it's the——devil." We thought that she was right, as we pictured to our selves that man of letters satisfying the magistrate's demand for his wife's misconduct, and taking the degraded, half-naked creature once more home to his children.

We saw him about twelve o'clock on that day, and he had then, too evidently, been endeavouring to support his misery by the free use of alcohol. We did not speak of it down in the parlour; but even Mrs. Grimes, we think, would have admitted that he had taken more than was good for him. He was sitting up in the bedroom with his head hanging upon his hand, with a swarm of our learned friend's papers spread on the table before him. Mrs. Grimes, when he entered the house, had gone up-stairs to give them out to him; but he had made no attempt to settle himself to his work. "This kind of thing must come to an end," he said to us with a thick, husky voice. We muttered something to him as to the need there was that he should exert a manly courage in his troubles. "Manly!" he said. "Well, yes; manly. A man should be a man, of course. There are some things which a man can't bear. I've borne more than enough, and I'll have an end of it."

We shall never forget that scene. After awhile he got up, and became almost violent. Talk of bearing! Who had borne half as much as he? There were things a man should not bear. As for manliness, he believed that the truly manly thing would be to put an end to the lives of his wife, his children, and himself at one swoop. Of course the judgment of a mealy-mouthed world would be against him, but what would that matter to him when he and they had vanished out of this miserable place into the infinite realms of nothingness? Was he fit to live, or were they? Was there any chance for his children but that of becoming thieves and prostitutes? And for that poor wretch of a woman, from out of whose bosom even her human instincts had been washed by gin,—would not death to her be, indeed, a charity? There was but one drawback to all this. When he should have destroyed them, how would it be with him if he should afterwards fail to make sure work with his own life? In such case it was not hanging that he would fear, but the self-reproach that would come upon him in that he had succeeded in sending others out of their misery, but had flinched when his own turn had come. Though he was drunk when he said these horrid things, or so nearly drunk that he could not perfect the articulation of his words, still there was a marvellous eloquence with him.

When we attempted to answer, and told him of that canon which had been set against self-slaughter, he laughed us to scorn. There was something terrible to us in the audacity of the arguments which he used, when he asserted for himself the right to shuffle off from his shoulders a burden which they had not been made broad enough to bear. There was an intensity and a thorough hopelessness of suffering in his case, an openness of acknowledged degradation, which robbed us for the time of all that power which the respectable ones of the earth have over the disreputable. When we came upon him with our wise saws, our wisdom was shattered instantly, and flung back upon us in fragments. What promise could we dare to hold out to him that further patience would produce any result that could be beneficial? What further harm could any such doing on his part bring upon him? Did we think that were he brought out to stand at the gallows' foot with the knowledge that ten minutes would usher him into what folks called eternity, his sense of suffering would be as great as it had been when he conducted that woman out of court and along the streets to his home, amidst the jeering congratulations of his neighbours? "When you have fallen so low," said he, "that you can fall no lower, the ordinary trammels of the world cease to bind you." Though his words were knocked against each other with the dulled utterances of intoxication, his intellect was terribly clear, and his scorn for himself, and for the world that had so treated him, was irrepressible.

We must have been over an hour with him up there in the bedroom, and even then we did not leave him. As it was manifest that he could do no work on that day, we collected the papers together, and proposed that he should take a walk with us. He was patient as we shovelled together the Doctor's pages, and did not object to our suggestion. We found it necessary to call up Mrs. Grimes to assist us in putting away the "Opus magnum," and were astonished to find how much she had come to know about the work. Added to the Doctor's manuscript there were now the pages of Mackenzie's indexes,—and there were other pages of reference, for use in making future indexes,—as to all of which Mrs. Grimes seemed to be quite at home. We have no doubt that she was familiar with the names of Greek tragedians, and could have pointed out to us in print the performances of the chorus. "A little fresh air'll do you a deal of good, Mr. Mackenzie," she said to the unfortunate man,— "only take a biscuit in your pocket." We got him out into the street, but he angrily refused to take the biscuit which she endeavoured to force into his hands.

That was a memorable walk. Turning from the end of Liquorpond Street up Gray's Inn Lane towards Holborn, we at once came upon the entrance into a miserable court. "There," said he; "it is down there that I live. She is sleeping it off now, and the children are hanging about her, wondering whether mother has got money to have another go at it when she rises. I'd take you down to see it all, only it'd sicken you." We did not offer to go down the court, abstaining rather for his sake than for our own. The look of the place was as of a spot squalid, fever-stricken, and utterly degraded. And this man who was our companion had been born and bred a gentleman,—had been nourished with that soft and gentle care which comes of wealth and love combined,—had received the education which the country gives to her most favoured sons, and had taken such advantage of that education as is seldom taken by any of those favoured ones;—and Cucumber Court, with a drunken wife and four half-clothed, half-starved children, was the condition to which he had brought himself! The world knows nothing higher nor brighter than had been his outset in life,—nothing lower nor more debased than the result. And yet he was one whose time and intellect had been employed upon the pursuit of knowledge,—who even up to this day had high ideas of what should be a man's career,—who worked very hard and had always worked,—who as far as we knew had struck upon no rocks in the pursuit of mere pleasure. It had all come to him from that idea of his youth that it would be good for him "to take refuge from the conventional thraldom of so-called gentlemen amidst the liberty of the lower orders." His life, as he had himself owned, had indeed been a mistake.

We passed on from the court, and crossing the road went through the squares of Gray's Inn, down Chancery Lane, through the little iron gate into Lincoln's Inn, round through the old square,—than which we know no place in London more conducive to suicide; and the new square,—which has a gloom of its own, not so potent, and savouring only of madness, till at last we found ourselves in the Temple Gardens. I do not know why we had thus clung to the purlieus of the Law, except it was that he was telling us how in his early days, when he had been sent away from Cambridge,—as on this occasion he acknowledged to us, for an

attempt to pull the tutor's nose, in revenge for a supposed insult,—
he had intended to push his fortunes as a barrister. He pointed up
to a certain window in a dark corner of that suicidal old court, and
told us that for one year he had there sat at the feet of a great
Gamaliel in Chancery, and had worked with all his energies. Of
course we asked him why he had left a prospect so alluring.
Though his answers to us were not quite explicit, we think that he
did not attempt to conceal the truth. He learned to drink, and that
Gamaliel took upon himself to rebuke the failing, and by the end
of that year he had quarrelled irreconcilably with his family. There
had been great wrath at home when he was sent from Cambridge,
greater wrath when he expressed his opinion upon certain questions of religious faith, and wrath to the final severance of all family
relations when he told the chosen Gamaliel that he should get
drunk as often as he pleased. After that he had "taken refuge among
the lower orders," and his life, such as it was, had come of it.

In Fleet Street, as we came out of the Temple, we turned into
an eating-house and had some food. By this time the exercise and
the air had carried off the fumes of the liquor which he had taken,
and I knew that it would be well that he should eat. We had a mutton chop and a hot potato and a pint of beer each, and sat down to
table for the first and last time as mutual friends. It was odd to see
how in his converse with us on that day he seemed to possess a
double identity. Though the hopeless misery of his condition was
always present to him, was constantly on his tongue, yet he could
talk about his own career and his own character as though they
belonged to a third person. He could even laugh at the wretched
mistake he had made in life, and speculate as to its consequences.
For himself he was well aware that death was the only release that
he could expect. We did not dare to tell him that if his wife should
die, then things might be better with him. We could only suggest
to him that work itself, if he would do honest work, would console
him for many sufferings. "You don't know the filth of it," he said
to us. Ah, dear; how well we remember the terrible word, and the
gesture with which he pronounced it, and the gleam of his eyes as
he said it! His manner to us on this occasion was completely
changed, and we had a gratification in feeling that a sense had come
back upon him of his old associations. "I remember this room so
well," he said,—"when I used to have friends and money." And,
indeed, the room was one which had been made memorable by

Genius. "I did not think ever to have found myself here again." We observed, however, that he could not eat the food that was placed before him. A morsel or two of the meat he swallowed, and struggled to eat the crust of his bread, but he could not make a clean plate of it, as we did,—regretting that the nature of chops did not allow of ampler dimensions. His beer was quickly finished, and we suggested to him a second tankard. With a queer, half-abashed twinkle of the eye, he accepted our offer, and then the second pint disappeared also. We had our doubts on the subject, but at last decided against any further offer. Had he chosen to call for it he must have had a third; but he did not call for it. We left him at the door of the tavern, and he then promised that in spite of all that he had suffered and all that he had said he would make another effort to complete the Doctor's work. "Whether I go or stay," he said, "I'd like to earn the money that I've spent." There was something terrible in that idea of his going! Whither was he to go?

The Doctor heard nothing of the misfortune of these three or four inauspicious days; and the work was again going on prosperously when he came up again to London at the end of the second month. He told us something of his banker, and something of his lawyer, and murmured a word or two as to a new curate whom he needed; but we knew that he had come up to London because he could not bear a longer absence from the great object of his affections. He could not endure to be thus parted from his manuscript, and was again childishly anxious that a portion of it should be in the printer's hands. "At sixty-five, sir," he said to us, "a man has no time to dally with his work." He had been dallying with his work all his life, and we sincerely believed that it would be well with him if he could be contented to dally with it to the end. If all that Mackenzie said of it was true, the Doctor's erudition was not equalled by his originality, or by his judgment. Of that question, however, we could take no cognizance. He was bent upon publishing, and as he was willing and able to pay for his whim and was his own master, nothing that we could do would keep him out of the printer's hands.

He was desirous of seeing Mackenzie, and was anxious even to see him once at his work. Of course he could meet his assistant in our editorial room, and all the papers could easily be brought backwards and forwards in the old despatch-box. But in the interest of all parties we hesitated as to taking our revered and reverend friend to the Spotted Dog. Though we had told him that his work was being done at a public-house, we thought that his mind had conceived the idea of some modest inn, and that he would be shocked at being introduced to a place which he would regard simply as a gin-shop. Mrs. Grimes, or if not Mrs. Grimes, then Mr. Grimes, might object to another visitor to their bed-room; and Mackenzie himself would be thrown out of gear by the appearance of those clerical gaiters upon the humble scene of his labours. We, therefore, gave him such reasons as were available for submitting, at any rate for the present, to having the papers brought up to him at our room. And we ourselves went down to the Spotted Dog to make an appointment with Mackenzie for the following day. We had last seen him about a week before, and then the task was progressing well. He had told us that another fortnight would finish it. We had inquired also of Mrs. Grimes about the man's wife. All she could tell us was that the woman had not again troubled them at the Spotted Dog. She expressed her belief, however, that the drunkard had been more than once in the hands of the police since the day on which Mackenzie had walked with us through the squares of the Inns of Court.

It was late when we reached the public-house on the occasion to which we now allude, and the evening was dark and rainy. It was then the end of January, and it might have been about six o'clock. We knew that we should not find Mackenzie at the public-house; but it was probable that Mrs. Grimes could send for him, or, at least, could make the appointment for us. We went into the little parlour, where she was seated with her husband, and we could immediately see, from the countenance of both of them, that something was amiss. We began by telling Mrs. Grimes that the Doctor had come to town. "Mackenzie ain't here, sir," said Mrs. Grimes, and we almost thought that the very tone of her voice was altered. We explained that we had not expected to find him at that hour, and asked if she could send for him. She only shook her head. Grimes was standing with his back to the fire and his hands in his trousers pockets. Up to this moment he had not spoken a word. We asked if the man was drunk. She again shook her head. Could she bid him to come to us to-morrow, and bring the box and the papers with him? Again she shook her head.

"I've told her that I won't have no more of it." said Grimes; "nor yet I won't. He was drunk this morning,—as drunk as an owl."

"He was sober, John, as you are, when he came for the papers this afternoon at two o'clock." So the box and the papers had all been taken away!

"And she was here yesterday rampaging about the place, without as much clothes on as would cover her nakedness," said Mr. Grimes. "I won't have no more of it. I've done for that man what his own flesh and blood wouldn't do. I know that; and I won't have no more of it. Mary Anne, you'll have that table cleared out after breakfast to-morrow." When a man, to whom his wife is usually Polly, addresses her as Mary Anne, then it may be surmised that that man is in earnest. We knew that he was in earnest, and she knew it also.

"He wasn't drunk, John,—no, nor yet in liquor, when he come and took away that box this afternoon." We understood this reiterated assertion. It was in some sort excusing to us her own breach of trust in having allowed the manuscript to be withdrawn from her own charge, or was assuring us that, at the worst, she had not been guilty of the impropriety of allowing the man to take it away when he was unfit to have it in his charge. As for blaming her, who could have thought of it? Had Mackenzie at any time chosen to pass downstairs with the box in his hands, it was not to be expected that she should stop him violently. And now that he had done so we could not blame her; but we felt that a great weight had fallen upon our own hearts. If evil should come to the manuscript would not the Doctor's wrath fall upon us with a crushing weight? Something must be done at once. And we suggested that it would be well that somebody should go round to Cucumber Court. "I'd go as soon as look," said Mrs. Grimes, "but he won't let me."

"You don't stir a foot out of this to-night;—not that way," said Mr. Grimes.

"Who wants to stir?" said Mrs. Grimes.

We felt that there was something more to be told than we had yet heard, and a great fear fell upon us. The woman's manner to us was altered, and we were sure that this had come not from altered feelings on her part, but from circumstances which had frightened her. It was not her husband that she feared, but the truth of something that her husband had said to her. "If there is anything more to tell, for God's sake tell it," we said, addressing ourselves rather to the man than to the woman. Then Grimes did tell us his story. On the previous evening Mackenzie had received three or four

sovereigns from Mrs. Grimes, being, of course, a portion of the
Doctor's payments; and early on that morning all Liquorpond
Street had been in a state of excitement with the drunken fury of
Mackenzie's wife. She had found her way into the Spotted Dog,
and was being actually extruded by the strength of Grimes himself,—of Grimes, who had been brought down, half dressed, from
his bed-room by the row,—when Mackenzie himself, equally
drunk, appeared upon the scene. "No, John;—not equally drunk,"
said Mrs. Grimes. "Bother!" exclaimed her husband, going on with
his story. The man had struggled to take the woman by the arm,
and the two had fallen and rolled in the street together. "I was
looking out of the window, and it was awful to see," said Mrs.
Grimes. We felt that it was "awful to hear." A man,—and such a
man, rolling in the gutter with a drunken woman,—himself
drunk,—and that woman his wife! "There ain't to be no more of
it at the Spotted Dog; that's all," said John Grimes, as he finished
his part of the story.

Then, at last, Mrs. Grimes became voluble. All this had occurred
before nine in the morning. "The woman must have been at it all
night," she said. "So must the man," said John. "Anyways he came
back about dinner, and he was sober then. I asked him not to go
up, and offered to make him a cup of tea. It was just as you'd gone
out after dinner, John."

"He won't have no more tea here," said John.

"And he didn't have any then. He wouldn't, he said, have any
tea, but went up-stairs. What was I to do? I couldn't tell him as he
shouldn't. Well;—during the row in the morning John had said
something as to Mackenzie not coming about the premises any
more."

"Of course I did," said Grimes.

"He was a little cut, then, no doubt," continued the lady; "and
I didn't think as he would have noticed what John had said."

"I mean it to be noticed now."

"He had noticed it then, sir, though he wasn't just as he should
be at that hour of the morning. Well;—what does he do? He goes
up-stairs and packs up all the papers at once. Leastways, that's as I
suppose. They ain't there now. You can go and look if you please,
sir. Well; when he came down, whether I was in the kitchen,—
though it isn't often as my eyes is off the bar, or in the tap-room,
or busy drawing, which I do do sometimes, sir, when there are a

many calling for liquor, I can't say;—but if I ain't never to stand upright again, I didn't see him pass out with the box. But Miss Wilcox did. You can ask her." Miss Wilcox was the young lady in the bar, whom we did not think ourselves called upon to examine, feeling no doubt whatever as to the fact of the box having been taken away by Mackenzie. In all this Mrs. Grimes seemed to defend herself, as though some serious charge was to be brought against her; whereas all that she had done had been done out of pure charity; and in exercising her charity towards Mackenzie she had shown an almost exaggerated kindness towards ourselves.

"If there's anything wrong, it isn't your fault," we said.

"Nor yet mine," said John Grimes.

"No, indeed," we replied.

"It ain't none of our faults," continued he; "only this;—you can't wash a blackamoor white, nor it ain't no use trying. He don't come here any more, that's all. A man in drink we don't mind. We has to put up with it. And they ain't that tarnation desperate as is a woman. As long as a man can keep his legs he'll try to steady hisself; but there is women who, when they've liquor, gets a fury for rampaging. There ain't a many as can beat this one, sir. She's that strong, it took four of us to hold her; though she can't hardly do a stroke of work, she's that weak when she's sober."

We had now heard the whole story, and, while hearing it, had determined that it was our duty to go round into Cucumber Court and seek the manuscript and the box. We were unwilling to pry into the wretchedness of the man's home; but something was due to the Doctor; and we had to make that appointment for the morrow, if it were still possible that such an appointment should be kept. We asked for the number of the house, remembering well the entrance into the court. Then there was a whisper between John and his wife, and the husband offered to accompany us. "It's a roughish place," he said, "but they know me." "He'd better go along with you," said Mrs. Grimes. We, of course, were glad of such companionship, and glad also to find that the landlord, upon whom we had inflicted so much trouble, was still sufficiently our friend to take this trouble on our behalf.

"It's a dreary place enough," said Grimes, as he led us up the narrow archway. Indeed it was a dreary place. The court spread itself a little in breadth, but very little, when the passage was passed, and there were houses on each side of it. There was neither gutter nor, as far as we saw, drain, but the broken flags were slippery with moist mud, and here and there, strewed about between the houses, there were the remains of cabbages and turnip-tops. The place swarmed with children, over whom one ghastly gas-lamp at the end of the court threw a flickering and uncertain light. There was a clamour of scolding voices, to which it seemed that no heed·was paid; and there was a smell of damp, rotting nastiness, amidst which it seemed to us to be almost impossible that life should be continued. Grimes led the way, without further speech, to the middle house on the left hand of the court, and asked a man who was sitting on the low threshold of the door whether Mackenzie was within. "So that be you, Muster Grimes; be it?" said the man, without stirring. "Yes; he's there I guess, but they've been and took her." Then we passed on into the house. "No matter about that," said the man, as we apologised for kicking him in our passage. He had not moved, and it had been impossible to enter without kicking him.

It seemed that Mackenzie held the two rooms on the ground floor, and we entered them at once. There was no light, but we could see the glimmer of a fire in the grate; and presently we became aware of the presence of children. Grimes asked after Mackenzie, and a girl's voice told us that he was in the inner room. The publican then demanded a light, and the girl, with some hesitation, lit the end of a farthing candle, which was fixed in a small bottle. We endeavoured to look round the room by the glimmer which this afforded, but could see nothing but the presence of four children, three of whom seemed to be seated in apathy on the floor. Grimes, taking the candle in his hand, passed at once into the other room, and we followed him. Holding the bottle something over his head, he contrived to throw a gleam of light upon one of the two beds with which the room was fitted, and there we saw the body of Julius Mackenzie stretched in the torpor of dead intoxication. His head lay against the wall, his body was across the bed, and his feet dangled on to the floor. He still wore his dirty boots, and his clothes as he had worn them in the morning. No sight so piteous, so wretched, and at the same time so eloquent had we ever seen before. His eyes were closed, and the light of his face was therefore quenched. His mouth was open, and the slaver had fallen upon his beard. His dark, clotted hair had been pulled over his face by the unconscious movement of his hands. There came from him a stertorous sound of breathing, as though he were being choked by the attitude in which he lay; and even in his drunkenness there was an uneasy twitching as of pain about his face. And there sat, and had been sitting for hours past, the four children in the other room, knowing the condition of the parent whom they most respected, but not even endeavouring to do anything for his comfort. What could they do? They knew, by long training and thorough experience, that a fit of drunkenness had to be got out of by sleep. To them there was nothing shocking in it. It was but a periodical misfortune. "She'll have to own he's been and done it now," said Grimes, looking down upon the man, and alluding to his wife's good-natured obstinacy. He handed the candle to us, and, with a mixture of tenderness and roughness, of which the roughness was only in the manner and the tenderness was real, he raised Mackenzie's head and placed it on the bolster, and lifted the man's legs on to the bed. Then he took off the man's boots, and the old silk handkerchief from the neck, and pulled the trousers straight, and arranged the folds of the coat. It was almost as though he were laying out one that was dead. The eldest girl was now standing by us, and Grimes asked her how long her father had been in that condition. "Jack Hoggart brought him in just afore it was dark," said the girl. Then it was explained to us that Jack Hoggart was the man whom we had seen sitting on the door-step.

"And your mother?" asked Grimes.

"The perlice took her afore dinner."

"And you children;—what have you had to eat?" In answer to this the girl only shook her head. Grimes took no immediate notice of this, but called the drunken man by his name, and shook his shoulder, and looked round to a broken ewer which stood on the little table, for water to dash upon him;—but there was no water in the jug. He called again, and repeated the shaking, and at last Mackenzie opened his eyes, and in a dull, half-conscious manner looked up at us. "Come, my man," said Grimes, "Shake this off and have done with it."

"Hadn't you better try to get up?" we asked.

There was a faint attempt at rising, then a smile,—a smile which was terrible to witness, so sad was all which it said; then a look of utter, abject misery, coming, as we thought, from a momentary remembrance of his degradation; and after that he sank back in the dull, brutal, painless, death-like apathy of absolute unconsciousness.

"It'll be morning afore he'll move," said the girl.

"She's about right," said Grimes. "He's got it too heavy for us to do anything but just leave him. We'll take a look for the box and the papers."

And the man upon whom we were looking down had been born a gentleman, and was a finished scholar,—one so well educated, so ripe in literary acquirement, that we knew few whom we could call his equal. Judging of the matter by the light of our reason, we cannot say that the horror of the scene should have been enhanced to us by these recollections. Had the man been a shoemaker or a coalheaver there would have been enough of tragedy in it to make an angel weep,—that sight of the child standing by the bedside of her drunken father, while the other parent was away in custody,—and in no degree shocked at what she saw, because the thing was so common to her! But the thought of what the man had been, of what he was, of what he might have been, and the steps by which he had brought himself to the foul degradation which we witnessed, filled us with a dismay which we should hardly have felt had the gifts which he had polluted and the intellect which he had wasted been less capable of noble uses.

Our purpose in coming to the court was to rescue the Doctor's papers from danger, and we turned to accompany Grimes into the other room. As we did so the publican asked the girl if she knew anything of a black box which her father had taken away from the Spotted Dog. "The box is here," said the girl.

"And the papers?" asked Grimes. Thereupon the girl shook her head, and we both hurried into the outer room. I hardly know who first discovered the sight which we encountered, or whether it was shown to us by the child. The whole fire-place was strewn with half-burnt sheets of manuscript. There were scraps of pages of which almost the whole had been destroyed, others which were hardly more than scorched, and heaps of paper-ashes all lying tumbled together about the fender. We went down on our knees to examine them, thinking at the moment that the poor creature might in his despair have burned his own work and have spared that of the Doctor. But it was not so. We found scores of charred pages of the Doctor's elaborate handwriting. By this time Grimes had found the open box, and we perceived that the sheets remaining in it were tumbled and huddled together in absolute confusion. There were pages of the various volumes mixed with those which

Mackenzie himself had written, and they were all crushed, and rolled, and twisted, as though they had been thrust thither as waste-paper,—out of the way. "'Twas mother as done it," said the girl, "and we put 'em back again when the perlice took her."

There was nothing more to learn,—nothing more by the hearing which any useful clue could be obtained. What had been the exact course of the scenes which had been enacted there that morning it little booted us to inquire. It was enough and more than enough that we knew that the mischief had been done. We went down on our knees before the fire, and rescued from the ashes with our hands every fragment of manuscript that we could find. Then we put the mass all together into the box, and gazed upon the wretched remnants almost in tears. "You'd better go and get a bit of some'at to eat," said Grimes, handing a coin to the elder girl. "It's hard on them to starve 'cause their father's drunk, sir." Then he took the closed box in his hand, and we followed him out into the street. "I'll send or step up and look after him to-morrow," said Grimes, as he put us and the box into a cab. We little thought, when we made to the drunkard that foolish request to arise, that we should never speak to him again.

As we returned to our office in the cab that we might deposit the box there ready for the following day, our mind was chiefly occupied in thinking over the undeserved grievances which had fallen upon our selves. We had been moved by the charitable desire to do services to two different persons,—to the learned Doctor and to the rednosed drunkard, and this had come of it! There had been nothing for us to gain by assisting either the one or the other. We had taken infinite trouble, attempting to bring together two men who wanted each other's services,—working hard in sheer benevolence;—and what had been the result? We had spent half an hour on our knees in the undignified and almost disreputable work of raking among Mrs. Mackenzie's cinders, and now we had to face the anger, the dismay, the reproach, and,—worse than all,—the agony of the Doctor. As to Mackenzie,—we asserted to ourselves again and again that nothing further could be done for him. He had made his bed, and he must lie upon it; but, oh! why,—why had we attempted to meddle with a being so degraded? We got out of the cab at our office door, thinking of the Doctor's countenance as we should see it on the morrow. Our heart sank within us, and we asked ourselves, if it was so bad with us now, how it would be with us when we returned to the place on the following morning.

But on the following morning we did return. No doubt each individual reader to whom we address ourselves has at some period felt that indescribable load of personal, short-lived care, which causes the heart to sink down into the boots. It is not great grief that does it;—nor is it excessive fear; but the unpleasant operation comes from the mixture of the two. It is the anticipation of some imperfectly-understood evil that does it,—some evil out of which there might perhaps be an escape if we could only see the way. In this case we saw no way out of it. The Doctor was to be with us at one o'clock, and he would come with smiles, expecting to meet his learned colleague. How should we break it to the Doctor? We might indeed send to him, putting off the meeting, but the advantage coming from that would be slight, if any. We must see the injured Grecian sooner or later; and we had resolved, much as we feared, that the evil hour should not be postponed. We spent an hour that morning in arranging the fragments. Of the first volume about a third had been destroyed. Of the second nearly every page had been either burned or mutilated. Of the third but little had been injured. Mackenzie's own work had fared better than the Doctor's; but there was no comfort in that. After what had passed I thought it quite improbable that the Doctor would make any use of Mackenzie's work. So much of the manuscript as could still be placed in continuous pages, we laid out upon the table, volume by volume,—that in the middle sinking down from its original goodly bulk almost to the dimensions of a poor sermon;—and the half-burned bits we left in the box. Then we sat ourselves down at our accustomed table, and pretended to try to work. Our ears were very sharp, and we heard the Doctor's step upon our stairs within a minute or two of the appointed time. Our heart went to the very toes of our boots. We shuffled in our chair, rose from it, and sat down again,—and were conscious that we were not equal to the occasion. Hitherto we had, after some mild literary form, patronised the Doctor,—as a man of letters in town will patronise his literary friend from the country;—but we now feared him as a truant school-boy fears his master. And yet it was so necessary that we should wear some air of self-assurance!

In a moment he was with us, wearing that bland smile which we knew so well, and which at the present moment almost overpowered us. We had been sure that he would wear that smile, and had especially feared it. "Ah," said he, grasping us by the hand, "I thought I should have been late. I see that our friend is not here yet."

"Doctor," we replied, "a great misfortune has happened."

"A great misfortune! Mr. Mackenzie is not dead?"

"No;—he is not dead. Perhaps it would have been better that he had died long since. He has destroyed your manuscript." The Doctor's face fell, and his hands at the same time, and he stood looking at us. "I need not tell you, Doctor, what my feelings are, and how great my remorse."

"Destroyed it!" Then we took him by the hand and led him to the table. He turned first upon the appetising and comparatively uninjured third volume, and seemed to think that we had hoaxed him. "This is not destroyed," he said, with a smile. But before I could explain anything, his hands were among the fragments in the box. "As I am a living man, they have burned it!" he exclaimed. "I—I—I—" Then he turned from us, and walked twice the length of the room, backwards and forwards, while we stood still, patiently waiting the explosion of his wrath. "My friend," he said, when his walk was over, "a great man underwent the same sorrow. Newton's manuscript was burned. I will take it home with me, and we will say no more about it." I never thought very much of the Doctor as a divine, but I hold him to have been as good a Christian as I ever met.

But that plan of his of saying no more about it could not quite be carried out. I was endeavouring to explain to him, as I thought it necessary to do, the circumstances of the case, and he was protesting his indifference to any such details, when there came a knock at the door, and the boy who waited on us below ushered Mrs. Grimes into the room. As the reader is aware, we had, during the last two months, become very intimate with the landlady of the Spotted Dog, but we had never hitherto had the pleasure of seeing her outside her own house. "Oh, Mr.——" she began, and then she paused, seeing the Doctor.

We thought it expedient that there should be some introduction. "Mrs. Grimes," we said, "this is the gentleman whose invaluable manuscript has been destroyed by that unfortunate drunkard."

"Oh, then;—you're the Doctor, sir?" The Doctor bowed and smiled. His heart must have been very heavy, but he bowed po-

litely and smiled sweetly. "Oh, dear," she said, "I don't know how
to tell you!"

"To tell us what?" asked the Doctor.

"What has happened since?" we demanded. The woman stood
shaking before us, and then sank into a chair. Then arose to us at
the moment some idea that the drunken woman, in her mad rage,
had done some great damage to the Spotted Dog,—had set fire to
the house, or injured Mr. Grimes personally, or perhaps run amuck
amidst the jugs and pitchers, window glass, and gas lights.
Something had been done which would give the Grimeses pecuniary claim on me or on the Doctor, and the woman had been sent
hither to make the first protest. Oh,—when should I see the last of
the results of my imprudence in having attempted to befriend such
a one as Julius Mackenzie! "If you have anything to tell, you had
better tell it," we said, gravely.

"He's been, and—"

"Not destroyed himself?" asked the Doctor.

"Oh yes, sir. He have indeed,—from ear to ear,—and is now a
lying at the Spotted Dog!"

And so, after all, that was the end of Julius Mackenzie! We need
hardly say that our feelings, which up to that moment had been
very hostile to the man, underwent a sudden revulsion. Poor,
overburdened, struggling, ill-used, abandoned creature! The world
had been hard upon him, with a severity which almost induced one
to make complaint against Omnipotence. The poor wretch had
been willing to work, had been industrious in his calling, had had
capacity for work; and he had also struggled gallantly against his evil
fate, had recognised and endeavoured to perform his duty to his
children and to the miserable woman who had brought him to his
ruin! And that sin of drunkenness had seemed to us to be in him
rather the reflex of her vice than the result of his own vicious
tendencies. Still it might be doubtful whether she had not learned
the vice from him. They had both in truth been drunkards as long
as they had been known in the neighbourhood of the Spotted Dog;
but it was stated by all who had known them there that he was
never seen to be drunk unless when she had disgraced him by the
public exposure of her own abomination. Such as he was he had
now come to his end! This was the upshot of his loud claims for
liberty from his youth upwards;—liberty as against his father and

family; liberty as against his college tutor; liberty as against all pastors, masters, and instructors; liberty as against the conventional thraldom of the world! He was now lying a wretched corpse at the Spotted Dog, with his throat cut from ear to ear, till the coroner's jury should have decided whether or not they would call him a suicide!

Mrs. Grimes had come to tell us that the coroner was to be at the Spotted Dog at four o'clock, and to say that her husband hoped that we would be present. We had seen Mackenzie so lately, and had so much to do with the employment of the last days of his life, that we could not refuse this request, though it came accompanied by no legal summons. Then Mrs. Grimes again became voluble, and poured out to us her biography of Mackenzie as far as she knew it. He had been married to the woman ten years, and certainly had been a drunkard before he married her. "As for her, she'd been well-nigh suckled on gin," said Mrs. Grimes, "though he didn't know it, poor fellow." Whether this was true or not, she had certainly taken to drink soon after her marriage, and then his life had been passed in alternate fits of despondency and of desperate efforts to improve his own condition and that of his children. Mrs. Grimes declared to us that when the fit came on them,—when the woman had begun and the man had followed,—they would expend upon drink in two days what would have kept the family for a fortnight. "They say as how it was nothing for them to swallow forty shillings' worth of gin in forty-eight hours." The Doctor held up his hands in horror. "And it didn't, none of it, come our way," said Mrs. Grimes. "Indeed, John wouldn't let us serve it for 'em."

She sat there for half an hour, and during the whole time she was telling us of the man's life; but the reader will already have heard more than enough of it. By what immediate demon the woman had been instigated to burn the husband's work almost immediately on its production within her own home, we never heard. Doubtless there had been some terrible scene in which the man's sufferings must have been carried almost beyond endurance. "And he had feelings, sir, he had," said Mrs. Grimes; "he knew as a woman should be decent, and a man's wife especial; I'm sure we pitied him so, John and I, that we could have cried over him. John would say a hard word to him at times, but he'd have walked round London to do him a good turn. John ain't to say edicated hisself, but he do respect learning."

When she had told us all, Mrs. Grimes went, and we were left alone with the Doctor. He at once consented to accompany us to the Spotted Dog, and we spent the hour that still remained to us in discussing the fate of the unfortunate man. We doubt whether an allusion was made during the time to the burned manuscript. If so, it was certainly not made by the Doctor himself. The tragedy which had occurred in connection with it had made him feel it to be unfitting even to mention his own loss. That such a one should have gone to his account in such a manner, without hope, without belief, and without fear,—as Burley said to Bothwell, and Bothwell boasted to Burley,—that was the theme of the Doctor's discourse. "The mercy of God is infinite," he said, bowing his head, with closed eyes and folded hands. To threaten while the life is in the man is human. To believe in the execution of those threats when the life has passed away is almost beyond the power of humanity.

At the hour fixed we were at the Spotted Dog, and found there a crowd assembled. The coroner was already seated in Mrs. Grimes' little parlour, and the body as we were told had been laid out in the tap-room. The inquest was soon over. The fact that he had destroyed himself in the low state of physical suffering and mental despondency which followed his intoxication was not doubted. At the very time that he was doing it, his wife was being taken from the lock-up house to the police office in the police van. He was not penniless, for he had sent the children out with money for their breakfasts, giving special caution as to the youngest, a little toddling thing of three years old;—and then he had done it. The eldest girl, returning to the house, had found him lying dead upon the floor. We were called upon for our evidence, and went into the tap-room accompanied by the Doctor. Alas! the very table which had been dragged up-stairs into the landlady's bed-room with the charitable object of assisting Mackenzie in his work,—the table at which we had sat with him conning the Doctor's pages,—had now been dragged down again and was used for another purpose. We had little to say as to the matter, except that we had known the man to be industrious and capable, and that we had, alas! seen him utterly prostrated by drink on the evening before his death.

The saddest sight of all on this occasion was the appearance of Mackenzie's wife,—whom we had never before seen. She had been brought there by a policeman, but whether she was still in custody

we did not know. She had been dressed, either by the decency of
the police or by the care of her neighbours, in an old black gown,
which was a world too large and too long for her. And on her head
there was a black bonnet which nearly enveloped her. She was a
small woman, and, as far as we could judge from the glance we got
of her face, pale, and worn, and wan. She had not such outward
marks of a drunkard's career as those which poor Mackenzie always
carried with him. She was taken up to the coroner, and what answers she gave to him were spoken in so low a voice that they did
not reach us. The policeman, with whom we spoke, told us that
she did not feel it much,—that she was callous now and beyond the
power of mental suffering. "She's frightened just this minute, sir;
but it isn't more than that," said the policeman. We gave one
glance along the table at the burden which it bore, but we saw
nothing beyond the outward lines of that which had so lately been
the figure of a man. We should have liked to see the countenance
once more. The morbid curiosity to see such horrid sights is strong
with most of us. But we did not wish to be thought to wish to see
it,—especially by our friend the Doctor,—and we abstained from
pushing our way to the head of the table. The Doctor himself remained quiescent in the corner of the room the farthest from the
spectacle. When the matter was submitted to them, the jury lost not
a moment in declaring their verdict. They said that the man had
destroyed himself while suffering under temporary insanity produced by intoxication. And that was the end of Julius Mackenzie,
the scholar.

On the following day the Doctor returned to the country, taking
with him our black box, to the continued use of which, as a sar-
cophagus, he had been made very welcome. For our share in bringing upon him the great catastrophe of his life, he never uttered to
us, either by spoken or written word, a single reproach. That idea
of suffering as the great philosopher had suffered seemed to comfort
him. "If Newton bore it, surely I can," he said to us with his bland
smile, when we renewed the expression of our regret. Something
passed between us, coming more from us than from him, as to the
expediency of finding out some youthful scholar who could go
down to the rectory, and reconstruct from its ruins the edifice of
our friend's learning. The Doctor had given us some encourage-
ment, and we had begun to make inquiry, when we received the
following letter:—

"———Rectory, ——— ———, 18–.

"DEAR MR. ———,—You were so kind as to say that you would endeavour to find for me an assistant in arranging and reconstructing the fragments of my work on The Metres of the Greek Dramatists. Your promise has been an additional kindness."

Dear, courteous, kind old gentleman! For we knew well that no slightest sting of sarcasm was intended to be conveyed in these words.

"Your promise has been an additional kindness; but looking upon the matter carefully, and giving to it the best consideration in my power, I have determined to relinquish the design. That which has been destroyed cannot be replaced; and it may well be that it was not worth replacing. I am old now, and never could do again that which perhaps I was never fitted to do with any fair prospect of success. I will never turn again to the ashes of my unborn child; but will console myself with the memory of my grievance, knowing well, as I do so, that consolation from the severity of harsh but just criticism might have been more difficult to find. When I think of the end of my efforts as a scholar, my mind reverts to the terrible and fatal catastrophe of one whose scholarship was infinitely more finished and more ripe than mine.

"Whenever it may suit you to come into this part of the country, pray remember that it will give very great pleasure to myself and to my daughter to welcome you at our parsonage.

"Believe me to be,
"My dear Mr. ———,
"Yours very sincerely,
"——— ———."

We never have found the time to accept the Doctor's invitation, and our eyes have never again rested on the black box containing the ashes of the unborn child to which the Doctor will never turn again. We can picture him to ourselves standing, full of thought, with his hand upon the lid, but never venturing to turn the lock. Indeed, we do not doubt but that the key of the box is put away among other secret treasures, a lock of his wife's hair, perhaps, and the little shoe of the boy who did not live long enough to stand at his father's knee. For a tender, soft-hearted man was the Doctor, and one who fed much on the memories of the past.

We often called upon Mr. and Mrs. Grimes at the Spotted Dog, and would sit there talking of Mackenzie and his family. Mackenzie's widow soon vanished out of the neighbourhood, and no one there knew what was the fate of her or of her children. And then also Mr. Grimes went and took his wife with him. But they could not be said to vanish. Scratching his head one day, he told me with a dolorous voice that he had——made his fortune. "We've got as snug a little place as ever you see, just two mile out of Colchester," said Mrs. Grimes triumphantly,—"with thirty acres of land just to amuse John. And as for the Spotted Dog, I'm that sick of it, another year'd wear me to a dry bone." We looked at her, and saw no tendency that way. And we looked at John, and thought that he was not triumphant.

Who followed Mr. and Mrs. Grimes at the Spotted Dog we have never visited Liquorpond Street to see.

MARY GRESLEY

WE HAVE KNOWN many prettier girls than Mary Gresley, and many handsomer women,—but we never knew girl or woman gifted with a face which in supplication was more suasive, in grief more sad, in mirth more merry. It was a face that compelled sympathy, and it did so with the conviction on the mind of the sympathiser that the girl was altogether unconscious of her own power. In her intercourse with us there was, alas! much more of sorrow than of mirth, and we may truly say that in her sufferings we suffered; but still there came to us from our intercourse with her much of delight mingled with the sorrow; and that delight arose, partly no doubt from her woman's charms, from the bright eye, the beseeching mouth, the soft little hand, and the feminine grace of her unpretending garments; but chiefly, we think, from the extreme humanity of the girl. She had little, indeed none, of that which the world calls society, but yet she was pre-eminently social. Her troubles were very heavy, but she was making ever an unconscious effort to throw them aside, and to be jocund in spite of their weight. She would even laugh at them, and at herself as bearing them. She was a little fair-haired creature, with broad brow and small nose and dimpled chin, with no brightness of complexion, no luxuriance of hair, no swelling glory of bust and shoulders; but with a pair of eyes which, as they looked at you, would be gemmed always either with a tear or with some spark of laughter, and with a mouth in the corners of which was ever lurking some little spark of humour, unless when some unspoken prayer seemed to be hanging on her lips. Of woman's vanity she had absolutely none. Of her corporeal self, as having charms to rivet man's love, she thought no more than does a dog. It was a fault with her that she lacked that quality of womanhood. To be loved was to her all the world; unconscious desire for the admiration of men was as strong in her as in other women; and her instinct taught her, as such instincts do teach all women, that such love and admiration was to be the fruit of what feminine gifts she possessed; but the gifts on which she depended,— depending on them without thinking on the matter,—were her softness, her trust, her woman's weakness, and that power of sup- plicating by her eye without putting her petition into words which was absolutely irresistible. Where is the man of fifty, who in the course of his life has not learned to love some woman simply be- cause it has come in his way to help her, and to be good to her in her struggles? And if added to that source of affection there be brightness, some spark of humour, social gifts, and a strong flavour of that which we have ventured to call humanity, such love may become almost a passion without the addition of much real beauty.

But in thus talking of love we must guard ourselves somewhat from miscomprehension. In love with Mary Gresley, after the com- mon sense of the word, we never were, nor would it have become us to be so. Had such a state of being unfortunately befallen us, we certainly should be silent on the subject. We were married and old; she was very young, and engaged to be married, always talking to us of her engagement as a thing fixed as the stars. She looked upon us, no doubt,—after she had ceased to regard us simply in our edi- torial capacity,—as a subsidiary old uncle whom Providence had supplied to her, in order that if it were possible, the troubles of her life might be somewhat eased by assistance to her from that special quarter. We regarded her first almost as a child, and then as a young woman to whom we owed that sort of protecting care which a greybeard should ever be ready to give to the weakness of feminine adolescence. Nevertheless we were in love with her, and we think such a state of love to be a wholesome and natural condition. We might, indeed, have loved her grandmother,—but the love would have been very different. Had circumstances brought us into con- nection with her grandmother, we hope we should have done our duty, and had that old lady been our friend we should, we trust, have done it with alacrity. But in our intercourse with Mary Gresley there was more than that. She charmed us. We learned to love the hue of that dark grey stuff frock which she seemed always to wear. When she would sit in the low armchair opposite to us, looking up into our eyes as we spoke to her words which must often have stabbed her little heart, we were wont to caress her with that inward undemonstrative embrace that one spirit is able to confer upon another. We thought of her constantly, perplexing our mind for her succour. We forgave all her faults. We exaggerated her virtues. We exerted ourselves for her with a zeal that was perhaps fatuous. Though we attempted sometimes to look black at her, telling her that our time was too precious to be wasted in conversation with her, she soon learned to know how welcome she was to us. Her glove,—which, by-the-bye, was never tattered, though she was very poor,—was an object of regard to us. Her grandmother's gloves would have been as unacceptable to us as any other morsel of old kid or cotton. Our heart bled for her. Now the heart may suffer much for the sorrows of a male friend, but it may hardly for such be said to bleed. We loved her, in short, as we should not have loved her, but that she was young and gentle, and could smile,—and, above all, but that she looked at us with those, bright, beseeching, tear-laden eyes.

Sterne, in his latter days, when very near his end, wrote passionate love-letters to various women, and has been called hard names by Thackeray,—not for writing them, but because he thus showed himself to be incapable of that sincerity which should have bound him to one love. We do not ourselves much admire the sentimentalism of Sterne, finding the expression of it to be mawkish, and thinking that too often he misses the pathos for which he strives from a want of appreciation on his own part of that which is really vigorous in language and touching in sentiment. But we think that Thackeray has been somewhat wrong in throwing that blame on Sterne's heart which should have been attributed to his taste. The love which he declared when he was old and sick and dying,—a worn-out wreck of a man,—disgusts us, not because it was felt, or not felt, but because it was told;—and told as though the teller meant to offer more than that warmth of sympathy which woman's strength and woman's weakness combined will ever produce in the hearts of certain men. This is a sympathy with which neither age, nor crutches, nor matrimony, nor position of any sort need consider itself to be incompatible. It is unreasoning, and perhaps irrational. It gives to outward form and grace that which only inward merit can deserve. It is very dangerous because, unless watched, it leads to words which express that which is not intended. But, though it may be controlled, it cannot be killed. He, who is of his nature open to such impression, will feel it while breath remains to him. It was that which destroyed the character and happiness of Swift, and which made Sterne contemptible. We do not doubt that such unreasoning sympathy, exacted by feminine attraction, was always strong in Johnson's heart;—but Johnson was strong all over, and could guard himself equally from misconduct and from ridicule. Such sympathy with women, such incapability of withstanding the feminine magnet was very strong with Goethe,—who could guard himself from ridicule, but not from misconduct. To us the child of whom we are speaking,—for she was so then,—was ever a child. But she bore in her hand the power of that magnet, and we admit that the needle within our bosom was swayed by it. Her story,—such as we have to tell it,—was as follows.

Mary Gresley, at the time when we first knew her, was eighteen years old, and was the daughter of a medical practitioner, who had lived and died in a small town in one of the northern counties. For facility in telling our story we will call that town Cornboro. Dr. Gresley, as he seemed to have been called though without proper claim to the title, had been a diligent man, and fairly successful,—except in this, that he died before he had been able to provide for those whom he left behind him. The widow still had her own modest fortune, amounting to some eighty pounds a year; and that, with the furniture of her house, was her whole wealth, when she found herself thus left with the weight of the world upon her shoulders. There was one other daughter older than Mary, whom we never saw, but who was always mentioned as poor Fanny. There had been no sons, and the family consisted of the mother and the two girls. Mary had been only fifteen when her father died, and up to that time had been regarded quite as a child by all who had known her. Mrs. Gresley, in the hour of her need, did as widows do in such cases. She sought advice from her clergyman and neighbours, and was counselled to take a lodger into her house. No lodger could be found so fitting as the curate, and when Mary was seventeen years old, she and the curate were engaged to be married. The curate paid thirty pounds a year for his lodgings, and on this, with their own little income, the widow and her two daughters had managed to live. The engagement was known to them all as soon as it had been known to Mary. The love-making, indeed, had gone on beneath the eyes of the mother. There had been not only no deceit, no privacy, no separate interests, but, as far as we ever knew, no question as to prudence in the making of the engagement. The two young people had been brought together, had loved each other, as was so natural, and had become engaged as a matter of course. It was an event as easy to be foretold, or at least as easy to be believed, as the pairing of two birds. From what we heard of this curate, the Rev. Arthur Donne,—for we never saw him,—we fancy that he was a simple, pious, commonplace young man, imbued with a strong idea that in being made a priest he had been invested with a nobility and with some special capacity beyond that of other men, slight in body, weak in health, but honest, true, and warm-hearted. Then, the engagement having been completed, there arose the question of matrimony. The salary of the curate was a hundred a year. The whole income of the vicar, an old man, was, after payment made to his curate, two hundred a year. Could the curate, in such circumstances, afford to take to himself a penniless wife of seventeen? Mrs. Gresley was willing that the marriage should take place, and that they should all do as best they might on their joint income. The vicar's wife, who seems to have been a strong-minded, sage, though somewhat hard woman, took Mary aside, and told her that such a thing must not be. There would come, she said, children, and destitution, and ruin. She knew perhaps more than Mary knew when Mary told us her story, sitting opposite to us in the low armchair. It was the advice of the vicar's wife that the engagement should be broken off; but that, if the breaking-off of the engagement were impossible, there should be an indefinite period of waiting. Such engagements cannot be broken off. Young hearts will not consent to be thus torn asunder. The vicar's wife was too strong for them to get themselves married in her teeth, and the period of indefinite waiting was commenced.

And now for a moment we will go further back among Mary's youthful days. Child as she seemed to be, she had in very early years taken a pen in her hand. The reader need hardly be told that had not such been the case there would not have arisen any cause for friendship between her and us. We are telling an Editor's tale, and it was in our editorial capacity that Mary first came to us. Well;—in her earliest attempts, in her very young days, she wrote,—heaven knows what; poetry first, no doubt; then, God help her, a tragedy; after that, when the curate-influence first commenced, tales for the conversion of the ungodly;—and at last, before her engagement was a fact, having tried her wing at fiction, in the form of those false little dialogues between Tom the Saint and Bob the Sinner, she had completed a novel in one volume. She was then seventeen, was engaged to be married, and had completed her novel! Passing her in the street you would almost have taken her for a child to whom you might give an orange.

Hitherto her work had come from ambition,—or from a feeling of restless piety inspired by the curate. Now there arose in her young mind the question whether such talent as she possessed might not be turned to account for ways and means, and used to shorten, perhaps absolutely to annihilate, that uncertain period of waiting. The first novel was seen by "a man of letters" in her neighbourhood, who pronounced it to be very clever;—not indeed fit as yet for publication, faulty in grammar, faulty even in spelling,—how I loved the tear that shone in her eye as she confessed this delinquency!—faulty of course in construction, and faulty in character;—but still clever. The man of letters had told her that she must begin again.

Unfortunate man of letters in having thrust upon him so terrible a task! In such circumstances what is the candid, honest, soft-hearted man of letters to do? "Go, girl, and mend your stockings. Learn to make a pie. If you work hard, it may be that some day your intellect will suffice to you to read a book and understand it. For the writing of a book that shall either interest or instruct a brother human being many gifts are required. Have you just reason to believe that they have been given to you?" That is what the candid, honest man of letters says who is not soft-hearted;—and in ninety-nine cases out of a hundred it will probably be the truth. The soft hearted man of letters remembers that this special case submitted to him may be the hundredth; and, unless the blotted manuscript is conclusive against such possibility, he reconciles it to his conscience to tune his counsel to that hope. Who can say that he is wrong? Unless such evidence be conclusive, who can venture to declare that this aspirant may not be the one who shall succeed? Who in such emergency does not remember the day in which he also was one of the hundred of whom the ninety-and-nine must fail;—and will not remember also the many convictions on his own mind that he certainly would not be the one appointed? The man of letters in the neighbourhood of Cornboro to whom poor Mary's manuscript was shown was not sufficiently hard-hearted to make any strong attempt to deter her. He made no reference to the easy stockings, or the wholesome pie,—pointed out the manifest faults which he saw, and added, we do not doubt with much more energy than he threw into his words of censure,—his comfortable assurance that there was great promise in the work. Mary Gresley that evening burned the manuscript, and began another, with the dictionary close at her elbow.

Then, during her work, there occurred two circumstances which brought upon her,—and, indeed, upon the household to which she belonged,—intense sorrow and greatly-increased trouble. The first of these applied more especially to herself. The Rev. Arthur Donne did not approve of novels,—of other novels than those dialogues between Tom and Bob, of the falsehood of which he was unconscious,—and expressed a desire that the writing of them should be abandoned. How far the lover went in his attempt to enforce obedience we, of course, could not know; but he pronounced the edict, and the edict, though not obeyed, created tribulation. Then there came forth another edict which had to be obeyed,—an edict from the probable successor of the late Dr. Gresley,—ordering the poor curate to seek employment in some clime more congenial to his state of health than that in which he was then living. He was told that his throat and lungs and general apparatus for living and preaching were not strong enough for those hyperborean regions, and that he must seek a southern climate. He did do so, and, before I became acquainted with Mary, had transferred his services to a small town in Dorsetshire. The engagement, of course, was to be as valid as ever, though matrimony must be postponed, more indefinitely even than heretofore. But if Mary could write novels and sell them, then how glorious would it be to follow her lover into Dorsetshire! The Rev. Arthur Donne went, and the curate who came in his place was a married man, wanting a house, and not lodgings. So Mary Gresley persevered with her second novel, and completed it before she was eighteen.

The literary friend in the neighbourhood,—to the chance of whose acquaintance I was indebted for my subsequent friendship with Mary Gresley,—found this work to be a great improvement on the first. He was an elderly man who had been engaged nearly all his life in the conduct of a scientific and agricultural periodical, and was the last man whom I should have taken as a sound critic on works of fiction;—but with spelling, grammatical construction, and the composition of sentences he was acquainted; and he assured

Mary that her progress had been great. Should she burn that second story? she asked him. She would if he so recommended, and begin another the next day. Such was not his advice. "I have a friend in London," said he, "who has to do with such things, and you shall go to him. I will give you a letter." He gave her the fatal letter, and she came to us.

She came up to town with her novel; but not only with her novel, for she brought her mother with her. So great was her eloquence, so excellent her suasive power either with her tongue or by that look of supplication in her face, that she induced her mother to abandon her home in Cornboro, and trust herself to London lodgings. The house was let furnished to the new curate, and when I first heard of the Gresleys they were living on the second floor in a small street near to the Euston Square station. Poor Fanny, as she was called, was left in some humble home at Cornboro, and Mary travelled up to try her fortune in the great city. When we came to know her well we expressed our doubts as to the wisdom of such a step. Yes; the vicar's wife had been strong against the move. Mary confessed as much. That lady had spoken most forcible words, had uttered terrible predictions, had told sundry truths. But Mary had prevailed, and the journey was made, and the lodgings were taken.

We can now come to the day on which we first saw her. She did not write, but came direct to us with her manuscript in her hand. "A young woman, sir, wants to see you," said the clerk, in that tone to which we were so well accustomed, and which indicated the dislike which he had learned from us to the reception of unknown visitors.

"Young woman! What young woman?"

"Well, sir; she is a very young woman;—quite a girl like."

"I suppose she has got a name. Who sent her? I cannot see any young woman without knowing why. What does she want?"

"Got a manuscript in her hand, sir."

"I've no doubt she has, and a ton of manuscripts in drawers and cupboards. Tell her to write. I won't see any woman, young or old, without knowing who she is." The man retired, and soon returned with an envelope belonging to the office, on which was written, "Miss Mary Gresley, late of Cornboro." He also brought me a note from "the man of letters" down in Yorkshire. "Of what sort is she?" I asked, looking at the introduction.

"She ain't amiss as to looks," said the clerk; "and she's modest-like." Now certainly it is the fact that all female literary aspirants are not "modest-like." We read our friend's letter through, while poor Mary was standing at the counter below. How eagerly should we have run to greet her, to save her from the gaze of the public, to welcome her at least with a chair and the warmth of our editorial fire, had we guessed then what were her qualities! It was not long before she knew the way up to our sanctum without any clerk to show her, and not long before we knew well the sound of that low but not timid knock at our door made always with the handle of the parasol, with which her advent was heralded. We will confess that there was always music to our ears in that light tap from the little round wooden knob. The man of letters in Yorkshire, whom we had known well for many years, had been never known to us with intimacy. We had bought with him and sold with him, had talked with him, and, perhaps, walked with him; but he was not one with whom we had eaten, or drunk, or prayed. A dull, well-instructed, honest man he was, fond of his money, and, as we had thought, as unlikely as any man to be waked to enthusiasm by the ambitious dreams of a young girl. But Mary had been potent even over him, and he had written to me, saying that Miss Gresley was a young lady of exceeding promise, in respect of whom he had a strong presentiment that she would rise, if not to eminence, at least to a good position as a writer. "But she is very young," he added. Having read this letter, we at last desired our clerk to send the lady up.

We remember her step as she came to the door, timid enough then,—hesitating, but yet with an assumed lightness as though she was determined to show us that she was not ashamed of what she was doing. She had on her head a light straw hat, such as then was very unusual in London,—and is not now, we believe, commonly worn in the streets of the metropolis by ladies who believe themselves to know what they are about. But it was a hat, worn upon her head, and not a straw plate done up with ribbons, and reaching down the incline of the forehead as far as the top of the nose. And she was dressed in a grey stuff frock, with a little black band round her waist. As far as our memory goes, we never saw her in any other dress, or with other hat or bonnet on her head. "And what can we do for you,—Miss Gresley?" we said, standing up and holding the literary gentleman's letter in our hand. We had almost said, "my dear," seeing her youth and remembering our own age. We were afterwards glad that we had not so addressed her; though it came before long that we did call her "my dear,"—in quite another spirit.

She recoiled a little from the tone of our voice, but recovered herself at once. "Mr.——thinks that you can do something for me. I have written a novel, and I have brought it to you."

"You are very young, are you not, to have written a novel?"

"I am young," she said, "but perhaps older than you think. I am eighteen." Then for the first time there came into her eye that gleam of a merry humour which never was allowed to dwell there long, but which was so alluring when it showed itself.

"That is a ripe age," we said laughing, and then we bade her seat herself. At once we began to pour forth that long and dull and ugly lesson which is so common to our life, in which we tried to explain to our unwilling pupil that of all respectable professions for young women literature is the most uncertain, the most heart-breaking, and the most dangerous. "You hear of the few who are remunerated," we said; "but you hear nothing of the thousands that fail."

"It is so noble!" she replied.

"But so hopeless."

"There are those who succeed."

"Yes, indeed. Even in a lottery one must gain the prize; but they who trust to lotteries break their hearts."

"But literature is not a lottery. If I am fit, I shall succeed. Mr.——thinks I may succeed." Many more words of wisdom we spoke to her, and well do we remember her reply when we had run all our line off the reel, and had completed our sermon. "I shall go on all the same," she said. "I shall try, and try again,—and again."

Her power over us, to a certain extent, was soon established. Of course we promised to read the MS., and turned it over, no doubt with an anxious countenance, to see of what kind was the writing. There is a feminine scrawl of a nature so terrible that the task of reading it becomes worse than the treadmill. "I know I can write well,—though I am not quite sure about the spelling," said Mary, as she observed the glance of our eyes. She spoke truly. The writing was good, though the erasures and alterations were very numerous. And then the story was intended to fill only one volume. "I will copy it for you if you wish it," said Mary. "Though there are so many scratchings out, it has been copied once." We would not for worlds have given her such labour, and then we promised to read the tale. We forget how it was brought about, but she told us at that interview that her mother had obtained leave from the pastry-cook round the corner to sit there waiting till Mary should rejoin her. "I thought it would be trouble enough for you to have one of us here," she said with her little laugh when I asked her why she had not brought her mother on with her. I own that I felt that she had been wise; and when I told her that if she would call on me again that day week I would then have read at any rate so much of her work as would enable me to give her my opinion, I did not invite her to bring her mother with her. I knew that I could talk more freely to the girl without the mother's presence. Even when you are past fifty, and intend only to preach a sermon, you do not wish to have a mother present.

When she was gone we took up the roll of paper and examined it. We looked at the division into chapters, at the various mottoes the poor child had chosen, pronounced to ourselves the name of the story,—it was simply the name of the heroine, an easy-going, unaffected, well-chosen name,—and read the last page of it. On such occasions the reader of the work begins his task almost with a conviction that the labour which he is about to undertake will be utterly thrown away. He feels all but sure that the matter will be bad, that it will be better for all parties, writer, intended readers, and intended publisher, that the written words should not be conveyed into type,—that it will be his duty after some fashion to convey that unwelcome opinion to the writer, and that the writer will go away incredulous, and accusing mentally the Mentor of the moment of all manner of literary sins, among which ignorance, jealousy, and falsehood, will, in the poor author's imagination, be most prominent. And yet when the writer was asking for that opinion, declaring his especial desire that the opinion should be candid, protesting that his present wish is to have some gauge of his own capability, and that he has come to you believing you to be above others able to give him that gauge,—while his petition to you was being made, he was in every respect sincere. He had come desirous to measure himself, and had believed that you could measure him. When coming he did not think that you would declare him to be an Apollo. He had told himself, no doubt, how probable it was that you would point out to him that he was a dwarf. You find him to be an ordinary man, measuring perhaps five feet seven, and unable to reach the standard of the particular regiment in which he is ambitious of serving. You tell him so in what civillest words you know, and you are at once convicted in his mind of jealousy, ignorance, and falsehood! And yet he is perhaps a most excellent fellow, and capable of performing the best of service,—only in some other regiment! As we looked at Miss Gresley's manuscript, tumbling it through our hands, we expected even from her some such result. She had gained two things from us already by her outward and inward gifts, such as they were,—first that we would read her story, and secondly that we would read it quickly; but she had not as yet gained from us any belief that by reading it we could serve it.

We did read it,—the most of it before we left our editorial chair on that afternoon, so that we lost altogether the daily walk so essential to our editorial health, and were put to the expense of a cab on our return home. And we incurred some minimum of domestic discomfort from the fact that we did not reach our own door till twenty minutes after our appointed dinner hour. "I have this moment come from the office as hard as a cab could bring me," we said in answer to the mildest of reproaches, explaining nothing as to the nature of the cause which had kept us so long at our work.

We must not allow our readers to suppose that the intensity of our application had arisen from the overwhelming interest of the story. It was not that the story entranced us, but that our feeling for the writer grew as we read the story. It was simple, unaffected, and almost painfully unsensational. It contained, as I came to perceive afterwards, little more than a recital of what her imagination told her might too probably be the result of her own engagement. It was the story of two young people who became engaged and could not be married. After a course of years the man, with many true arguments, asked to be absolved. The woman yields with an expressed conviction that her lover is right, settles herself down for maiden life, then breaks her heart and dies. The character of the man was utterly untrue to nature. That of the woman was true, but commonplace. Other interest, or other character there was none. The dialogues between the lovers were many and tedious, and hardly a word was spoken between them which two lovers really would have uttered. It was clearly not a work as to which I could tell my little friend that she might depend upon it for fame or fortune. When I had finished it I was obliged to tell myself that I could not advise her even to publish it. But yet I could not say that she had mistaken her own powers or applied herself to a profession beyond her reach. There were a grace and delicacy in her work which were charming. Occasionally she escaped from the trammels of grammar, but only so far that it would be a pleasure to point out to her her errors. There was not a word that a young lady should not have written; and there were throughout the whole evident signs of honest work. We had six days to think it over between our completion of the task and her second visit.

She came exactly at the hour appointed, and seated herself at once in the arm-chair before us as soon as the young man had closed the door behind him. There had been no great occasion for nervousness at her first visit, and she had then, by an evident effort, overcome the diffidence incidental to a meeting with a stranger. But now she did not attempt to conceal her anxiety. "Well," she said, leaning forward, and looking up into our face, with her two hands folded together.

Even though Truth, standing full panoplied at our elbow, had positively demanded it, we could not have told her then to mend her stockings and bake her pies and desert the calling that she had chosen. She was simply irresistible, and would, we fear, have constrained us into falsehood had the question been between falsehood and absolute reprobation of her work. To have spoken hard, heart-breaking words to her, would have been like striking a child when it comes to kiss you. We fear that we were not absolutely true at first, and that by that absence of truth we made subsequent pain more painful. "Well," she said, looking up into our face. "Have you read it?" We told her that we had read every word of it. "And it is no good?"

We fear that we began by telling her that it certainly was good,—after a fashion, very good,—considering her youth and necessary inexperience, very good indeed. As we said this she shook her head, and sent out a spark or two from her eyes, intimating her conviction that excuses or quasi praise founded on her youth would avail her nothing. "Would anybody buy it from me?" she asked. No;—we did not think that any publisher would pay her money for it. "Would they print it for me without costing me anything?" Then we told her the truth as nearly as we could. She lacked experience; and if, as she had declared to us before, she was determined to persevere, she must try again, and must learn more of that lesson of the world's ways which was so necessary to those who attempted to teach that lesson to others. "But I shall try again at once," she said. We shook our head, endeavouring to shake it kindly. "Currer Bell was only a young girl when she succeeded," she added. The injury which Currer Bell did after this fashion was almost equal to that perpetrated by Jack Sheppard, and yet Currer Bell was not very young when she wrote.

She remained with us then for above an hour;—for more than two probably, though the time was not specially marked by us; and before her visit was brought to a close she had told us of her engagement with the curate. Indeed, we believe that the greater part of her little history as hitherto narrated was made known to us on that occasion. We asked after her mother early in the interview, and learned that she was not on this occasion kept waiting at the pastrycook's shop. Mary had come alone, making use of some friendly omnibus, of which she had learned the route. When she told us that she and her mother had come up to London solely with the view of forwarding her views in her intended profession, we ventured to ask whether it would not be wiser for them to return to Cornboro, seeing how improbable it was that she would have matter fit for the press within any short period. Then she explained that they had calculated that they would be able to live in London for twelve months, if they spent nothing except on absolute necessaries. The poor girl seemed to keep back nothing from us. "We have clothes that will carry us through, and we shall be very careful. I came in an omnibus;—but I shall walk if you will let me come again." Then she asked me for advice. How was she to set about further work with the best chance of turning it to account?

It had been altogether the fault of that retired literary gentleman down in the north, who had obtained what standing he had in the world of letters by writing about guano and the cattle plague! Divested of all responsibility, and fearing no further trouble to himself, he had ventured to tell this girl that her work was full of promise. Promise means probability, and in this case there was nothing beyond a remote chance. That she and her mother should have left their little household gods, and come up to London on such a chance, was a thing terrible to the mind. But we felt before these two hours were over that we could not throw her off now. We had become old friends, and there had been that between us which gave her a positive claim upon our time. She had sat in our arm-chair, leaning forward with her elbows on her knees and her hands stretched out, till we, caught by the charm of her unstudied intimacy, had wheeled round our chair, and had placed ourselves, as nearly as the circumstances would admit, in the same position. The magnetism had already begun to act upon us. We soon found ourselves taking it for granted that she was to remain in London and begin another book. It was impossible to resist her. Before the interview was over, we, who had been conversant with all these matters before she was born; we, who had latterly come to regard our own editorial fault as being chiefly that of personal harshness; we, who had repulsed aspirant novelists by the score,—we had consented to be a party to the creation, if not to the actual writing, of this new book!

It was to be done after this fashion. She was to fabricate a plot, and to bring it to us, written on two sides of a sheet of letter paper. On the reverse sides we were to criticise this plot, and prepare emendations. Then she was to make out skeletons of the men and women who were afterwards to be clothed with flesh and made alive with blood, and covered with cuticles. After that she was to arrange her proportions; and at last, before she began to write the story, she was to describe in detail such part of it as was to be told in each chapter. On every advancing wavelet of the work we were to give her our written remarks. All this we promised to do because of the quiver in her lip, and the alternate tear and sparkle in her eye. "Now that I have found a friend, I feel sure that I can do it," she said, as she held our hand tightly before she left us.

In about a month, during which she had twice written to us and twice been answered, she came with her plot. It was the old story, with some additions and some change. There was matrimony instead of death at the end, and an old aunt was brought in for the purpose of relenting and producing an income. We added a few details, feeling as we did so that we were the very worst of botchers. We doubt now whether the old, sad, simple story was not the better of the two. Then, after another lengthened interview, we sent our pupil back to create her skeletons. When she came with the skeletons we were dear friends and learned to call her Mary. Then it was that she first sat at our editorial table, and wrote a love-letter to the curate. It was then mid-winter, wanting but a few days to Christmas, and Arthur, as she called him, did not like the cold weather. "He does not say so," she said, "but I fear he is ill. Don't you think there are some people with whom everything is unfortunate?" She wrote her letter, and had recovered her spirits before she took her leave.

We then proposed to her to bring her mother to dine with us on Christmas Day. We had made a clean breast of it at home in regard to our heart-flutterings, and had been met with a suggestion that some kindness might with propriety be shown to the old lady as well as to the young one. We had felt grateful to the old lady for not coming to our office with her daughter, and had at once assented. When we made the suggestion to Mary there came first a blush over all her face, and then there followed the well-known smile before the blush was gone. "You'll all be dressed fine," she said. We protested that not a garment would be changed by any of the family after the decent church-going in the morning. "Just as I am?" she asked. "Just as you are," we said, looking at the dear grey frock, adding some mocking assertion that no possible combination of millinery could improve her. "And mamma will be just the same? Then we will come," she said. We told her an absolute falsehood, as to some necessity which would take us in a cab to Euston Square on the afternoon of that Christmas Day, so that we could call and bring them both to our house without trouble or expense. "You shan't do anything of the kind," she said. However, we swore to our falsehood,—perceiving, as we did so, that she did not believe a word of it; but in the matter of the cab we had our own way.

We found the mother to be what we had expected,—a weak, ladylike, lachrymose old lady, endowed with a profound admiration for her daughter, and so bashful that she could not at all enjoy her plum-pudding. We think that Mary did enjoy hers thoroughly. She made a little speech to the mistress of the house, praising ourselves with warm words and tearful eyes, and immediately won the heart of a new friend. She allied herself warmly to our daughters, put up with the schoolboy pleasantries of our sons, and before the evening was over was dressed up as a ghost for the amusement of some neighbouring children who were brought in to play snap-dragon. Mrs. Gresley, as she drank her tea and crumbled her bit of cake, seated on a distant sofa, was not so happy, partly because she remembered her old gown, and partly because our wife was a stranger to her. Mary had forgotten both circumstances before the dinner was half over. She was the sweetest ghost that ever was seen.

How pleasant would be our ideas of departed spirits if such ghosts would visit us frequently!

They repeated their visits to us not unfrequently during the twelve months; but as the whole interest attaching to our inter-course had reference to circumstances which took place in that editorial room of ours, it will not be necessary to refer further to the hours, very pleasant to ourselves, which she spent with us in our domestic life. She was ever made welcome when she came, and was known by us as a dear, well-bred, modest, clever little girl. The novel went on. That catalogue of the skeletons gave us more trouble than all the rest, and many were the tears which she shed over it, and sad were the misgivings by which she was afflicted, though never vanquished! How was it to be expected that a girl of eighteen should portray characters such as she had never known? In her intercourse with the curate all the intellect had been on her side. She had loved him because it was requisite to her to love some one; and now, as she had loved him, she was as true as steel to him. But there had been almost nothing for her to learn from him. The plan of the novel went on, and as it did so we became more and more despondent as to its success. And through it all we knew how contrary it was to our own judgment to expect, even to dream of, anything but failure. Though we went on working with her, find-ing it to be quite impossible to resist her entreaties, we did tell her from day to day that, even presuming she were entitled to hope for ultimate success, she must go through an apprenticeship of ten years before she could reach it. Then she would sit silent, repressing her tears, and searching for arguments with which to support her cause.

"Working hard is apprenticeship," she said to us once.

"Yes, Mary; but the work will be more useful, and the appren-ticeship more wholesome, if you will take them for what they are worth."

"I shall be dead in ten years," she said.

"If you thought so you would not intend to marry Mr. Donne. But even were it certain that such would be your fate, how can that alter the state of things? The world would know nothing of that; and if it did, would the world buy your book out of pity?"

"I want no one to pity me," she said; "but I want you to help me." So we went on helping her. At the end of four months she had not put pen to paper on the absolute body of her projected novel; and yet she had worked daily at it, arranging its future construction.

During the next month, when we were in the middle of March, a gleam of real success came to her. We had told her frankly that we would publish nothing of hers in the periodical which we were ourselves conducting. She had become too dear to us for us not to feel that were we to do so, we should be doing it rather for her sake than for that of our readers. But we did procure for her the publication of two short stories elsewhere. For these she received twelve guineas, and it seemed to her that she had found an El Dorado of literary wealth. I shall never forget her ecstasy when she knew that her work would be printed, or her renewed triumph when the first humble cheque was given into her hands. There are those who will think that such a triumph, as connected with literature, must be sordid. For ourselves, we are ready to acknowledge that money payment for work done is the best and most honest test of success. We are sure that it is so felt by young barristers and young doctors, and we do not see why rejoicing on such realisation of long-cherished hope should be more vile with the literary aspirant than with them. "What do you think I'll do first with it?" she said. We thought she meant to send something to her lover, and we told her so. "I'll buy mamma a bonnet to go to church in. I didn't tell you before, but she hasn't been these three Sundays because she hasn't one fit to be seen." I changed the cheque for her, and she went off and bought the bonnet.

Though I was successful for her in regard to the two stories, I could not go beyond that. We could have filled pages of periodicals with her writing had we been willing that she should work without remuneration. She herself was anxious for such work, thinking that it would lead to something better. But we opposed it, and, indeed, would not permit it, believing that work so done can be serviceable to none but those who accept it that pages may be filled without cost.

During the whole winter, while she was thus working, she was in a state of alarm about her lover. Her hope was ever that when warm weather came he would again be well and strong. We know nothing sadder than such hope founded on such source. For does not the winter follow the summer, and then again comes the killing spring? At this time she used to read us passages from his letters, in which he seemed to speak of little but his own health. In her literary ambition he never seemed to have taken part since she had declared her intention of writing profane novels. As regarded him, his sole merit to us seemed to be in his truth to her. He told her that in his opinion they two were as much joined together as though the service of the Church had bound them; but even in saying that he spoke ever of himself and not of her. Well;—May came, dangerous, doubtful, deceitful May, and he was worse. Then, for the first time, the dread word, Consumption, passed her lips. It had already passed ours, mentally, a score of times. We asked her what she herself would wish to do. Would she desire to go down to Dorsetshire and see him? She thought awhile, and said that she would wait a little longer.

The novel went on, and at length, in June, she was writing the actual words on which, as she thought, so much depended. She had really brought the story into some shape in the arrangement of her chapters; and sometimes even I began to hope. There were moments in which with her hope was almost certainty. Towards the end of June Mr. Donne declared himself to be better. He was to have a holiday in August, and then he intended to run up to London and see his betrothed. He still gave details, which were distressing to us, of his own symptoms; but it was manifest that he himself was not desponding, and she was governed in her trust or in her despair altogether by him. But when August came the period of his visit was postponed. The heat had made him weak, and he was to come in September.

Early in August we ourselves went away for our annual recreation;—not that we shoot grouse, or that we have any strong opinion that August and September are the best months in the year for holiday-making,—but that everybody does go in August. We ourselves are not specially fond of August. In many places to which one goes a-touring mosquitoes bite in that month. The heat, too, prevents one from walking. The inns are all full, and the railways crowded. April and May are twice pleasanter months in which to see the world and the country. But fashion is everything, and no man or woman will stay in town in August for whom there exists any practicability of leaving it. We went on the 10th,—just as though we had a moor, and one of the last things we did before our departure was to read and revise the last-written chapter of Mary's story.

About the end of September we returned, and up to that time the lover had not come to London. Immediately on our return we wrote to Mary, and the next morning she was with us. She had seated herself on her usual chair before she spoke, and we had taken her hand and asked after herself and her mother. Then, with something of mirth in our tone, we demanded the work which she had done since our departure. "He is dying," she replied.

She did not weep as she spoke. It was not on such occasions as this that the tears filled her eyes. But there was in her face a look of fixed and settled misery which convinced us that she at least did not doubt the truth of her own assertion. We muttered something as to our hope that she was mistaken. "The doctor, there, has written to tell mamma that it is so. Here is his letter." The doctor's letter was a good letter, written with more of assurance than doctors can generally allow themselves to express. "I fear that I am justified in telling you," said the doctor, "that it can only be a question of weeks." We got up and took her hand. There was not a word to be uttered.

"I must go to him," she said, after a pause.

"Well;—yes. It will be better."

"But we have no money." It must be explained now that offers of slight, very slight, pecuniary aid had been made by us both to Mary and to her mother on more than one occasion. These had been refused with adamantine firmness, but always with something of mirth, or at least of humour, attached to the refusal. The mother would simply refer to the daughter, and Mary would declare that they could manage to see the twelvemonth through and go back to Cornboro, without becoming absolute beggars. She would allude to their joint wardrobe, and would confess that there would not have been a pair of boots between them but for that twelve guineas; and indeed she seemed to have stretched that modest incoming so as to cover a legion of purchases. And of these things she was never ashamed to speak. We think there must have been at least two grey frocks, because the frock was always clean, and never absolutely shabby. Our girls at home declared that they had seen three. Of her frock, as it happened, she never spoke to us, but the new boots and the new gloves, "and ever so many things that I can't tell you about, which we really couldn't have gone without," all came out of the twelve guineas. That she had taken, not only with delight, but with triumph. But pecuniary assistance from ourselves she had always refused. "It would be a gift," she would say.

"Have it as you like."

"But people don't give other people money."

"Don't they? That's all you know about the world."

"Yes; to beggars. We hope we needn't come to that." It was thus that she always answered us,—but always with something of laughter in her eye, as though their poverty was a joke. Now, when the demand upon her was for that which did not concern her personal comfort, which referred to a matter felt by her to be vitally important, she declared, without a minute's hesitation, that she had not money for the journey.

"Of course you can have money," we said. "I suppose you will go at once?"

"Oh yes;—at once. That is, in a day or two,—after he shall have received my letter. Why should I wait?" We sat down to write a cheque, and she, seeing what we were doing, asked how much it was to be. "No;—half that will do," she said. "Mamma will not go. We have talked it over and decided it. Yes; I know all about that. I am going to see my lover,—my dying lover; and I have to beg for the money to take me to him. Of course I am a young girl; but in such a condition am I to stand upon the ceremony of being taken care of? A housemaid wouldn't want to be taken care of at eighteen." We did exactly as she bade us, and then attempted to comfort her while the young man went to get money for the cheque. What consolation was possible? It was simply necessary to admit with frankness that sorrow had come from which there could be no present release. "Yes," she said. "Time will cure it,—in a way. One dies in time, and then of course it is all cured." "One hears of this kind of thing often," she said afterwards, still leaning forward in her chair, still with something of the old expression in her eyes,—something almost of humour in spite of her grief; "but it is the girl who dies. When it is the girl, there isn't, after all, so much harm done. A man goes about the world and can shake it off; and then, there are plenty of girls." We could not tell her how infinitely more important, to our thinking, was her life than that of him whom she was going to see now for the last time; but there did spring up within our mind a feeling, greatly opposed to that conviction which formerly we had endeavoured to impress upon herself,—that she was destined to make for herself a successful career.

She went, and remained by her lover's bed-side for three weeks. She wrote constantly to her mother, and once or twice to ourselves. She never again allowed herself to entertain a gleam of hope, and she spoke of her sorrow as a thing accomplished. In her last interview with us she had hardly alluded to her novel, and in her letters she never mentioned it. But she did say one word which made us guess what was coming. "You will find me greatly changed in one thing," she said; "so much changed that I need never have troubled you." The day for her return to London was twice postponed, but at last she was brought to leave him. Stern necessity was too strong for her. Let her pinch herself as she might, she must live down in Dorsetshire,—and could not live on his means, which were as narrow as her own. She left him; and on the day after her arrival in London she walked across from Euston Square to our office.

"Yes," she said, "it is all over. I shall never see him again on this side of heaven's gates." We do not know that we ever saw a tear in her eyes produced by her own sorrow. She was possessed of some wonderful strength which seemed to suffice for the bearing of any burden. Then she paused, and we could only sit silent, with our eyes fixed upon the rug. "I have made him a promise," she said at last. Of course we asked her what was the promise, though at the moment we thought that we knew. "I will make no more attempt at novel writing."

"Such a promise should not have been asked,—or given," we said vehemently.

"It should have been asked,—because he thought it right," she answered. "And of course it was given. Must he not know better than I do? Is he not one of God's ordained priests? In all the world is there one so bound to obey him as I?" There was nothing to be said for it at such a moment as that. There is no enthusiasm equal to that produced by a death-bed parting. "I grieve greatly," she said, "that you should have had so much vain labour with a poor girl who can never profit by it."

"I don't believe the labour will have been vain," we answered, having altogether changed those views of ours as to the futility of the pursuit which she had adopted.

"I have destroyed it all," she said.

"What;—burned the novel?"

"Every scrap of it. I told him that I would do so, and that he should know that I had done it. Every page was burned after I got home last night, and then I wrote to him before I went to bed."

"Do you mean that you think it wicked that people should write novels?" we asked.

"He thinks it to be a misapplication of God's gifts, and that has been enough for me. He shall judge for me, but I will not judge for others. And what does it matter? I do not want to write a novel now."

They remained in London till the end of the year for which the married curate had taken their house, and then they returned to Cornboro. We saw them frequently while they were still in town, and despatched them by the train to the north just when the winter was beginning. At that time the young clergyman was still living down in Dorsetshire, but he was lying in his grave when Christmas came. Mary never saw him again, nor did she attend his funeral. She wrote to us frequently then, as she did for years afterwards. "I should have liked to have stood at his grave," she said; "but it was a luxury of sorrow that I wished to enjoy, and they who cannot earn luxuries should not have them. They were going to manage it for me here, but I knew I was right to refuse it." Right, indeed! As far as we knew her, she never moved a single point from what was right.

All these things happened many years ago. Mary Gresley, on her return to Cornboro, apprenticed herself, as it were, to the married curate there, and called herself, I think, a female Scripture reader. I know that she spent her days in working hard for the religious aid of the poor around her. From time to time we endeavoured to instigate her to literary work; and she answered our letters by sending us wonderful little dialogues between Tom the Saint and Bob the Sinner. We are in no humour to criticise them now; but we can assert, that though that mode of religious teaching is most distasteful to us, the literary merit shown even in such works as these was very manifest. And there came to be apparent in them a gleam of humour which would sometimes make us think that she was sitting opposite to us and looking at us, and that she was Tom the Saint, and that we were Bob the Sinner. We said what we could to turn her from her chosen path, throwing into our letters all the eloquence and all the thought of which we were masters; but our eloquence and our thought were equally in vain.

At last, when eight years had passed over her head after the death of Mr. Donne, she married a missionary who was going out to some forlorn country on the confines of African colonisation; and there she died. We saw her on board the ship in which she sailed, and before we parted there had come that tear into her eyes, the old look of supplication on her lips, and the gleam of mirth across her face. We kissed her once,—for the first and only time,—as we bade God bless her!

THE TWO HEROINES OF PLUMPLINGTON

CHAPTER I

THE TWO GIRLS

IN THE LITTLE town of Plumplington last year, just about this time of the year,—it was in November,—the ladies and gentlemen forming the Plumplington Society were much exercised as to the affairs of two young ladies. They were both the only daughters of two elderly gentlemen, well known and greatly respected in Plumplington. All the world may not know that Plumplington is the second town in Barsetshire, and though it sends no member to Parliament, as does Silverbridge, it has a population of over 20,000 souls, and three separate banks. Of one of these Mr. Greenmantle is the manager, and is reputed to have shares in the bank. At any rate he is known to be a warm man. His daughter Emily is supposed to be the heiress of all he possesses, and has been regarded as a fitting match by many of the sons of the country gentlemen around It was rumoured a short time since that young Harry Gresham was likely to ask her hand in marriage, and Mr. Greenmantle was supposed at the time to have been very willing to entertain the idea. Whether Mr. Gresham has ever asked or not, Emily Greenmantle did not incline her ear that way, and it came out while the affair was being discussed in Plumplington circles that the young lady much preferred one Mr. Philip Hughes. Now Philip Hughes was a very promising young man, but was at the time no more than a cashier in her father's bank. It become known at once that Mr. Greenmantle was very angry. Mr. Greenmantle was a man who carried himself with a dignified and handsome demeanour, but he was one of whom those who knew him used to declare that it would be found very difficult to turn him from his purpose. It might not be possible that he should succeed with Harry Gresham, but it was considered out of the question that he should give his girl and his money to such a man as Philip Hughes.

The other of these elderly gentlemen is Mr. Hickory Peppercorn. It cannot be said that Mr. Hickory Peppercorn had ever been put on a par with Mr. Greenmantle. No one could suppose that Mr. Peppercorn had ever sat down to dinner in company with Mr. and Miss Greenmantle. Neither did Mr. or Miss Peppercorn expect to be asked on the festive occasion of one of Mr. Greenmantle's dinners. But Miss Peppercorn was not unfrequently made welcome to Miss Greenmantle's five o'clock tea-table; and in many of the affairs of the town the two young ladies were seen associated together. They were both very active in the schools, and stood nearly equal in the good graces of old Dr. Freeborn. There was, perhaps, a little jealousy on this account in the bosom of Mr. Greenmantle, who was pervaded perhaps by an idea that Dr. Freeborn thought too much of himself. There never was a quarrel, as Mr. Greenmantle was a good churchman; but there was a jealousy. Mr. Greenmantle's family sank into insignificance if you looked beyond his grandfather; but Dr. Freeborn could talk glibly of his ancestors in the time of Charles I. And it certainly was the fact that Dr. Freeborn would speak of the two young ladies in one and the same breath.

Now Mr. Hickory Peppercorn was in truth nearly as warm a man as his neighbour, and he was one who was specially proud of being warm. He was a foreman,—or rather more than foreman,—a kind of top sawyer in the brewery establishment of Messrs. Du Boung and Co., a firm which has an establishment also in the town of Silverbridge. His position in the world may be described by declaring that he always wears a dark coloured tweed coat and trousers, and a chimney-pot hat. It is almost impossible to say too much that is good of Mr. Peppercorn. His one great fault has been already designated. He was and still is very fond of his money. He does not talk much about it; but it is to be feared that it dwells too constantly on his mind. As a servant to the firm he is honesty and constancy itself. He is a man of such a nature that by means of his very presence all the partners can be allowed to go to bed if they wish it.

And there is not a man in the establishment who does not know him to be good and true. He understands all the systems of brewing, and his very existence in the brewery is a proof that Messrs. Du Boung and Co. are prosperous.

He has one daughter, Polly, to whom he is so thoroughly devoted that all the other girls in Plumplington envy her. If anything is to be done Polly is asked to go to her father, and if Polly does go to her father the thing is done. As far as money is concerned it is not known that Mr. Peppercorn ever refused Polly anything. It is the pride of his heart that Polly shall be, at any rate, as well dressed as Emily Greenmantle. In truth nearly double as much is spent on her clothes, all of which Polly accepts without a word to show her pride. Her father does not say much, but now and again a sigh does escape him. Then it came out, as a blow to Plumplington, that Polly too had a lover. And the last person in Plumplington who heard the news was Mr. Peppercorn. It seemed from his demeanour, when he first heard the tidings, that he had not expected that any such accident would ever happen. And yet Polly Peppercorn was a very pretty, bright girl of one-and-twenty of whom the wonder was,—if it was true,—that she had never already had a lover. She looked to be the very girl for lovers, and she looked also to be one quite able to keep a lover in his place.

Emily Greenmantle's lover was a two-months'-old story when Polly's lover became known to the public. There was a young man in Barchester who came over on Thursdays dealing with Mr. Peppercorn for malt. He was a fine stalwart young fellow, six-feet-one, with bright eyes and very light hair and whiskers, with a pair of shoulders which would think nothing of a sack of wheat, a hot temper, and a thoroughly good heart. It was known to all Plumplington that he had not a shilling in the world, and that he earned forty shillings a week from Messrs. Mealing's establishment at Barchester. Men said of him that he was likely to do well in the world, but nobody thought that he would have the impudence to make up to Polly Peppercorn.

But all the girls saw it and many of the old women, and some even of the men. And at last Polly told him that if he had anything to say to her he must say it to her father. "And you mean to have him, then?" said Bessy Rolt in surprise. Her lover was by at the moment, though not exactly within hearing of Bessy's question. But Polly when she was alone with Bessy spoke up her mind freely.

"Of course I mean to have him, if he pleases. What else? You don't suppose I would go on with a young man like that and mean nothing. I hate such ways."

"But what will your father say?"

"Why shouldn't he like it? I heard papa say that he had but 7*s*. 6*d*. a week when he first came to Du Boungs. He got poor mamma to marry him, and he never was a good-looking man."

"But he had made some money."

"Jack has made no money as yet, but he is a good-looking fellow. So they're quits. I believe that father would do anything for me, and when he knows that I mean it he won't let me break my heart."

But a week after that a change had come over the scene. Jack had gone to Mr. Hickory Peppercorn, and Mr. Peppercorn had given him a rough word or two. Jack had not borne the rough word well, and old Hickory, as he was called, had said in his wrath, "Impudent cub! you've got nothing. Do you know what my girl will have?"

"I've never asked."

"You knew she was to have something."

"I know nothing about it. I'm ready to take the rough and the smooth together. I'll marry the young lady and wait till you give her something." Hickory couldn't turn him out on the spur of the moment because there was business to be done, but warned him not to go into his private house. "If you speak another word to Polly, old as I am, I'll measure you across the back with my stick." But Polly, who knew her father's temper, took care to keep out of her father's sight on that occasion.

Polly after that began the battle in a fashion that had been invented by herself. No one heard the words that were spoken between her and her father,—her father who had so idolized her; but it appeared to the people of Plumplington that Polly was holding her own. No disrespect was shown to her father, not a word was heard from her mouth that was not affectionate or at least decorous. But she took upon herself at once a certain lowering of her own social standing. She never drank tea with Emily Greenmantle, or accosted her in the street with her old friendly manner. She was terribly humble to Dr. Freeborn, who however would not acknowledge her humility on any account. "What's come over you?" said the Doctor. "Let me have none of your stage plays or I shall take you and shake you."

"You can shake me if you like it, Dr. Freeborn," said Polly, "but I know who I am and what my position is."

"You are a determined young puss," said the Doctor, "but I am not going to help you in opposing your own father." Polly said not a word further, but looked very demure as the Doctor took his departure.

But Polly performed her greatest stroke in reference to a change in her dress. All her new silks, that had been the pride of her father's heart, were made to give way to old stuff gowns. People wondered where the old gowns, which had not been seen for years, had been stowed away. It was the same on Sundays as on Mondays and Tuesdays. But the due gradation was kept between Sundays and week-days. She was quite well enough dressed for a brewer's foreman's daughter on one day as on the other, but neither on one day nor on the other was she at all the Polly Peppercorn that Plumplington had known for the last couple of years. And there was not a word said about it. But all Plumplington knew that Polly was fitting herself, as regarded her outside garniture, to be the wife of Jack Hollycombe with 40s. a week. And all Plumplington said that she would carry her purpose, and that Hickory Peppercorn would break down under stress of the artillery brought to bear against him. He could not put out her clothes for her, or force her into wearing them as her mother might have done, had her mother been living. He could only tear his hair and greet, and swear to himself that under no such artillery as this would he give way. His girl should never marry Jack Hollycombe. He thought he knew his girl well enough to be sure that she would not marry without his consent. She might make him very unhappy by wearing dowdy clothes, but she would not quite break his heart. In the meantime Polly took care that her father should have no opportunity of measuring Jack's back.

With the affairs of Miss Greenmantle much more ceremony was observed, though I doubt whether there was more earnestness felt in the matter. Mr. Peppercorn was very much in earnest, as was Polly,—and Jack Hollycombe. But Peppercorn talked about it publicly, and Polly showed her purpose, and Jack exhibited the triumphant lover to all eyes. Mr. Greenmantle was silent as death in respect to the great trouble that had come upon him. He had spoken to no one on the subject except to the peccant lover, and just a word or two to old Dr. Freeborn. There was no trouble in the town that did not reach Dr. Freeborn's ears; and Mr. Greenmantle, in spite of his little jealousy, was no exception. To the Doctor he had said a word or two as to Emily's bad behaviour. But in the stiffness of his back, and the length of his face, and the continual frown which was gathered on his brows, he was eloquent to all the town. Peppercorn had no powers of looking as he looked. The gloom of the bank was awful. It was felt to be so by the two junior clerks, who hardly knew whether to hate or to pity most Mr. Philip Hughes. And if Mr. Greenmantle's demeanour was hard to bear down below, within the bank, what must it have been upstairs in the family sitting-room? It was now, at this time, about the middle of November; and with Emily everything had been black and clouded for the last two months past. Polly's misfortune had only begun about the first of November. The two young ladies had had their own ideas about their own young men from nearly the same date. Philip Hughes and Jack Hollycombe had pushed themselves into prominence about the same time. But Emily's trouble had declared itself six weeks before Polly had sent her young man to her father. The first scene which took place with Emily and Mr. Greenmantle, after young Hughes had declared himself, was very impressive. "What is this, Emily?"

"What is what, papa?" A poor girl when she is thus cross-questioned hardly knows what to say.

"One of the young men in the bank has been to me." There was in this a great slur intended. It was acknowledged by all Plumplington that Mr. Hughes was the cashier, and was hardly more fairly designated as one of the young men than would have been Mr. Greenmantle himself,—unless in regard to age.

"Philip, I suppose," said Emily. Now Mr. Greenmantle had certainly led the way into this difficulty himself. He had been allured by some modesty in the young man's demeanour,—or more probably by something pleasant in his manner which had struck Emily also,—to call him Philip. He had, as it were, shown a parental regard for him, and those who had best known Mr. Greenmantle had been sure that he would not forget his manifest good intentions towards the young man. As coming from Mr. Greenmantle the use of the christian name had been made. But certainly he had not intended that it should be taken up in this manner. There had been an ingratitude in it, which Mr. Greenmantle had felt very keenly.

"I would rather that you should call the young man Mr. Hughes in anything that you may have to say about him."

"I thought you called him Philip, papa."

"I shall never do so again,—never. What is this that he has said to me? Can it be true?"

"I suppose it is true, papa."

"You mean that you want to marry him?"

"Yes, papa."

"Goodness gracious me!" After this Emily remained silent for a while. "Can you have realised the fact that the young man has— nothing; literally nothing!" What is a young lady to say when she is thus appealed to? She knew that though the young man had nothing, she would have a considerable portion of her own. She was her father's only child. She had not "cared for" young Gresham, whereas she had "cared for" young Hughes. What would be all the world to her if she must marry a man she did not care for? That, she was resolved, she would not do. But what would all the world be to her if she were not allowed to marry the man she did love? And what good would it be to her to be the only daughter of a rich man if she were to be baulked in this manner? She had thought it all over, assuming to herself perhaps greater privileges than she was entitled to expect.

But Emily Greenmantle was somewhat differently circumstanced from Polly Peppercorn. Emily was afraid of her father's sternness, whereas Polly was not in the least afraid of her governor, as she was wont to call him. Old Hickory was, in a good-humoured way, afraid of Polly. Polly could order the things, in and about the house, very much after her own fashion. To tell the truth Polly had but slight fear but that she would have her own way, and when she laid by her best silks she did not do it as a person does bid farewell to those treasures which are not to be seen again. They could be made to do very well for the future Mrs. Hollycombe. At any rate, like a Marlborough or a Wellington, she went into the battle thinking of victory and not of defeat. But Wellington was a long time before he had beaten the French, and Polly thought that there might be some trouble also for her. With Emily there was no prospect of ultimate victory.

Mr. Greenmantle was a very stern man, who could look at his daughter as though he never meant to give way. And, without say- ing a word, he could make all Plumplington understand that such was to be the case. "Poor Emily," said the old Doctor to his old wife; "I'm afraid there's a bad time coming for her." "He's a nasty cross old man," said the old woman. "It always does take three generations to make a 'gentleman.'" For Mrs. Freeborn's ancestors had come from the time of James I.

"You and I had better understand each other," said Mr. Greenmantle, standing up with his back to the fireplace, and looking as though he were all poker from the top of his head to the heels of his boots. "You cannot marry Mr. Philip Hughes." Emily said nothing but turned her eyes down upon the ground. "I don't suppose he thinks of doing so without money."

"He has never thought about money at all."

"Then what are you to live upon? Can you tell me that? He has £220 from the bank. Can you live upon that? Can you bring up a family?" Emily blushed as she still looked upon the ground. "I tell you fairly that he shall never have the spending of my money. If you mean to desert me in my old age,—go."

"Papa, you shouldn't say that."

"You shouldn't think it." Then Mr. Greenmantle looked as though he had uttered a clenching argument. "You shouldn't think it. Now go away, Emily, and turn in your mind what I have said to you."

CHAPTER II

"DOWN I SHALL GO"

Then there came about a conversation between the two young ladies which was in itself very interesting. They had not met each other for about a fortnight when Emily Greenmantle came to Mr. Peppercorn's house. She had been thoroughly unhappy, and among her causes for sorrow had been the severance which seemed to have taken place between her and her friend. She had discussed all her troubles with Dr. Freeborn, and Dr. Freeborn had advised her to see Polly. "Here's Christmas-time coming on and you are all going to quarrel among yourselves. I won't have any such nonsense. Go and see her."

"It's not me, Dr. Freeborn," said Emily. "I don't want to quarrel with anybody; and there is nobody I like better than Polly." Thereupon Emily went to Mr. Peppercorn's house when

Peppercorn would be certainly at the brewery, and there she found Polly at home.

Polly was dressed very plainly. It was manifest to all eyes that the Polly Peppercorn of to-day was not the same Polly Peppercorn that had been seen about Plumplington for the last twelve months. It was equally manifest that Polly intended that everybody should see the difference. She had not meekly put on her poorer dress so that people should see that she was no more than her father's child; but it was done with some ostentation. "If father says that Jack and I are not to have his money I must begin to reduce myself by times." That was what Polly intended to say to all Plumplington. She was sure that her father would have to give way under such shots as she could fire at him.

"Polly, I have not seen you, oh, for such a long time."

Polly did not look like quarrelling at all. Nothing could be more pleasant than the tone of her voice. But yet there was something in her mode of address which at once excited Emily Greenmantle's attention. In bidding her visitor welcome she called her Miss Greenmantle. Now on that matter there had been some little trouble heretofore, in which the banker's daughter had succeeded in getting the better of the banker. He had suggested that Miss Peppercorn was safer than Polly; but Emily had replied that Polly was a nice dear girl, very much in Dr. Freeborn's good favours, and in point of fact that Dr. Freeborn wouldn't allow it. Mr. Greenmantle had frowned, but had felt himself unable to stand against Dr. Freeborn in such a matter. "What's the meaning of the Miss Greenmantle?" said Emily sorrowfully.

"It's what I'm come to," said Polly, without any show of sorrow, "and it's what I mean to stick to as being my proper place. You have heard all about Jack Hollycombe. I suppose I ought to call him John as I'm speaking to you."

"I don't see what difference it will make."

"Not much in the long run; but yet it will make a difference. It isn't that I should not like to be just the same to you as I have been, but father means to put me down in the world, and I don't mean to quarrel with him about that. Down I shall go."

"And therefore I'm to be called Miss Greenmantle."

"Exactly. Perhaps it ought to have been always so as I'm so poorly minded as to go back to such a one as Jack Hollycombe. Of course it is going back. Of course Jack is as good as father was at his age. But father has put himself up since that and has put me up. I'm such poor stuff that I wouldn't stay up. A girl has to begin where her husband begins; and as I mean to be Jack's wife I have to fit myself for the place."

"I suppose it's the same with me, Polly."

"Not quite. You're a lady bred and born, and Mr. Hughes is a gentleman. Father tells me that a man who goes about the country selling malt isn't a gentleman. I suppose father is right. But Jack is a good enough gentleman to my thinking. If he had a share of father's money he would break out in quite a new place."

"Mr. Peppercorn won't give it to him?"

"Well! That's what I don't know. I do think the governor loves me. He is the best fellow anywhere for downright kindness. I mean to try him. And if he won't help me I shall go down as I say. You may be sure of this,—that I shall not give up Jack."

"You wouldn't marry him against your father's wishes?"

Here Polly wasn't quite ready with her answer. "I don't know that father has a right to destroy all my happiness," she said at last. "I shall wait a long time first at any rate. Then if I find that Jack can remain constant,—I don't know what I shall do."

"What does he say?"

"Jack? He's all sugar and promises. They always are for a time. It takes a deal of learning to know whether a young man can be true. There is not above one in twenty that do come out true when they are tried."

"I suppose not," said Emily sorrowfully.

"I shall tell Mr. Jack that he's got to go through the ordeal. Of course he wants me to say that I'll marry him right off the reel and that he'll earn money enough for both of us. I told him only this morning—"

"Did you see him?"

"I wrote him,—out quite plainly. And I told him that there were other people had hearts in their bodies besides him and me. I'm not going to break father's heart,—not if I can help it. It would go very hard with him if I were to walk out of this house and marry Jack Hollycombe, quite plain like."

"I would never do it," said Emily with energy.

"You are a little different from me, Miss Greenmantle. I suppose my mother didn't think much about such things, and as long as she got herself married decent, didn't trouble herself much what her people said."

"Didn't she?"

"I fancy not. Those sort of cares and bothers always come with money. Look at the two girls in this house. I take it they only act just like their mothers, and if they're good girls, which they are, they get their mothers' consent. But the marriage goes on as a matter of course. It's where money is wanted that parents become stern and their children become dutiful. I mean to be dutiful for a time. But I'd rather have Jack than father's money."

"Dr. Freeborn says that you and I are not to quarrel. I am sure I don't see why we should."

"What Dr. Freeborn says is very well." It was thus that Polly carried on the conversation after thinking over the matter for a moment or two. "Dr. Freeborn is a great man in Plumplington, and has his own way in everything. I'm not saying a word against Dr. Freeborn, and goodness knows I don't want to quarrel with you, Miss Greenmantle."

"I hope not."

"But I do mean to go down if father makes me, and if Jack proves himself a true man."

"I suppose he'll do that," said Miss Greenmantle. "Of course you think he will."

"Well, upon the whole I do," said Polly. "And though I think father will have to give up, he won't do it just at present, and I shall have to remain just as I am for a time."

"And wear—" Miss Greenmantle had intended to inquire whether it was Polly's purpose to go about in her second-rate clothes, but had hesitated, not quite liking to ask the question.

"Just that," said Polly. "I mean to wear such clothes as shall be suitable for Jack's wife. And I mean to give up all my airs. I've been thinking a deal about it, and they're wrong. Your papa and my father are not the same."

"They are not the same, of course," said Emily.

"One is a gentleman, and the other isn't. That's the long and the short of it. I oughtn't to have gone to your house drinking tea and the rest of it; and I oughtn't to have called you Emily. That's the long and the short of that," said she, repeating herself.

"Dr. Freeborn thinks—"

"Dr. Freeborn mustn't quite have it all his own way. Of course Dr. Freeborn is everything in Plumplington; and when I'm Jack's wife I'll do what he tells me again."

"I suppose you'll do what Jack tells you then."

"Well, yes; not exactly. If Jack were to tell me not to go to church,—which he won't,—I shouldn't do what he told me. If he said he'd like to have a leg of mutton boiled, I should boil it. Only legs of mutton wouldn't be very common with us, unless father comes round."

"I don't see why all that should make a difference between you and me."

"It will have to do so," said Polly with perfect self-assurance. "Father has told me that he doesn't mean to find money to buy legs of mutton for Jack Hollycombe. Those were his very words. I'm determined I'll never ask him. And he said he wasn't going to find clothes for Jack Hollycombe's brats. I'll never go to him to find a pair of shoes for Jack Hollycombe or one of his brats. I've told Jack as much, and Jack says that I'm right. But there's no knowing what's inside a young man till you've tried him. Jack may fall off, and if so there's an end of him. I shall come round in time, and wear my fine clothes again when I settle down as an old maid. But father will never make me wear them, and I shall never call you anything but Miss Greenmantle, unless he consent to my marrying Jack."

Such was the eloquence of Polly Peppercorn as spoken on that occasion. And she certainly did fill Miss Greenmantle's mind with a strong idea of her persistency. When Polly's last speech was finished the banker's daughter got up, and kissed her friend, and took her leave. "You shouldn't do that," said Polly with a smile. But on this one occasion she returned the caress; and then Miss Greenmantle went her way thinking over all that had been said to her.

"I'll do it too, let him persuade me ever so." This was Polly's soliloquy to herself when she was left alone, and the "him" spoken of on this occasion was her father. She had made up her own mind as to the line of action she would follow, and she was quite resolved never again to ask her father's permission for her marriage. Her father and Jack might fight that out among themselves, as best they could. There had already been one scene on the subject between herself and her father in which the brewer's foreman had acted the part of stern parent with considerable violence. He had not beaten his girl, nor used bad words to her, nor, to tell the truth, had he threatened her with any deprivation of those luxuries to which she had become accustomed; but he had sworn by all the oaths which he knew by heart that if she chose to marry Jack Hollycombe she should go "bare as a tinker's brat." "I don't want anything better," Polly had said. "He'll want something else though," Peppercorn had replied, and had bounced out of the room and banged the door.

Miss Greenmantle, in whose nature there was perhaps something of the lugubrious tendencies which her father exhibited, walked away home from Mr. Peppercorn's house with a sad heart. She was very sorry for Polly Peppercorn's grief, and she was very sorry also for her own. But she had not that amount of high spirits which sustained Polly in her troubles. To tell the truth Polly had some hope that she might get the better of her father, and thereby do a good turn both to him and to herself. But Emily Greenmantle had but little hope. Her father had not sworn at her, nor had he banged the door, but he had pressed his lips together till there was no lip really visible. And he had raised his forehead on high till it looked as though one continuous poker descended from the crown of his head passing down through his entire body. "Emily, it is out of the question. You had better leave me." From that day to this not a word had been spoken on the "subject." Young Gresham had been once asked to dine at the bank, but that had been the only effort made by Mr. Greenmantle in the matter.

Emily had felt as she walked home that she had not at her command weapons so powerful as those which Polly intended to use against her father. No change in her dress would be suitable to her, and were she to make any it would be altogether inefficacious. Nor would her father be tempted by his passion to throw in her teeth the lack of either boots or legs of mutton which might be the consequence of her marriage with a poor man. There was something almost vulgar in these allusions which made Emily feel that there had been some reason for her papa's exclusiveness,—but she let that go by. Polly was a dear girl, though she had found herself able to speak of the brats' feet without even a blush. "I suppose there will be brats, and why shouldn't she,—when she's talking only to me. It must be so I suppose." So Emily had argued to herself, making the excuse altogether on behalf of her friend. But she was sure that if her father had heard Polly he would have been offended.

But what was Emily to do on her own behalf? Harry Gresham had come to dinner, but his coming had been altogether without effect. She was quite sure that she could never care for Harry Gresham, and she did not quite believe that Harry Gresham cared very much for her. There was a rumour about in the country that Harry Gresham wanted money, and she knew well that Harry Gresham's father and her own papa had been closeted together. She did not care to be married after such a fashion as that. In truth Philip Hughes was the only young man for whom she did care.

She had always felt her father to be the most impregnable of men,—but now on this subject of her marriage he was more impregnable than ever. He had never yet entirely digested that poker which he had swallowed when he had gone so far as to tell his daughter that it was "entirely out of the question." From that hour her home had been terrible to her as a home, and had not been in the least enlivened by the presence of Harry Gresham. And now how was she to carry on the battle? Polly had her plans all drawn out, and was preparing herself for the combat seriously. But for Emily, there was no means left for fighting.

And she felt that though a battle with her father might be very proper for Polly, it would be highly unbecoming for herself. There was a difference in rank between herself and Polly of which Polly clearly understood the strength. Polly would put on her poor clothes, and go into the kitchen, and break her father's heart by preparing for a descent into regions which would be fitting for her were she to marry her young man without a fortune. But to Miss Greenmantle this would be impossible. Any marriage, made now or later, without her father's leave, seemed to her out of the question. She would only ruin her "young man" were she to attempt it, and the attempt would be altogether inefficacious. She could only be unhappy, melancholy,—and perhaps morose; but she could not be so unhappy and melancholy,—or morose, as was her father. At such weapons he could certainly beat her. Since that unhappy word had been spoken, the poker within him had not been for a moment lessened in vigour. And she feared even to appeal to Dr. Freeborn. Dr. Freeborn could do much,—almost everything in Plumplington,—but there was a point at which her father would turn even against Dr. Freeborn. She did not think that the Doctor would ever dare to take up the cudgels against her father on behalf of Philip Hughes. She felt that it would be more becoming for her to abstain and to suffer in silence than to apply to any human being for assistance. But she could be miserable;—outwardly miserable as

well as inwardly;—and very miserable she was determined that she
would be! Her father no doubt would be miserable too; but she was
sad at heart as she bethought herself that her father would rather
like it. Though he could not easily digest a poker when he had
swallowed it, it never seemed to disagree with him. A state of misery in which he would speak to no one seemed to be almost to his
taste. In this way poor Emily Greenmantle did not see her way to
the enjoyment of a happy Christmas.

CHAPTER III

MR. GREENMANTLE IS MUCH PERPLEXED

That evening Mr. Greenmantle and his daughter sat down to dinner together in a very unhappy humour. They always dined at
half-past seven; not that Mr. Greenmantle liked to have his dinner
at that hour better than any other, but because it was considered to
be fashionable. Old Mr. Gresham, Harry's father, always dined at
half-past seven, and Mr. Greenmantle rather followed the habits of
a county gentleman's life. He used to dine at this hour when there
was a dinner-party, but of late he had adopted it for the family
meal. To tell the truth there had been a few words between him
and Dr. Freeborn while Emily had been talking over matters with
Polly Peppercorn. Dr. Freeborn had not ventured to say a word as
to Emily's love affairs; but had so discussed those of Jack
Hollycombe and Polly as to leave a strong impression on the mind
of Mr. Greenmantle. He had quite understood that the Doctor had
been talking at himself, and that when Jack's name had been mentioned, or Polly's, the Doctor had intended that the wisdom spoken
should be intended to apply to Emily and to Philip Hughes. "It's
only because he can give her a lot of money," the Doctor had said.
"The young man is a good young man, and steady. What is
Peppercorn that he should want anything better for his child?
Young Hollycombe has taken her fancy, and why shouldn't she
have him?"

"I suppose Mr. Peppercorn may have his own views," Mr.
Greenmantle had answered.

"Bother his views," the Doctor had said. "He has no one else to
think of but the girl and his views should be confined to making

her happy. Of course he'll have to give way at last, and will only make himself ridiculous. I shouldn't say a word about it only that the young man is all that he ought to be."

Now in this there was not a word which did not apply to Mr. Greenmantle himself. And the worst of it was the fact that Mr. Greenmantle felt that the Doctor intended it.

But as he had taken his constitutional walk before dinner, a walk which he took every day of his life after bank hours, he had sworn to himself that he would not be guided, or in the least affected, by Dr. Freeborn's opinion in the matter. There had been an underlying bitterness in the Doctor's words which had much aggravated the banker's ill-humour. The Doctor would not so have spoken of the marriage of one of his own daughters,—before they had all been married. Birth would have been considered by him almost before anything. The Peppercorns and the Greenmantles were looked down upon almost from an equal height. Now Mr. Greenmantle considered himself to be infinitely superior to Mr. Peppercorn, and to be almost, if not altogether, equal to Dr. Freeborn. He was much the richer man of the two, and his money was quite sufficient to outweigh a century or two of blood.

Peppercorn might do as he pleased. What became of Peppercorn's money was an affair of no matter. The Doctor's argument was no doubt good as far as Peppercorn was concerned. Peppercorn was not a gentleman. It was that which Mr. Greenmantle felt so acutely. The one great line of demarcation in the world was that which separated gentlemen from non-gentlemen. Mr. Greenmantle assured himself that he was a gentleman, acknowledged to be so by all the county. The old Duke of Omnium had customarily asked him to dine at his annual dinner at Gatherum Castle. He had been in the habit of staying occasionally at Greshambury, Mr. Gresham's county seat, and Mr. Gresham had been quite willing to forward the match between Emily and his younger son. There could be no doubt that he was on the right side of the line of demarcation. He was therefore quite determined that his daughter should not marry the Cashier in his own bank.

As he sat down to dinner he looked sternly at his daughter, and thought with wonder at the viciousness of her taste. She looked at him almost as sternly as she thought with awe of his cruelty. In her eyes Philip Hughes was quite as good a gentleman as her father. He was the son of a clergyman who was now dead, but had been intimate with Dr. Freeborn. And in the natural course of events might succeed her father as manager of the Bank. To be manager of the Bank at Plumplington was not very much in the eyes of the world; but it was the position which her father filled. Emily vowed to herself as she looked across the table into her father's face, that she would be Mrs. Philip Hughes,—or remain unmarried all her life. "Emily, shall I help you to a mutton cutlet?" said her father with solemnity.

"No thank you, papa," she replied with equal gravity.

"On what then do you intend to dine?" There had been a sole of which she had also declined to partake. "There is nothing else, unless you will dine off rice pudding."

"I am not hungry, papa." She could not decline to wear her customary clothes as did her friend Polly, but she could at any rate go without her dinner. Even a father so stern as was Mr. Greenmantle could not make her eat. Then there came a vision across her eyes of a long sickness, produced chiefly by inanition, in which she might wear her father's heart out. And then she felt that she might too probably lack the courage. She did not care much for her dinner; but she feared that she could not persevere to the breaking of her father's heart. She and her father were alone together in the world, and he in other respects had always been good to her. And now a tear trickled from her eye down her nose as she gazed upon the empty plate. He ate his two cutlets one after another in solemn silence and so the dinner was ended.

He, too, had felt uneasy qualms during the meal. "What shall I do if she takes to starving herself and going to bed, all along of that young rascal in the outer bank?" It was thus that he had thought of it, and he too for a moment had begun to tell himself that were she to be perverse she must win the battle. He knew himself to be strong in purpose, but he doubted whether he would be strong enough to stand by and see his daughter starve herself. A week's starvation or a fortnight's he might bear, and it was possible that she might give way before that time had come.

Then he retired to a little room inside the bank, a room that was half private and half official, to which he would betake himself to spend his evening whenever some especially gloomy fit would fall upon him. Here, within his own bosom, he turned over all the circumstances of the case. No doubt he had with him all the laws of God and man. He was not bound to give his money to any such interloper as was Philip Hughes. On that point he was quite clear. But what step had he better take to prevent the evil? Should he resign his position at the bank, and take his daughter away to live in the south of France? It would be a terrible step to which to be driven by his own Cashier. He was as efficacious to do the work of the bank as ever he had been, and he would leave this enemy to occupy his place. The enemy would then be in a condition to marry a wife without a fortune; and who could tell whether he might not show his power in such a crisis by marrying Emily! How terrible in such a case would be his defeat! At any rate he might go for three months on sick leave. He had been for nearly forty years in the bank, and had never yet been absent for a day on sick leave. Thinking of all this he remained alone till it was time for him to go to bed.

On the next morning he was dumb and stiff as ever, and after breakfast sat dumb and stiff, in his official room behind the bank counter, thinking over his great trouble. He had not spoken a word to Emily since yesterday's dinner beyond asking her whether she would take a bit of fried bacon. "No thank you, papa," she had said; and then Mr. Greenmantle had made up his mind that he must take her away somewhere at once, lest she should be starved to death. Then he went into the bank and sat there signing his name, and meditating the terrible catastrophe which was to fall upon him. Hughes, the Cashier, had become Mr. Hughes, and if any young man could be frightened out of his love by the stern look and sterner voice of a parent, Mr. Hughes would have been so frightened.

Then there came a knock at the door, and Mr. Peppercorn having been summoned to come in, entered the room. He had expressed a desire to see Mr. Greenmantle personally, and having proved his eagerness by a double request, had been allowed to have his way. It was quite a common affair for him to visit the bank on matters referring to the brewery; but now it was evident to any one with half an eye that such at present was not Mr. Peppercorn's business. He had on the clothes in which he habitually went to church instead of the light-coloured pepper and salt tweed jacket in which he was accustomed to go about among the malt and barrels. "What can I do for you, Mr. Peppercorn?" said the banker. But the aspect was the aspect of a man who had a poker still fixed within his head and gullet.

"'Tis nothing about the brewery, sir, or I shouldn't have troubled you. Mr. Hughes is very good at all that kind of thing." A further frown came over Mr. Greenmantle's face, but he said nothing. "You know my daughter Polly, Mr. Greenmantle?"

"I am aware that there is a Miss Peppercorn," said the other. Peppercorn felt that an offence was intended. Mr. Greenmantle was of course aware. "What can I do on behalf of Miss Peppercorn?"

"She's as good a girl as ever lived."

"I do not in the least doubt it. If it be necessary that you should speak to me respecting Miss Peppercorn, will it not be well that you should take a chair?"

Then Mr. Peppercorn sat down, feeling that he had been snubbed. "I may say that my only object in life is to do every mortal thing to make my girl happy." Here Mr. Greenmantle simply bowed. "We sit close to you in church, where, however, she comes much more reg'lar than me, and you must have observed her scores of times."

"I am not in the habit of looking about among young ladies at church time, but I have occasionally been aware that Miss Peppercorn has been there."

"Of course you have. You couldn't help it. Well, now, you know the sort of appearance she has made."

"I can assure you, Mr. Peppercorn, that I have not observed Miss Peppercorn's dress in particular. I do not look much at the raiment worn by young ladies even in the outer world,—much less in church. I have a daughter of my own——"

"It's her as I'm coming to." Then Mr. Greenmantle frowned more severely than ever. But the brewer did not at the moment say a word about the banker's daughter, but reverted to his own. "You'll see next Sunday that my girl won't look at all like herself."

"I really cannot promise——"

"You cannot help yourself, Mr. Greenmantle. I'll go bail that every one in church will see it. Polly is not to be passed over in a crowd;—at least she didn't used to be. Now it all comes of her wanting to get herself married to a young man who is altogether beneath her. Not as I mean to say anything against John Hollycombe as regards his walk of life. He is an industrious young man, as can earn forty shillings a week, and he comes over here from Barchester selling malt and such like. He may rise himself to £3 some of these days if he looks sharp about it. But I can give my girl—; well; what is quite unfit that he should think of looking for with a wife. And it's monstrous of Polly wanting to throw herself away in such a fashion. I don't believe in a young man being so covetous."

"But what can I do, Mr. Peppercorn?"

"I'm coming to that. If you'll see her next Sunday you'll think of what my feelings must be. She's a-doing of it all just because she wants to show me that she thinks herself fit for nothing better than to be John Hollycombe's wife. When I tell her that I won't have it,—this sudden changing of her toggery, she says it's only fitting. It ain't fitting at all. I've got the money to buy things for her, and I'm willing to pay for it. Is she to go poor just to break her father's heart?"

"But what can I do, Mr. Peppercorn?"

"I'm coming to that. The world does say, Mr. Greenmantle, that your young lady means to serve you in the same fashion."

Hereupon Mr. Greenmantle waxed very wroth. It was terrible to his ideas that his daughter's affairs should be talked of at all by the people at Plumplington at large. It was worse again that his daughter and the brewer's girl should be lumped together in the scandal of the town. But it was worse, much worse, that this man Peppercorn should have dared to come to him, and tell him all about it. Did the man really expect that he, Mr. Greenmantle, should talk unreservedly as to the love affairs of his Emily? "The world, Mr. Peppercorn, is very impertinent in its usual scandalous conversations as to its betters. You must forgive me if I do not intend on this occasion to follow the example of the world. Good morning, Mr. Peppercorn."

"It's Dr. Freeborn as has coupled the two girls together."

"I cannot believe it."

"You ask him. It's he who has said that you and I are in a boat together."

"I'm not in a boat with any man."

"Well,—in a difficulty. It's the same thing. The Doctor seems to think that young ladies are to have their way in everything. I don't see it. When a man has made a tidy bit of money, as have you and I, he has a right to have a word to say as to who shall have the spending of it. A girl hasn't the right to say that she'll give it all to this man or to that. Of course, it's natural that my money should go to Polly. I'm not saying anything against it. But I don't mean that John Hollycombe shall have it. Now if you and I can put our heads together, I think we may be able to see our way out of the wood."

"Mr. Peppercorn, I cannot consent to discuss with you the affairs of Miss Greenmantle."

"But they're both alike. You must admit that."

"I will admit nothing, Mr. Peppercorn."

"I do think, you know, that we oughtn't to be done by our own daughters."

"Really, Mr. Peppercorn——"

"Dr. Freeborn was saying that you and I would have to give way at last."

"Dr. Freeborn knows nothing about it. If Dr. Freeborn coupled the two young ladies together he was I must say very impertinent; but I don't think he ever did so. Good morning, Mr. Peppercorn. I am fully engaged at present and cannot spare time for a longer interview." Then he rose up from his chair, and leant upon the table with his hands by way of giving a certain signal that he was to be left alone. Mr. Peppercorn, after pausing a moment, searching for an opportunity for another word, was overcome at last by the rigid erectness of Mr. Greenmantle and withdrew.

CHAPTER IV

JACK HOLLYCOMBE

Mr. Peppercorn's visit to the bank had been no doubt inspired by Dr. Freeborn. The Doctor had not actually sent him to the bank, but had filled his mind with the idea that such a visit might be made with good effect. "There are you two fathers going to make two fools of yourselves," the Doctor had said. "You have each of you got a daughter as good as gold, and are determined to break their hearts because you won't give your money to a young man who happens to want it."

"Now, Doctor, do you mean to tell me that you would have married your young ladies to the first young man that came and asked for them?"

"I never had much money to give my girls, and the men who came happened to have means of their own."

"But if you'd had it, and if they hadn't, do you mean to tell me you'd never have asked a question?"

"A man should never boast that in any circumstances of his life he would have done just what he ought to do,—much less when he has never been tried. But if the lover be what he ought to be in morals and all that kind of thing, the girl's father ought not to refuse to help them. You may be sure of this,—that Polly means to have her own way. Providence has blessed you with a girl that knows her own mind." On receipt of this compliment Mr. Peppercorn scratched his head. "I wish I could say as much for my friend Greenmantle. You two are in a boat together, and ought to make up your mind as to what you should do." Peppercorn resolved that he would remember the phrase about the boat, and began to think that it might be good that he should see Mr. Greenmantle. "What on earth is it you two want? It is not as though you were dukes, and looking for proper alliances for two ducal spinsters."

Now there had no doubt been a certain amount of intended venom in this. Dr. Freeborn knew well the weak points in Mr. Greenmantle's character, and was determined to hit him where he was weakest. He did not see the difference between the banker and the brewer nearly so clearly as did Mr. Greenmantle. He would probably have said that the line of demarcation came just below himself. At any rate, he thought that he would be doing best for Emily's interest if he made her father feel that all the world was on her side. Therefore it was that he so contrived that Mr. Peppercorn should pay his visit to the bank.

On his return to the brewery the first person that Peppercorn saw standing in the doorway of his own little sanctum was Jack Hollycombe. "What is it you're wanting?" he asked gruffly.

"I was just desirous of saying a few words to yourself, Mr. Peppercorn."

"Well, here I am!" There were two or three brewers and porters about the place, and Jack did not feel that he could plead his cause well in their presence. "What is it you've got to say,—because I'm busy? There ain't no malt wanted for the next week; but you know that, and as we stand at present you can send it in without any more words, as it's needed."

"It ain't about malt or anything of that kind."

"Then I don't know what you've got to say. I'm very busy just at present, as I told you."

"You can spare me five minutes inside."

"No I can't." But then Peppercorn resolved that neither would it suit him to carry on the conversation respecting his daughter in the presence of the workmen, and he thought that he perceived that Jack Hollycombe would be prepared to do so if he were driven. "Come in if you will," he said; "we might as well have it out." Then he led the way into the room, and shut the door as soon as Jack had followed him. "Now what is it you have got to say? I suppose it's about that young woman down at my house."

"It is, Mr. Peppercorn."

"Then let me tell you that the least said will be soonest mended. She's not for you,—with my consent. And to tell you the truth I think that you have a mortal deal of brass coming to ask for her. You've no edication suited to her edication,—and what's wus, no money." Jack had shown symptoms of anger when his deficient education had been thrown in his teeth, but had cheered up somewhat when the lack of money had been insisted upon. Them two things are so against you that you haven't a leg to stand on. My word! what do you expect that I should say when such a one as you comes a-courting to a girl like that?"

"I did, perhaps, think more of what she might say."

"I daresay;—because you knew her to be a fool like yourself. I suppose you think yourself to be a very handsome young man."

"I think she's a very handsome young woman. As to myself I never asked the question."

"That's all very well. A man can always say as much as that for himself. The fact is you're not going to have her."

"That's just what I want to speak to you about, Mr. Peppercorn."

"You're not going to have her. Now I've spoken my intentions, and you may as well take one word as a thousand. I'm not a man as was ever known to change my mind when I'd made it up in such a matter as this."

"She's got a mind too, Mr. Peppercorn."

"She have, no doubt. She have a mind and so have you. But you haven't either of you got the money. The money is here," and Mr. Peppercorn slapped his breeches pocket. "I've had to do with earning it, and I mean to have to do with giving it away. To me there is no idea of honesty at all in a chap like you coming and asking a girl to marry you just because you know that she's to have a fortune."

"That's not my reason."

"It's uncommon like it. Now you see there's somebody else that's got to be asked. You think I'm a goodnatured fellow. So I am, but I'm not soft like that.

"I never thought anything of the kind, Mr. Peppercorn."

"Polly told you so, I don't doubt. She's right in thinking so, because I'd give Polly anything in reason. Or out of reason for the matter of that, because she is the apple of my eye." This was indiscreet on the part of Mr. Peppercorn, as it taught the young man to think that he himself must be in reason or out of reason, and that in either case Polly ought to be allowed to have him. "But there's one thing I stop at; and that is a young man who hasn't got either edication, or money,—nor yet manners."

"There's nothing against my manner, I hope, Mr. Peppercorn."

"Yes; there is. You come a-interfering with me in the most delicate affair in the world. You come into my family, and want to take away my girl. That I take it is the worst of manners."

"How is any young lady to get married unless some young fellow comes after her?"

"There'll be plenty to come after Polly. You leave Polly alone, and you'll find that she'll get a young man suited to her. It's like your impudence to suppose that there's no other young man in the world so good as you. Why;—dash my wig; who are you? What are you? You're merely acting for them corn-factors over at Barsester."

"And you're acting for them brewers here at Plumplington. What's the difference?"

"But I've got the money in my pocket, and you've got none. That's the difference. Put that in your pipe and smoke it. Now if you'll please to remember that I'm very busy, you'll walk yourself off. You've had it out with me, which I didn't intend; and I've explained my mind very fully. She's not for you;—at any rate my money's not."

"Look here, Mr. Peppercorn."

"Well?"

"I don't care a farthing for your money."

"Don't you, now?"

"Not in the way of comparing it with Polly herself. Of course money is a very comfortable thing. If Polly's to be my wife—"

"Which she ain't."

"I should like her to have everything that a lady can desire."

"How kind you are."

"But in regard to money for myself I don't value it that." Here Jack Hollycombe snapped his fingers. "My meaning is to get the girl I love."

"Then you won't."

"And if she's satisfied to come to me without a shilling, I'm satisfied to take her in the same fashion. I don't know how much you've got, Mr. Peppercorn, but you can go and found a Hiram's Hospital with every penny of it." At this moment a discussion was going on respecting a certain charitable institution in Barchester,—and had been going on for the last forty years,—as to which Mr. Hollycombe was here expressing the popular opinion of the day. "That's the kind of thing a man should do who don't choose to leave his money to his own child." Jack was now angry, having had his deficient education twice thrown in his teeth by one whom he conceived to be so much less educated than himself. "What I've got to say to you, Mr. Peppercorn, is that Polly means to have me, and if she's got to wait—why, I'm so minded that I'll wait for her as long as ever she'll wait for me." So saying Jack Hollycombe left the room.

Mr. Peppercorn thrust his hat back upon his head, and stood with his back to the fire, with the tails of his coat appearing over his hands in his breeches pockets, glaring out of his eyes with anger which he did not care to suppress. This man had presented to him a picture of his future life which was most unalluring. There was nothing he desired less than to give his money to such an abominable institution as Hiram's Hospital. Polly, his own dear daughter Polly, was intended to be the recipient of all his savings. As he went about among the beer barrels, he had been a happy man as he thought of Polly bright with the sheen which his money had provided for her. But it was of Polly married to some gentleman that he thought at these moments;—of Polly surrounded by a large family of little gentlemen and little ladies. They would all call him grandpapa; and in the evenings of his days he would sit by the fire in that gentleman's parlour, a welcome guest because of the means which he had provided; and the little gentlemen and the little ladies would surround him with their prattle and their noises and caresses. He was not a man whom his intimates would have supposed to be gifted with a strong imagination, but there was the picture firmly set before his mind's eye. "Edication," however, in the intended son-in-law was essential. And the son-in-law must be a gentleman. Now Jack Hollycombe was not a gentleman, and was not educated up to that pitch which was necessary for Polly's husband.

But Mr. Peppercorn, as he thought of it all, was well aware that Polly had a decided will of her own. And he knew of himself that his own will was less strong than his daughter's. In spite of all the severe things which he had just said to Jack Hollycombe, there was present to him a dreadful weight upon his heart, as he thought that Polly would certainly get the better of him. At this moment he hated Jack Hollycombe with most un-Christian rancour. No misfortune that could happen to Jack, either sudden death, or forgery with flight to the antipodes, or loss of his good looks,—which Mr. Peppercorn most unjustly thought would be equally efficacious with Polly,—would at the present moment of his wrath be received otherwise than as a special mark of good-fortune. And yet he was well aware that if Polly were to come and tell him that she had by some secret means turned herself into Mrs. Jack Hollycombe, he knew very well that for Polly's sake he would have to take Jack with all his faults, and turn him into the dearest son-in-law that the world could have provided for him. This was a very trying position, and justified him in standing there for a quarter of an hour with his back to the fire, and his coat-tails over his arms, as they were thrust into his trousers pockets.

In the meantime Jack had succeeded in obtaining a few minutes' talk with Polly,—or rather the success had been on Polly's side, for she had managed the business. On coming out from the brewery Jack had met her in the street, and had been taken home by her. "You might as well come in, Jack," she had said, "and have a few words with me. You have been talking to father about it, I suppose."

"Well; I have. He says I am not sufficiently educated. I suppose he wants to get some young man from the colleges."

"Don't you be stupid, Jack. You want to have your own way, I suppose."

"I don't want him to tell me I'm uneducated. Other men that I've heard of ain't any better off than I am."

"You mean himself,—which isn't respectful."

"I'm educated up to doing what I've got to do. If you don't want more, I don't see what he's got to do with it."

"As the times go of course a man should learn more and more. You are not to compare him to yourself; and it isn't respectful. If you want to say sharp things against him, Jack, you had better give it all up;—for I won't bear it."

"I don't want to say anything sharp."

"Why can't you put up with him? He's not going to have his own way. And he is older than you. And it is he that has got the money. If you care about it——"

"You know I care."

"Very well. Suppose I do know, and suppose I don't. I hear you say you do, and that's all I've got to act upon. Do you bide your time if you've got the patience, and all will come right. I shan't at all think so much of you if you can't bear a few sharp words from him.

"He may say whatever he pleases."

"You ain't educated,—not like Dr. Freeborn, and men of that class."

"What do I want with it?" said he.

"I don't know that you do want it. At any rate I don't want it; and that's what you've got to think about at present. You just go on, and let things be as they are. You don't want to be married in a week's time."

"Why not?" he asked.

"At any rate I don't; and I don't mean to. This time five years will do very well."

"Five years! You'll be an old woman."

"The fitter for you, who'll still be three years older. If you've patience to wait leave it to me."

"I haven't over much patience."

"Then go your own way and suit yourself elsewhere."

"Polly, you're enough to break a man's heart. You know that I can't go and suit myself elsewhere. You are all the world to me, Polly."

"Not half so much as a quarter of malt if you could get your own price for it. A young woman is all very well just as a play-thing; but business is business;—isn't it, Jack?"

"Five years! Fancy telling a fellow that he must wait five years."

"That'll do for the present, Jack. I'm not going to keep you here idle all the day. Father will be angry when I tell him that you've been here at all."

"It was you that brought me."

"Yes, I did. But you're not to take advantage of that. Now I say, Jack, hands off. I tell you I won't. I'm not going to be kissed once a week for five years. Well. Mark my words, this is the last time I ever ask you in here. No; I won't have it. Go away." Then she succeeded in turning him out of the room and closing the house door behind his back. "I think he's the best young man I see about anywhere. Father twits him about his education. It's my belief there's nothing he can't do that he's wanted for. That's the kind of education a man ought to have. Father says it's because he's handsome I like him. It does go a long way, and he is handsome. Father has got ideas of fashion into his head which will send him crazy before he has done with them." Such was the soliloquy in which Miss Peppercorn indulged as soon as she had been left by her lover.

"Educated! Of course I'm not educated. I can't talk Latin and Greek as some of those fellows pretend to,—though for the matter of that I never heard it. But two and two make four, and ten and ten make twenty. And if a fellow says that it don't he is trying on some dishonest game. If a fellow understands that, and sticks to it, he has education enough for my business,—or for Peppercorn's either." Then he walked back to the inn yard where he had left his horse and trap.

As he drove back to Barchester he made up his mind that Polly Peppercorn would be worth waiting for. There was the memory of that kiss upon his lips which had not been made less sweet by the severity of the words which had accompanied it. The words indeed had been severe; but there had been an intention and a purpose about the kiss which had altogether redeemed the words. "She is just one in a thousand, that's about the truth. And as for waiting for her;—I'll wait like grim death, only I hope it won't be necessary!" It was thus he spoke of the lady of his love as he drove himself into the town under Barchester Towers.

CHAPTER V

DR. FREEBORN AND PHILIP HUGHES

Things went on at Plumplington without any change for a fortnight,—that is without any change for the better. But in truth the ill-humour both of Mr. Greenmantle and of Mr. Peppercorn had increased to such a pitch as to add an additional blackness to the general haziness and drizzle and gloom of the November weather. It was now the end of November, and Dr. Freeborn was becoming a little uneasy because the Christmas attributes for which he was desirous were still altogether out of sight. He was a man specially anxious for the mundane happiness of his parishioners and who would take any amount of personal trouble to insure it; but he was in fault perhaps in this, that he considered that everybody ought to be happy just because he told them to be so. He belonged to the Church of England certainly, but he had no dislike to Papists or Presbyterians, or dissenters in general, as long as they would arrange themselves under his banner as "Freebornites." And he had such force of character that in Plumplington,—beyond which he was not ambitious that his influence should extend,—he did in general prevail. But at the present moment he was aware that Mr. Greenmantle was in open mutiny. That Peppercorn would yield he had strong hope. Peppercorn he knew to be a weak, good fellow, whose affection for his daughter would keep him right at last. But until he could extract that poker from Mr. Greenmantle's throat, he knew that nothing could be done with him.

At the end of the fortnight Mr. Greenmantle called at the Rectory about half an hour before dinner time, when he knew that the Doctor would be found in his study before going up to dress for dinner. "I hope I am not intruding, Dr. Freeborn," he said. But the rust of the poker was audible in every syllable as it fell from his mouth.

"Not in the least. I've a quarter of an hour before I go and wash my hands."

"It will be ample. In a quarter of an hour I shall be able sufficiently to explain my plans." Then there was a pause, as though Mr. Greenmantle had expected that the explanation was to begin with the Doctor. "I am thinking," the banker continued after a while, "of taking my family abroad to some foreign residence." Now it was well known to Dr. Freeborn that Mr. Greenmantle's family consisted exclusively of Emily.

"Going to take Emily away?" he said.

"Such is my purpose,—and myself also."

"What are they to do at the bank?"

"That will be the worst of it, Dr. Freeborn. The bank will be the great difficulty."

"But you don't mean that you are going for good?"

"Only for a prolonged foreign residence;—that is to say for six months. For forty years I have given but very little trouble to the Directors. For forty years I have been at my post and have never suggested any prolonged absence. If the Directors cannot bear with me after forty years I shall think them unreasonable men." Now in truth Mr. Greenmantle knew that the Directors would make no opposition to anything that he might propose; but he always thought it well to be armed with some premonitory grievance. "In fact my pecuniary matters are so arranged that should the Directors refuse I shall go all the same."

"You mean that you don't care a straw for the Directors."

"I do not mean to postpone my comfort to their views,—or my daughter's."

"But why does your daughter's comfort depend on your going away? I should have thought that she would have preferred Plumplington at present."

That was true, no doubt. And Mr. Greenmantle felt;—well; that he was not exactly telling the truth in putting the burden of his departure upon Emily's comfort. If Emily, at the present crisis of affairs, were carried away from Plumplington for six months, her comfort would certainly not be increased. She had already been told that she was to go, and she had clearly understood why. "I mean as to her future welfare," said Mr. Greenmantle very solemnly.

Dr. Freeborn did not care to hear about the future welfare of young people. What had to be said as to their eternal welfare he thought himself quite able to say. After all there was something of benevolent paganism in his disposition. He liked better to deal with their present happiness,—so that there was nothing immoral in it. As to the world to come he thought that the fathers and mothers of his younger flock might safely leave that consideration to him. "Emily is a remarkably good girl. That's my idea of her."

Mr. Greenmantle was offended even at this. Dr. Freeborn had no right, just at present, to tell him that his daughter was a good girl. Her goodness had been greatly lessened by the fact that in regard to her marriage she was anxious to run counter to her father. "She is a good girl. At least I hope so."

"Do you doubt it?"

"Well, no;—or rather yes. Perhaps I ought to say no as to her life in general."

"I should think so. I don't know what a father may want,—but I should think so. I never knew her miss church yet,—either morning or evening."

"As far as that goes she does not neglect her duties."

"What is the matter with her that she is to be taken off to some foreign climate for prolonged residence?" The Doctor among his other idiosyncrasies entertained an idea that England was the proper place for all Englishmen and Englishwomen who were not driven out of it by stress of pecuniary circumstances. "Has she got a bad throat or a weak chest?"

"It is not on the score of her own health that I propose to move her," said Mr. Greenmantle.

"You did say her comfort. Of course that may mean that she likes the French way of living. I did hear that we were to lose your services for a time, because you could not trust your own health."

"It is failing me a little, Dr. Freeborn. I am already very near sixty."

"Ten years my junior," said the Doctor.

"We cannot all hope to have such perfect health as you possess."

"I have never frittered it away," said the Doctor, "by prolonged residence in foreign parts." This quotation of his own words was most harassing to Mr. Greenmantle, and made him more than once inclined to bounce in anger out of the Doctor's study. "I suppose the truth is that Miss Emily is disposed to run counter to your wishes in regard to her marriage, and that she is to be taken away not from consumption or a weak throat, but from a dangerous lover." Here Mr. Greenmantle's face became black as thunder. "You see, Greenmantle, there is no good in our talking about this matter unless we understand each other."

"I do not intend to give my girl to the young man upon whom she thinks that her affections rest."

"I suppose she knows."

"No, Dr. Freeborn. It is often the case that a young lady does not know; she only fancies, and where that is the case absence is the best remedy. You have said that Emily is a good girl."

"A very good girl."

"I am delighted to hear you so express yourself. But obedience to parents is a trait in character which is generally much thought of. I have put by a little money, Dr. Freeborn."

"All Plumplington knows that."

"And I shall choose that it shall go somewhat in accordance with my wishes. The young man of whom she is thinking—"

"Philip Hughes, an excellent fellow. I've known him all my life. He doesn't come to church quite so regularly as he ought, but that will be mended when he's married."

"Hasn't got a shilling in the world," continued Mr. Greenmantle, finishing his sentence. "Nor is he—just,—just—just what I should choose for the husband of my daughter. I think that when I have said so he should take my word for it."

"That's not the way of the world, you know."

"It's the way of my world, Dr. Freeborn. It isn't often that I speak out, but when I do it's about something that I've a right to speak of. I've heard this affair of my daughter talked about all over the town. There was one Mr. Peppercorn came to me——"

"One Mr. Peppercorn? Why, Hickory Peppercorn is as well known in Plumplington as the church-steeple."

"I beg your pardon, Dr. Freeborn; but I don't find any reason in that for his interfering about my daughter. I must say that I took it as a great piece of impertinence. Goodness gracious me! If a man's own daughter isn't to be considered peculiar to himself I don't know what is. If he'd asked you about your daughters,—before they were married?" Dr. Freeborn did not answer this, but declared to himself that neither Mr. Peppercorn nor Mr. Greenmantle could have taken such a liberty. Mr. Greenmantle evidently was not aware of it, but in truth Dr. Freeborn and his family belonged altogether to another set. So at least Dr. Freeborn told himself. "I've come to you now, Dr. Freeborn, because I have not liked to leave Plumplington for a prolonged residence in foreign parts without acquainting you."

"I should have thought that unkind."

"You are very good. And as my daughter will of course go with me, and as this idea of a marriage on her part must be entirely given up;" the emphasis was here placed with much weight on the word entirely;—"I should take it as a great kindness if you would let my feelings on the subject be generally known. I will own that I should not have cared to have my daughter talked about, only that the mischief has been done."

"In a little place like this," said the Doctor, "a young lady's marriage will always be talked about."

"But the young lady in this case isn't going to be married."

"What does she say about it herself?"

"I haven't asked her, Dr. Freeborn. I don't mean to ask her. I shan't ask her."

"If I understand her feelings, Greenmantle, she is very much set upon it."

"I cannot help it."

"You mean to say then that you intend to condemn her to unhappiness merely because this young man hasn't got as much money at the beginning of his life as you have at the end of yours?"

"He hasn't got a shilling," said Mr. Greenmantle.

"Then why can't you give him a shilling? What do you mean to do with your money?" Here Mr. Greenmantle again looked offended. "You come and ask me, and I am bound to give you my opinion for what it's worth. What do you mean to do with your money? You're not the man to found a Hiram's Hospital with it. As sure as you are sitting there your girl will have it when you're dead. Don't you know that she will have it?"

"I hope so."

"And because she's to have it, she's to be made wretched about it all her life. She's to remain an old maid, or else to be married to some well-born pauper, in order that you may talk about your son-in-law. Don't get into a passion, Greenmantle, but only think whether I'm not telling you the truth. Hughes isn't a spendthrift."

"I have made no accusation against him."

"Nor a gambler, nor a drunkard, nor is he the sort of man to treat a wife badly. He's there at the bank so that you may keep him under your own eye. What more on earth can a man want in a son-in-law?"

Blood, thought Mr. Greenmantle to himself; an old family name; county associations, and a certain something which he felt quite sure Philip Hughes did not possess. And he knew well enough that Dr. Freeborn had married his own daughters to husbands who possessed these gifts; but he could not throw the fact back into the Rector's teeth. He was in some way conscious that the Rector had been entitled to expect so much for his girls, and that he, the banker, was not so entitled. The same idea passed through the Rector's mind. But the Rector knew how far the banker's courage would carry him. "Good night, Dr. Freeborn," said Mr. Greenmantle suddenly.

"Good night, Greenmantle. Shan't I see you again before you go?" To this the banker made no direct answer, but at once took his leave.

"That man is the greatest ass in all Plumplington," the Doctor said to his wife within five minutes of the time of which the hall door was closed behind the banker's back. "He's got an idea into his head about having some young county swell for his son-in-law."

"Harry Gresham. Harry is too idle to earn money by a profession and therefore wants Greenmantle's money to live upon. There's Peppercorn wants something of the same kind for Polly. People are such fools." But Mrs. Freeborn's two daughters had been married much after the same fashion. They had taken husbands nearly as old as their father, because Dr. Freeborn and his wife had thought much of "blood."

On the next morning Philip Hughes was summoned by the banker into the more official of the two back parlours. Since he had presumed to signify his love for Emily, he had never been asked to enjoy the familiarity of the other chamber. "Mr. Hughes, you may probably have heard it asserted that I am about to leave Plumplington for a prolonged residence in foreign parts." Mr. Hughes had heard it and so declared. "Yes, Mr. Hughes, I am about to proceed to the south of France. My daughter's health requires attention,—and indeed on my own behalf I am in need of some change as well. I have not as yet officially made known my views to the Directors."

"There will be, I should think, no impediment with them."

"I cannot say. But at any rate I shall go. After forty years of service in the Bank I cannot think of allowing the peculiar views of men who are all younger than myself to interfere with my comfort. I shall go."

"I suppose so, Mr. Greenmantle."

"I shall go. I say it without the slightest disrespect for the Board. But I shall go."

"Will it be permanent, Mr. Greenmantle?"

"That is a question which I am not prepared to answer at a moment's notice. I do not propose to move my furniture for six months. It would not, I believe, be within the legal power of the Directors to take possession of the Bank house for that period."

"I am quite sure they would not wish it."

"Perhaps my assurance on that subject may be of more avail. At any rate they will not remove me. I should not have troubled you on this subject were it not that your position in the Bank must be affected more or less."

"I suppose that I could do the work for six months," said Philip Hughes.

But this was a view of the case which did not at all suit Mr. Greenmantle's mind. His own duties at Plumplington had been, to his thinking, the most important ever confided to a Bank Manager. There was a peculiarity about Plumplington of which no one knew the intricate details but himself. The man did not exist who could do the work as he had done it. But still he had determined to go, and the work must be intrusted to some man of lesser competence. "I should think it probable," he said, "that some confidential clerk will be sent over from Barchester. Your youth, Mr. Hughes, is against you. It is not for me to say what line the Directors may determine to take."

"I know the people better than any one can do in Barchester."

"Just so. But you will excuse me if I say you may for that reason be the less efficient. I have thought it expedient, however, to tell you of my views. If you have any steps that you wish to take you can now take them."

Then Mr. Greenmantle paused, and had apparently brought the meeting to an end. But there was still something which he wished to say. He did think that by a word spoken in due season,—by a strong determined word, he might succeed in putting an end to this young man's vain and ambitious hopes. He did not wish to talk to the young man about his daughter; but, if the strong word might avail here was the opportunity. "Mr. Hughes," he began.

"Yes, sir."

"There is a subject on which perhaps it would be well that I should be silent." Philip, who knew the manager thoroughly, was now aware of what was coming, and thought it wise that he should say nothing at the moment. "I do not know that any good can be done by speaking of it." Philip still held his tongue. "It is a matter no doubt of extreme delicacy,—of the most extreme delicacy I may say. If I go abroad as I intend, I shall as a matter of course take with me—Miss Greenmantle."

"I suppose so."

"I shall take with me—Miss Greenmantle. It is not to be supposed that when I go abroad for a prolonged sojourn in foreign parts, that I should leave—Miss Greenmantle behind me."

"No doubt she will accompany you."

"Miss Greenmantle will accompany me. And it is not improbable that my prolonged residence may in her case be—still further prolonged. It may be possible that she should link her lot in life to some gentleman whom she may meet in those realms."

"I hope not," said Philip.

"I do not think that you are justified, Mr. Hughes, in hoping anything in reference to my daughter's fate in life."

"All the same, I do."

"It is very,—very,—! I do not wish to use strong language, and therefore I will not say impertinent."

"What am I to do when you tell me that she is to marry a foreigner?"

"I never said so. I never thought so. A foreigner! Good heavens! I spoke of a gentleman whom she might chance to meet in those realms. Of course I meant an English gentleman."

"The truth is, Mr. Greenmantle, I don't want your daughter to marry anyone unless she can marry me."

"A most selfish proposition."

"It's a sort of matter in which a man is apt to be selfish, and it's my belief that if she were asked she'd say the same thing. Of course you can take her abroad and you can keep her there as long as you please."

"I can;—and I mean to do it."

"I am utterly powerless to prevent you, and so is she. In this contention between us I have only one point in my favour."

"You have no point in your favour, sir."

"The young lady's good wishes. If she be not on my side,— why then I am nowhere. In that case you needn't trouble yourself to take her out of Plumplington. But if——"

"You may withdraw, Mr. Hughes," said the banker. "The interview is over." Then Philip Hughes withdrew, but as he went he shut the door after him in a very confident manner.

CHAPTER VI

THE YOUNG LADIES ARE TO
BE TAKEN ABROAD

How should Philip Hughes see Emily before she had been carried away to "foreign parts" by her stern father? As he regarded the matter it was absolutely imperative that he should do so. If she should be made to go, in her father's present state of mind, without having reiterated her vows, she might be persuaded by that foreign-living

English gentleman whom she would find abroad, to give him her hand. Emily had no doubt confessed her love to Philip, but she had not done so in that bold unshrinking manner which had been natural to Polly Peppercorn. And her lover felt it to be incumbent upon him to receive some renewal of her assurance before she was taken away for a prolonged residence abroad. But there was a difficulty as to this. If he were to knock at the door of the private house and ask for Miss Greenmantle, the servant, though she was in truth Philip's friend in the matter, would not dare to show him up. The whole household was afraid of Mr. Greenmantle, and would receive any hint that his will was to be set aside with absolute dismay. So Philip at last determined to take the bull by the horns and force his way into the drawing-room. Mr. Greenmantle could not be made more hostile than he was; and then it was quite on the cards, that he might be kept in ignorance of the intrusion. When therefore the banker was sitting in his own more private room, Philip passed through from the bank into the house, and made his way up-stairs with no one to announce him.

With no one to announce him he passed straight through into the drawing-room, and found Emily sitting very melancholy over a half-knitted stocking. It had been commenced with an idea that it might perhaps be given to Philip, but as her father's stern severity had been announced she had given up that fond idea, and had increased the size, so as to fit them for the paternal feet. "Good gracious, Philip," she exclaimed, "how on earth did you get here?"

"I came up-stairs from the bank."

Oh, yes; of course. But did you not tell Mary that you were coming?"

"I should never have been let up had I done so. Mary has orders not to let me put my foot within the house."

"You ought not to have come; indeed you ought not."

"And I was to let you go abroad without seeing you! Was that what I ought to have done? It might be that I should never see you again. Only think of what my condition must be."

"Is not mine twice worse?"

"I do not know. If it be twice worse than mine then I am the happiest man in all the world."

"Oh, Philip, what do you mean?"

"If you will assure me of your love——"

"I have assured you."

"Give me another assurance, Emily," he said, sitting down beside her on the sofa. But she started up quickly to her feet. "When you gave me the assurance before, then—then——"

"One assurance such as that ought to be quite enough."

"But you are going abroad."

"That can make no difference."

"Your father says, that you will meet there some Englishman who will——"

"My father knows nothing about it. I shall meet no Englishman, and no foreigner; at least none that I shall care about. You oughtn't to get such an idea into your head."

"That's all very well, but how am I to keep such ideas out? Of course there will be men over there; and if you come across some idle young fellow who has not his bread to earn as I do, won't it be natural that you should listen to him?"

"No, it won't be natural."

"It seems to me to be so. What have I got that you should continue to care for me?"

"You have my word, Philip. Is that nothing?" She had now seated herself on a chair away from the sofa, and he, feeling at the time some special anxiety to get her into his arms, threw himself down on his knees before her, and seized her by both her hands. At that moment the door of the drawing-room was opened, and Mr. Greenmantle appeared within the room. Philip Hughes could not get upon his feet quick enough to return the furious anger of the look which was thrown on him. There was a difficulty even in disembarrassing himself of poor Emily's hands; so that she, to her father, seemed to be almost equally a culprit with the young man. She uttered a slight scream, and then he very gradually rose to his legs.

"Emily," said the angry father, "retire at once to your chamber."

"But, papa, I must explain."

"Retire at once to your chamber, miss. As for this young man, I do not know whether the laws of his country will not punish him for this intrusion."

Emily was terribly frightened by this allusion to her country's laws. "He has done nothing, papa; indeed he has done nothing."

"His very presence here, and on his knees! Is that nothing? Mr. Hughes, I desire that you will retire. Your presence in the bank is required. I lay upon you my strict order never again to presume to come through that door. Where is the servant who announced you?"

"No servant announced me."

"And did you dare to force your way into my private house, and into my daughter's presence unannounced? It is indeed time that I should take her abroad to undergo a prolonged residence in some foreign parts. But the laws of the country which you have outraged will punish you. In the meantime why do you not withdraw? Am I to be obeyed?"

"I have just one word which I wish to say to Miss Greenmantle."

"Not a word. Withdraw! I tell you, sir, withdraw to the bank. There your presence is required. Here it will never be needed."

"Good-bye, Emily," he said, putting out his hand in his vain attempt to take hers.

"Withdraw, I tell you." And Mr. Greenmantle, with all the stiffness of the poker apparent about him, backed poor young Philip Hughes through the door-way on to the staircase, and then banged the door behind him. Having done this, he threw himself on to the sofa, and hid his face with his hands. He wished it to be understood that the honour of his family had been altogether disgraced by the lightness of his daughter's conduct.

But his daughter did not see the matter quite in the same light. Though she lacked something of that firmness of manner which Polly Peppercorn was prepared to exhibit, she did not intend to be altogether trodden on. "Papa," she said, "Why do you do that?"

"Good heavens!"

"Why do you cover up your face?"

"That a daughter of mine should have behaved so disgracefully!"

"I haven't behaved disgracefully, papa."

"Admitting a young man surreptitiously to my drawing-room!"

"I didn't admit him; he walked in."

"And on his knees! I found him on his knees."

"I didn't put him there. Of course he came,—because,—because——"

"Because what?" he demanded.

"Because he is my lover. I didn't tell him to come; but of course he wanted to see me before we went away."

"He shall see you no more."

"Why shouldn't he see me? He's a very good young man, and I am very fond of him. That's just the truth."

"You shall be taken away for a prolonged residence in foreign parts before another week has passed over your head."

"Dr. Freeborn quite approves of Mr. Hughes," pleaded Emily. But the plea at the present moment was of no avail. Mr. Greenmantle in his present frame of mind was almost as angry with Dr. Freeborn as with Emily or Philip Hughes. Dr. Freeborn was joined in this frightful conspiracy against him.

"I do not know," said he grandiloquently, "that Dr. Freeborn has any right to interfere with the private affairs of my family. Dr. Freeborn is simply the Rector of Plumplington,—nothing more."

"He wants to see the people around him all happy," said Emily.

"He won't see me happy," said Mr. Greenmantle with awful pride.

"He always wishes to have family quarrels settled before Christmas."

"He shan't settle anything for me." Mr. Greenmantle, as he so expressed himself, determined to maintain his own independence. "Why is he to interfere with my family quarrels because he's the Rector of Plumplington? I never heard of such a thing. When I shall have taken up my residence in foreign parts he will have no right to interfere with me."

"But, papa, he will be my clergyman all the same."

"He won't be mine, I can tell him that. And as for settling things by Christmas, it is all nonsense. Christmas, except for going to church and taking the Sacrament, is no more than any other day."

"Oh papa!"

"Well, my dear, I don't quite mean that. What I do mean is that Dr. Freeborn has no more right to interfere with my family at this time of the year than at any other. And when you're abroad, which you will be before Christmas, you'll find that Dr. Freeborn will have nothing to say to you there." "You had better begin to pack up at once," he said on the following day.

"Pack up?"

"Yes, pack up. I shall take you first to London, where you will stay for a day or two. You will go by the afternoon train to-morrow."

"To-morrow!"

"I will write and order beds to-day."

"But where are we to go?"

"That will be made known to you in due time," said Mr. Greenmantle.

"But I've got no clothes," said Emily.

"France is a land in which ladies delight to buy their dresses."

"But I shall want all manner of things,—boots and undercloth- ing,—and—and linen, papa."

"They have all those things in France."

"But they won't fit me. I always have my things made to fit me. And I haven't got any boxes."

"Boxes! what boxes? work-boxes?"

"To put my things in. I can't pack up unless I've got something to pack them in. As to going to-morrow, papa, it's quite impossi- ble. Of course there are people I must say good-bye to. The Freeborns——"

"Not the slightest necessity," said Mr. Greenmantle. "Dr. Freeborn will quite understand the reason. As to boxes, you won't want the boxes till you've bought the things to put in them."

"But, papa, I can't go without taking a quantity of things with me. I can't get everything new; and then I must have my dresses made to fit me." She was very lachrymose, very piteous, and full of entreaties; but still she knew what she was about. As the result of the interview, Mr. Greenmantle did almost acknowledge that they could not depart for a prolonged residence abroad on the morrow.

Early on the following morning Polly Peppercorn came to call. For the last month she had stuck to her resolution,—that she and Miss Greenmantle belonged to different sets in society, and could not be brought together, as Polly had determined to wear her second-rate dresses in preparation for a second-rate marriage,—and this visit was supposed to be something altogether out of the way. It was clearly a visit with a cause, as it was made at eleven o'clock in the morning. "Oh, Miss Greenmantle," she said, "I hear that you're going away to France,—you and your papa, quite at once."

"Who has told you?"

"Well, I can't quite say; but it has come round through Dr. Freeborn." Dr. Freeborn had in truth told Mr. Peppercorn, with the express view of exercising what influence he possessed so as to prevent the rapid emigration of Mr. Greenmantle. And Mr. Peppercorn had told his daughter, threatening her that something of the same kind would have to happen in his own family if she proved obstinate about her lover. "It's the best thing going," said Mr. Peppercorn, "when a girl is upsetting and determined to have her own way." To this Polly made no reply, but came away early on the following morning, so as to converse with her late friend, Miss Greenmantle.

"Papa says so; but you know it's quite impossible."

"What is Mr. Hughes to do?" asked Polly in a whisper.

"I don't know what anybody is to do. It's dreadful, the idea of going away from home in this sudden manner."

"Indeed it is."

"I can't do it. Only think, Polly, when I talk to him about clothes he tells me I'm to buy dresses in some foreign town. He knows nothing about a woman's clothes;—nor yet a man's for the matter of that. Fancy starting to-morrow for six months. It's the sort of thing that Ida Pfeiffer used to do."

"I didn't know her," said Polly.

"She was a great traveller, and went about everywhere almost without anything. I don't know how she managed it, but I'm sure that I can't."

"Dr. Freeborn says that he thinks it's all nonsense." As Polly said this she shook her head and looked uncommonly wise. Emily, however, made no immediate answer. Could it be true that Dr. Freeborn had thus spoken of her father? Emily did think that it was all nonsense, but she had not yet brought herself to express her thoughts openly. "To tell the truth, Miss Greenmantle," continued Polly, "Dr. Freeborn thinks that Mr. Hughes ought to be allowed to have his own way." In answer to this Emily could bring herself to say nothing; but she declared to herself that since the beginning of things Dr. Freeborn had always been as near an angel as any old gentleman could be. "And he says that it's quite out of the question that you should be carried off in this way."

"I suppose I must do what papa tells me."

"Well; yes. I don't know quite about that. I'm all for doing everything that papa likes, but when he talks of taking me to France, I know I'm not going. Lord love you, he couldn't talk to anybody there." Emily began to remember that her father's proficiency in the French language was not very great. "Neither could I for the matter of that," continued Polly. "Of course, I learned it at school, but when one can only read words very slowly one can't talk them at all. I've tried it, and I know it. A precious figure father and I would make finding our way about France."

"Does Mr. Peppercorn think of going?" asked Emily.

"He says so;—if I won't drop Jack Hollycombe. Now I don't mean to drop Jack Hollycombe; not for father nor for anyone. It's only Jack himself can make me do that."

"He won't, I suppose."

"I don't think he will. Now it's absurd, you know, the idea of our papas both carrying us off to France because we've got lovers in Plumplington. How all the world would laugh at them! You tell your papa what my papa is saying, and Dr. Freeborn thinks that that will prevent him. At any rate, if I were you, I wouldn't go and buy anything in a hurry. Of course, you've got to think of what would do for married life."

"Oh, dear, no!" exclaimed Emily.

"At any rate I should keep my mind fixed upon it. Dr. Freeborn says that there's no knowing how things may turn out." Having finished the purport of her embassy, Polly took her leave without even having offered one kiss to her friend.

Dr. Freeborn had certainly been very sly in instigating Mr. Peppercorn to proclaim his intention of following the example of his neighbour the banker. "Papa," said Emily when her father came in to luncheon, "Mr. Peppercorn is going to take his daughter to foreign parts."

"What for?"

"I believe he means to reside there for a time."

"What nonsense! He reside in France! He wouldn't know what to do with himself for an hour. I never heard anything like it. Because I am going to France is all Plumplington to follow me? What is Mr. Peppercorn's reason for going to France?" Emily hesitated; but Mr. Greenmantle pressed the question, "What object can such a man have?"

"I suppose it's about his daughter," said Emily. Then the truth flashed upon Mr. Greenmantle's mind, and he became aware that he must at any rate for the present abandon the idea. Then, too, there came across him some vague notion that Dr. Freeborn had instigated Mr. Peppercorn and an idea of the object with which he had done so.

"Papa," said Emily that afternoon, "am I to get the trunks I spoke about?"

"What trunks?"

"To put my things in, papa. I must have trunks if I am to go abroad for any length of time. And you will want a large portmanteau. You would get it much better in London than you would at Plumplington." But here Mr. Greenmantle told his daughter that she need not at present trouble her mind about either his travelling gear or her own.

A few days afterwards Dr. Freeborn sauntered into the bank, and spoke a few words to the cashier across the counter. "So Mr. Greenmantle, I'm told, is not going abroad," said the Rector.

"I've heard nothing more about it," said Philip Hughes.

"I think he has abandoned the idea. There was Hickory Peppercorn thinking of going, too, but he has abandoned it. What do they want to go travelling about France for?"

"What indeed, Dr. Freeborn;—unless the two young ladies have something to say to it."

"I don't think they wish it, if you mean that."

"I think their fathers thought of taking them out of harm's way."

"No doubt. But when the harm's way consists of a lover it's very hard to tear a young lady away from it." This was said so that Philip only could hear it. The two lads who attended the bank were away at their desks in distant parts of the office. "Do you keep your eyes open, Philip," said the Rector, "and things will run smoother yet than you expected."

"He is frightfully angry with me, Dr. Freeborn. I made my way up into the drawing-room the other day, and he found me there."

"What business had you to do that?"

"Well, I was wrong, I suppose. But if Emily was to be taken away suddenly I had to see her before she went. Think, Doctor, what a prolonged residence in a foreign country means. I mightn't see her again for years."

"And so he found you up in the drawing-room. It was very improper; that's all I can say. Nevertheless, if you'll behave yourself, I shouldn't be surprised if things were to run smoother before Christmas." Then the Doctor took his leave.

"Now, father," said Polly, "you're not going to carry me off to foreign parts."

"Yes, I am. As you're so wilful it's the only thing for you."

"What's to become of the brewery?"

"The brewery may take care of itself. As you won't want the money for your husband there'll be plenty for me. I'll give it up. I ain't going to slave and slave all my life and nothing come of it. If you won't oblige me in this the brewery may go and take care of itself."

"If you're like that, father, I must take care of myself. Mr. Greenmantle isn't going to take his daughter over."

"Yes, he is."

"Not a bit of it. He's as much as told Emily that she's not to get her things ready." Then there was a pause, during which Mr. Peppercorn showed that he was much disturbed. "Now, father, why don't you give way, and show yourself what you always were,—the kindest father that ever a girl had."

"There's no kindness in you, Polly. Kindness ought to be reciprocal."

"Isn't it natural that a girl should like her young man?"

"He's not your young man."

"He's going to be. What have you got to say against him? You ask Dr. Freeborn."

"Dr. Freeborn, indeed! He isn't your father!"

"He's not my father, but he's my friend. And he's yours, if you only knew it. You think of it, just for another day, and then say that you'll be good to your girl." Then she kissed him, and as she left him she felt that she was about to prevail.

CHAPTER VII

THE YOUNG LADIES ARE TO REMAIN AT HOME

Miss Emily Greenmantle had always possessed a certain character for delicacy. We do not mean delicacy of sentiment. That of course belonged to her as a young lady,—but delicacy of health. She was not strong and robust, as her friend Polly Peppercorn. When we say that she possessed that character, we intend to imply that she perhaps made a little use of it. There had never been much the matter with her, but she had always been a little delicate. It seemed to suit her, and prevented the necessity of over-exertion. Whereas Polly, who had never been delicate, felt herself always called upon to "run round," as the Americans say. "Running round" on the part of a young lady implies a readiness and a willingness to do everything that has to be done in domestic life. If a father wants his slippers or a mother her thimble, or the cook a further supply of sauces, the active young lady has to "run round." Polly did run round; but Emily was delicate and did not. Therefore when she did not get up one morning, and complained of a headache, the doctor was sent for. "She's not very strong, you know," the doctor said to her father. "Miss Emily always was delicate."

"I hope it isn't much," said Mr. Greenmantle.

"There is something I fear disturbing the even tenor of her thoughts," said the doctor, who had probably heard of the hopes entertained by Mr. Philip Hughes and favoured them. "She should be kept quite quiet. I wouldn't prescribe much medicine, but I'll tell Mixet to send her in a little draught. As for diet she can have pretty nearly what she pleases. She never had a great appetite." And so the doctor went his way. The reader is not to suppose that Emily Greenmantle intended to deceive her father, and play the old soldier. Such an idea would have been repugnant to her nature. But when her father told her that she was to be taken abroad for a prolonged residence, and when it of course followed that her lover was to be left behind, there came upon her a natural feeling that the best thing for her would be to lie in bed, and so to avoid all the troubles of life for the present moment.

"I am very sorry to hear that Emily is so ill," said Dr. Freeborn, calling on the banker further on in the day.

"I don't think it's much, Dr. Freeborn."

"I hope not; but I just saw Miller, who shook his head. Miller never shakes his head quite for nothing."

In the evening Mr. Greenmantle got a little note from Mrs. Freeborn. "I'm *so unhappy* to hear about *dear* Emily. The poor child always is *delicate*. *Pray* take care of her. She must see Dr. Miller twice every day. Changes do take place so *frequently*. If you think she would be better here, we would be *delighted* to have her. There is so much in having the attention of a *lady*."

"Of course I am nervous," said Mr. Philip Hughes next morning to the banker. "I hope you will excuse me, if I venture to ask for one word as to Miss Greenmantle's health."

"I am very sorry to hear that Miss Greenmantle has been taken so poorly," said Mr. Peppercorn, who met Mr. Greenmantle in the street. "It is not very much, I have reason to hope," said the father, with a look of anger. Why should Mr. Peppercorn be solicitous as to his daughter?

"I am told that Dr. Miller is rather alarmed." Then Polly called at the front door to make special inquiry after Miss Greenmantle's health.

Mr. Greenmantle wrote to Mrs. Freeborn thanking her for the offer, and expressing a hope that it might not be necessary to move Emily from her own bed. And he thanked all his other neighbours for the pertinacity of their inquiries,—feeling however all the while that there was something of a conspiracy being hatched against him. He did not quite think his daughter guilty, but in his answer made to the inquiry of Philip Hughes, he spoke as though he believed that the young man had been the instigator of it. When on the third day his daughter could not get up, and Dr. Miller had ordered a more potent draught, Mr. Greenmantle almost owned to himself that he had been beaten. He took a walk by himself and meditated on it. It was a cruel case. The money was his money, and the girl was his girl, and the young man was his clerk. He ought according to the rules of justice in the world to have had plenary power over them all. But it had come to pass that his power was nothing. What is a father to do when a young lady goes to bed and remains there? And how is a soft-hearted father to make any use of his own money when all his neighbours turn against him?

"Miss Greenmantle is to have her own way, father," Polly said to Mr. Peppercorn on one of these days. It was now the second week in December, and the whole ground was hard with frost. "Dr. Freeborn will be right after all. He never is much wrong. He declared that Emily would be given to Philip Hughes as a Christmas-box."

"I don't believe it a bit," said Mr. Peppercorn.

"It is so all the same. I knew that when she became ill her father wouldn't be able to stand his ground. There is no knowing what these delicate young ladies can do in that way. I wish I were delicate.

"You don't wish anything of the kind. It would be very wicked to wish yourself to be sickly. What should I do if you were running up a doctor's bill?"

"Pay it,—as Mr. Greenmantle does. You've never had to pay half-a-crown for a doctor for me, I don't know when."

"And now you want to be poorly."

"I don't think you ought to have it both ways, you know. How am I to frighten you into letting me have my own lover? Do you think that I am not as unhappy about him as Emily Greenmantle? There he is now going down to the brewery. You go after him and tell him that he shall have what he wants."

Mr. Peppercorn turned round and looked at her. "Not if I know," he said.

"Then I shall go to bed," said Polly, "and send for Dr. Miller tomorrow. I don't see why I'm not to have the same advantage as other girls. But, father, I wouldn't make you unhappy, and I wouldn't cost you a shilling I could help, and I wouldn't not wait upon you for anything. I wouldn't pretend to be ill,—not for Jack Hollycombe."

"I should find you out if you did."

"I wouldn't fight my battle except on the square for any earthly consideration. But, father—"

"What do you want of me?"

"I am broken-hearted about him. Though I look red in the face, and fat, and all that, I suffer quite as much as Emily Greenmantle. When I tell him to wait perhaps for years, I know I'm unreasonable. When a young man wants a wife, he wants one. He has made up his mind to settle down, and he doesn't expect a girl to bid him remain as he is for another four or five years."

"You've no business to tell him anything of the kind."

"When he asks me I have a business,—if it's true. Father!"

"Well!"

"It is true. I don't know whether it ought to be so, but it is true. I'm very fond of you."

"You don't show it."

"Yes, I am. And I think I do show it, for I do whatever you tell me. But I like him the best."

"What has he done for you?"

"Nothing;—not half so much as I have done for him. But I do like him the best. It's human nature. I don't take on to tell him so;—only once. Once I told him that I loved him better than all the rest,—and that if he chose to take my word for it, once spoken, he might have it. He did choose, and I'm not going to repeat it, till I tell him when I can be his own."

"He'll have to take you just as you stand."

"May be; but it will be worth while for him to wait just a little, till he shall see what you mean to do. What do you mean to do with it, father? We don't want it at once."

"He's not edicated as a gentleman should be."

"Are you?"

"No; but I didn't try to get a young woman with money. I made the money, and I've a right to choose the sort of son-in-law my daughter shall marry."

"No; never!" she said.

"Then he must take you just as you are; and I'll make ducks and drakes of the money after my own fashion. If you were married tomorrow what do you mean to live upon?"

"Forty shillings a week. I've got it all down in black and white."

"And when children come;—one after another, year by year."

"Do as others do. I'll go bail my children won't starve;—or his. I'd work for them down to my bare bones. But would you look on the while, making ducks and drakes of your money, or spending it at the pot-house, just to break the heart of your own child? It's not in you to do it. You'd have to alter your nature first. You speak of yourself as though you were strong as iron. There isn't a bit of iron about you;—but there's something a deal better. You are one of those men, father, who are troubled with a heart."

"You're one of those women," said he, "who trouble the world by their tongues." Then he bounced out of the house and banged the door.

He had seen Jack Hollycombe through the window going down to the brewery, and he now slowly followed the young man's steps. He went very slowly as he got to the entrance to the brewery yard, and there he paused for a while thinking over the condition of things. "Hang the fellow," he said to himself; "what on earth has he done that he should have it all his own way. I never had it all my way. I had to work for it;—and precious hard too. My wife had to cook the dinner with only just a slip of a girl to help make the bed. If he'd been a gentleman there'd have been something in it. A gentleman expects to have things ready to his hand. But he's to walk into all my money just because he's good-looking. And then Polly tells me, that I can't help myself because I'm good-natured. I'll let her know whether I'm good-natured! If he wants a wife he must support a wife;—and he shall." But though Mr. Peppercorn stood in the doorway murmuring after this fashion he knew very well that he was about to lose the battle. He had come down the street on purpose to signify to Jack Hollycombe that he might go up and settle the day with Polly; and he himself in the midst of all his objurgations was picturing to himself the delight with which he would see Polly restored to her former mode of dressing. "Well, Mr. Hollycombe, are you here?"

"Yes, Mr. Peppercorn, I am here."

"So I perceive,—as large as life. I don't know what on earth you're doing over here so often. You're wasting your employers' time, I believe."

"I came over to see Messrs. Grist and Grindall's young man."

"I don't believe you came to see any young man at all."

"It wasn't any young woman, as I haven't been to your house, Mr. Peppercorn."

"What's the good of going to my house? There isn't any young woman there can do you any good." Then Mr. Peppercorn looked round and saw that there were others within hearing to whom the conversation might be attractive. "Do you come in here. I've got something to say to you." Then he led the way into his own little parlour, and shut the door. "Now Mr. Hollycombe, I've got something to communicate."

"Out with it, Mr. Peppercorn."

"There's that girl of mine up there is the biggest fool that ever was since the world began."

"It's astonishing," said Jack, "what different opinions different people have about the same thing."

"I daresay. That's all very well for you; but I say she's a fool. What on earth can she see in you to make her want to give you all my money?"

"She can't do that unless you're so pleased."

"And she won't neither. If you like to take her, there she is."

"Mr. Peppercorn, you make me the happiest man in the world."

"I don't make you the richest;—and you're going to make yourself about the poorest. To marry a wife upon forty shillings a week! I did it myself, however,—upon thirty-five, and I hadn't any stupid old father-in-law to help me out. I'm not going to see her break her heart; and so you may go and tell her. But you needn't tell her as I'm going to make her any regular allowance. Only tell her to put on some decent kind of gown, before I come home to tea.

Since all this came up the slut has worn the same dress she bought three winters ago. She thinks I didn't know it."

And so Mr. Peppercorn had given way; and Polly was to be allowed to flaunt it again this Christmas in silks and satins. "Now you'll give me a kiss," said Jack when he had told his tale.

"I've only got it on your bare word," she answered, turning away from him.

"Why; he sent me here himself; and says you're to put on a proper frock to give him his tea in."

"No."

"But he did."

"Then, Jack, you shall have a kiss. I am sure the message about the frock must have come from himself. Jack, are you not the happiest young man in all Plumplington?"

"How about the happiest young woman," said Jack.

"Well, I don't mind owning up. I am. But it's for your sake. I could have waited, and not have been a bit impatient. But it's so different with a man. Did he say, Jack, what he meant to do for you?"

"He swore that he would not give us a penny."

"But that's rubbish. I am not going to let you marry till I know what's fixed. Nor yet will I put on my silk frock."

"You must. He'll be sure to go back if you don't do that. I should risk it all now, if I were you."

"And so make a beggar of you. My husband shall not be dependent on any man,—not even on father. I shall keep my clothes on as I've got 'em till something is settled."

"I wouldn't anger him if I were you," said Jack cautiously.

"One has got to anger him sometimes, and all for his own good. There's the frock hanging up-stairs, and I'm as fond of a bit of finery as any girl. Well;—I'll put it on to-night because he has made something of a promise; but I'll not continue it till I know what he means to do for you. When I'm married my husband will have to pay for my clothes, and not father."

"I guess you'll pay for them yourself."

"No, I shan't. It's not the way of the world in this part of England. One of you must do it, and I won't have it done by father,—not regular. As I begin so I must go on. Let him tell me what he means to do and then we shall know how we're to live. I'm not a bit afraid of you and your forty shillings."

"My girl!" Here was some little attempt at embracing, which, however, Polly checked.

"There's no good in all that when we're talking business. I look upon it now that we're to be married as soon as I please. Father has given way as to that, and I don't want to put you off."

"Why no! You ought not to do that when you think what I have had to endure."

"If you had known the picture which father drew just now of what we should have to suffer on your forty shillings a week!"

"What did he say, Polly?"

"Never mind what he said. Dry bread would be the best of it. I don't care about the dry bread;—but if there is to be anything better it must be all fixed. You must have the money for your own."

"I don't suppose he'll do that."

"Then you must take me without the money. I'm not going to have him giving you a five-pound note at the time and your having to ask for it. Nor yet am I going to ask for it. I don't mind it now. And to give him his due, I never asked him for a sovereign but what he gave me two. He's very generous."

"Is he now?"

"But he likes to have the opportunity. I won't live in the want of any man's generosity,—only my husband's. If he chooses to do anything extra that'll be as he likes it. But what we have to live upon,—to pay for meat and coals and such like,—that must be your own. I'll put on the dress to-night because I won't vex him. But before he goes to bed he must be made to understand all that. And you must understand it too, Jack. As we mean to go on so must we begin!" The interview ended, however, in an invitation given to Jack to stay in Plumplington and eat his supper. He knew the road so well that he could drive himself home in the dark.

"I suppose I'd better let them have two hundred a year to begin with," said Peppercorn to himself, sitting alone in his little parlour. "But I'll keep it in my own hands. I'm not going to trust that fellow further than I can see him."

But on this point he had to change his mind before he went to bed. He was gracious enough to Jack as they were eating their supper, and insisted on having a hot glass of brandy and water afterwards,—all in honour of Polly's altered dress. But as soon as Jack was gone Polly explained her views of the case, and spoke such undoubted wisdom as she sat on her father's knee, that he was forced to yield. I'll speak to Mr. Scribble about having it all properly settled." Now Mr. Scribble was the Plumplington attorney.

"Two hundred a year, father, which is to be Jack's own,—for ever. I won't marry him for less,—not to live as you propose."

"When I say a thing I mean it," said Peppercorn. Then Polly retired, having given him a final kiss.

About a fortnight after this Mr. Greenmantle came to the Rectory and desired to see Dr. Freeborn. Since Emily had been taken ill there had not been many signs of friendship between the Greenmantle and the Freeborn houses. But now there he was in the Rectory hall, and within five minutes had followed the Rectory footman into Dr. Freeborn's study. "Well, Greenmantle, I'm delighted to see you. How's Emily?"

Mr. Greenmantle might have been delighted to see the Doctor but he didn't look it. "I trust that she is somewhat better. She has risen from her bed to-day."

"I'm glad to hear that," said the Doctor.

"Yes; she got up yesterday, and to-day she seems to be restored to her usual health."

"That's good news. You should be careful with her and not let her trust too much to her strength. Miller said that she was very weak, you know."

"Yes; Miller has said so all through," said the father; "but I'm not quite sure that Miller has understood the case."

"He hasn't known all the ins and outs you mean,—about Philip Hughes." Here the Doctor smiled, but Mr. Greenmantle moved about uneasily as though the poker were at work. "I suppose Philip Hughes had something to do with her malady."

"The truth is—," began Mr. Greenmantle.

"What's the truth?" asked the Doctor. But Mr. Greenmantle looked as though he could not tell his tale without many efforts. "You heard what old Peppercorn has done with his daughter?— Settled £250 a year on her for ever, and has come to me asking me whether I can't marry them on Christmas Day. Why if they were to be married by banns there would not be time."

"I don't see why they shouldn't be married by banns," said Mr. Greenmantle, who amidst all these difficulties disliked nothing so much as that he should be put into the category with Mr. Peppercorn, or Emily with Polly Peppercorn.

"I say nothing about that. I wish everybody was married by banns. Why shouldn't they? But that's not to be. Polly came to me the next day, and said that her father didn't know what he was talking about."

"I suppose she expects a special licence like the rest of them," said Mr. Greenmantle.

"What the girls think mostly of is their clothes. Polly wouldn't mind the banns the least in the world; but she says she can't have her things ready. When a young lady talks about her things a man has to give up. Polly says that February is a very good month to be married in."

Mr. Greenmantle was again annoyed, and showed it by the knitting of his brow, and the increased stiffness of his head and shoulders. The truth may as well be told. Emily's illness had prevailed with him and he too had yielded. When she had absolutely refused to look at her chicken-broth for three consecutive days her father's heart had been stirred. For Mr. Greenmantle's character will not have been adequately described unless it be explained that the stiffness lay rather in the neck and shoulders than in the organism by which his feelings were conducted. He was in truth very like Mr. Peppercorn, though he would have been infuriated had he been told so. When he found himself alone after his defeat,—which took place at once when the chicken-broth had gone down untasted for the third time,—he was ungainly and ill-natured to look at. But he went to work at once to make excuses for Philip Hughes, and ended by assuring himself that he was a manly honest sort of fellow, who was sure to do well in his profession; and ended by assuring himself that it would be very comfortable to have his married daughter and her husband living with him. He at once saw Philip, and explained to him that he had certainly done very wrong in coming up to his drawing-room without leave. "There is an etiquette in those things which no doubt you will learn as you grow older." Philip thought that the etiquette wouldn't much matter as soon as he had married his wife. And he was wise enough to do no more than beg Mr. Greenmantle's pardon for the fault which he had committed. "But as I am informed by my daughter," continued Mr. Greenmantle, "that her affections are irrevocably settled upon you,"—here Philip could only bow,—"I am prepared to withdraw my opposition, which has only been entertained as long as I thought it necessary for my daughter's happiness. There need be no words now," he continued, seeing that Philip was about to speak, "but when I shall have made up my mind as to what it may be fitting that I shall do in regard to money, then I will see you again. In the meantime you're welcome to come into my drawing-room when it may suit you to pay your respects to Miss Greenmantle." It was speedily settled that the marriage should take place in February, and Mr. Greenmantle was now informed that Polly Peppercorn and Mr. Hollycombe were to be married in the same month!

He had resolved, however, after much consideration, that he would himself inform Dr. Freeborn that he had given way, and had now come for this purpose. There would be less of triumph to the enemy, and less of disgrace to himself, if he were to declare the truth. And there no longer existed any possibility of a permanent quarrel with the Doctor. The prolonged residence abroad had altogether gone to the winds. "I think I will just step over and tell the Doctor of this alteration in our plans." This he had said to Emily, and Emily had thanked him and kissed him, and once again had called him "her own dear papa." He had suffered greatly during the period of his embittered feelings, and now had his reward. For it is not to be supposed that when a man has swallowed a poker the evil results will fall only upon his companions. The process is painful also to himself. He cannot breathe in comfort so long as the poker is there.

"And so Emily too is to have her lover. I am delighted to hear it. Believe me she hasn't chosen badly. Philip Hughes is an excellent young fellow. And so we shall have the double marriage coming after all." Here the poker was very visible. "My wife will go and see her at once, and congratulate her; and so will I as soon as I have heard that she's got herself properly dressed for drawing-room visitors. Of course I may congratulate Philip."

"Yes, you may do that," said Mr. Greenmantle very stiffly.

"All the town will know all about it before it goes to bed to-night. It is better so. There should never be a mystery about such matters. Goodbye, Greenmantle, I congratulate you with all my heart."

CHAPTER VIII

CHRISTMAS-DAY

"Now I'll tell you what we'll do," said the Doctor to his wife a few days after the two marriages had been arranged in the manner thus described. It yet wanted ten days to Christmas, and it was known to all Plumplington that the Doctor intended to be more than ordinarily blithe during the present Christmas holidays. "We'll have these young people to dinner on Christmas-day, and their fathers shall come with them."

"Will that do, Doctor?" said his wife.

"Why should it not do?"

"I don't think that Mr. Greenmantle will care about meeting Mr. Peppercorn."

"If Mr. Peppercorn dines at my table," said the Doctor with a certain amount of arrogance, "any gentleman in England may meet him. What! not meet a fellow townsman on Christmas-day and on such an occasion as this!"

"I don't think he'll like it," said Mrs. Freeborn.

"Then he may lump it. You'll see he'll come. He'll not like to refuse to bring Emily here, especially as she is to meet her betrothed. And the Peppercorns and Jack Hollycombe will be sure to come. Those sort of vagaries as to meeting this man and not that, in sitting next to one woman and objecting to another, don't prevail on Christmas-day, thank God. They've met already at the Lord's Supper, or ought to have met; and they surely can meet afterwards at the parson's table. And we'll have Harry Gresham to show that there is no ill-will. I hear that Harry is already making up to the Dean's daughter at Barchester."

"He won't care whom he meets," said Mrs. Freeborn. "He has got a position of his own and can afford to meet anybody. It isn't quite so with Mr. Greenmantle. But of course you can have it as you please. I shall be delighted to have Polly and her husband at dinner with us."

So it was settled and the invitations were sent out. That to the Peppercorns was despatched first, so that Mr. Greenmantle might be informed whom he would have to meet. It was conveyed in a note from Mrs. Freeborn to Polly, and came in the shape of an order rather than of a request. "Dr. Freeborn hopes that your Papa and Mr. Hollycombe will bring you to dine with us on Christmas-day at six o'clock. We'll try and get Emily Greenmantle and her lover to meet you. You must come because the Doctor has set his heart upon it."

"That's very civil," said Mr. Peppercorn. "Shan't I get any dinner till six o'clock?"

"You can have lunch, father, of course. You must go."

"A bit of bread and cheese when I come out of church—just when I'm most famished! Of course I'll go. I never dined with the Doctor before."

"Nor did I; but I've drunk tea there. You'll find he'll make himself very pleasant. But what are we to do about Jack."

"He'll come of course."

"But what are we to do about his clothes?" said Polly. "I don't think he's got a dress coat; and I'm sure he hasn't a white tie. Let him come just as he pleases, they won't mind on Christmas-day as long as he's clean. He'd better come over and go to church with us; and then I'll see as to making him up tidy." Word was sent to say that Polly and her father and her lover would come, and the necessary order was at once despatched to Barchester.

"I really do not know what to say about it," said Mr. Greenmantle when the invitation was read to him. "You will meet Polly Peppercorn and her husband as is to be," Mrs. Freeborn had written in her note; "for we look on you and Polly as the two heroines of Plumplington for this occasion." Mr. Greenmantle had been struck with dismay as he read the words. Could he bring himself to sit down to dinner with Hickory Peppercorn and Jack Hollycombe; and ought he to do so? Or could he refuse the Doctor's invitation on such an occasion? He suggested at first that a letter should be prepared declaring that he did not like to take his Christmas dinner away from his own house. But to this Emily would by no means consent. She had plucked up her spirits greatly since the days of the chicken-broth, and was determined at the present moment to rule both her future husband and her father. "You must go, papa. I wouldn't not go for all the world."

"I don't see it, my dear; indeed I don't."

"The Doctor has been so kind. What's your objection, papa?"

"There are differences, my dear."

"But Dr. Freeborn likes to have them."

"A clergyman is very peculiar. The rector of a parish can always meet his own flock. But rank is rank you know, and it behoves me to be careful with whom I shall associate. I shall have Mr. Peppercorn slapping my back and poking me in the ribs some of these days. And moreover they have joined your name with that of the young lady in a manner that I do not quite approve. Though you each of you may be a heroine in your own way, you are not the two heroines of Plumplington. I do not choose that you shall appear together in that light."

"That is only his joke," said Emily.

"It is a joke to which I do not wish to be a party. The two heroines of Plumplington! It sounds like a vulgar farce."

Then there was a pause, during which Mr. Greenmantle was thinking how to frame the letter of excuse by which he would avoid the difficulty. But at last Emily said a word which settled him. "Oh, papa, they'll say that you were too proud, and then they'll laugh at you." Mr. Greenmantle looked very angry at this, and was preparing himself to use some severe language to his daughter. But he remembered how recently she had become engaged to be married, and he abstained. "As you wish it, we will go," he said. "At the present crisis of your life I would not desire to disappoint you in anything." So it happened that the Doctor's proposed guests all accepted; for Harry Gresham too expressed himself as quite delighted to meet Emily Greenmantle on the auspicious occasion.

"I shall be delighted also to meet Jack Hollycombe," Harry had said. "I have known him ever so long and have just given him an order for twenty quarters of oats."

They were all to be seen at the Parish Church of Plumplington on that Christmas morning;—except Harry Gresham, who, if he did so at all, went to church at Greshamsbury,—and the Plumplington world all looked at them with admiring eyes. As it happened the Peppercorns sat just behind the Greenmantles, and on this occasion Jack Hollycombe and Polly were exactly in the rear of Philip Hughes and Emily. Mr. Greenmantle as he took his seat observed that it was so, and his devotions were, we fear, disturbed by the fact. He walked up proudly to the altar among the earliest and most aristocratic recipients, and as he did so could not keep himself from turning round to see whether Hickory Peppercorn was treading on his kibes. But on the present occasion Hickory Peppercorn was very modest and remained with his future son-in-law nearly to the last.

At six o'clock they all met in the Rectory drawing-room. "Our two heroines," said the Doctor as they walked in, one just after the other, each leaning on her lover's arm. Mr. Greenmantle looked as though he did not like it. In truth he was displeased, but he could not help himself. Of the two young ladies Polly was by far the most self-possessed. As long as she had got the husband of her choice she did not care whether she were or were not called a heroine. And her father had behaved very well on that morning as to money. "If you come out like that, father," she had said, "I shall have to wear a silk dress every day." "So you ought," he said with true Christmas generosity. But the income then promised had been a solid assurance, and Polly was the best contented young woman in all Plumplington.

They all sat down to dinner, the Doctor with a bride on each side of him, the place of honour to his right having been of course accorded to Emily Greenmantle; and next to each young lady was her lover. Miss Greenmantle as was her nature was very quiet, but Philip Hughes made an effort and carried on, as best he could, a conversation with the Doctor. Jack Hollycombe till after pudding-time said not a word and Polly tried to console herself through his silence by remembering that the happiness of the world did not depend upon loquacity. She herself said a little word now and again, always with a slight effort to bring Jack into notice. But the Doctor with his keen power of observation understood them all, and told himself that Jack was to be a happy man. At the other end of the table Mr. Greenmantle and Mr. Peppercorn sat opposite to each other, and they too, till after pudding-time, were very quiet. Mr. Peppercorn felt himself to be placed a little above his proper position, and could not at once throw off the burden. And Mr. Greenmantle would not make the attempt. He felt that an injury had been done him in that he had been made to sit opposite to Hickory Peppercorn. And in truth the dinner party as a dinner party would have been a failure, had it not been for Harry Gresham, who, seated in the middle between Philip and Mr. Peppercorn, felt it incumbent upon him in his present position to keep up the rattle of the conversation. He said a good deal about the "two heroines," and the two heroes, till Polly felt herself bound to quiet him by saying that it was a pity that there was not another heroine also for him.

"I'm an unfortunate fellow," said Harry, "and am always left out in the cold. But perhaps I may be a hero too some of these days."

Then when the cloth had been removed,—for the Doctor always had the cloth taken off his table,—the jollity of the evening really began. The Doctor delighted to be on his legs on such an occasion and to make a little speech. He said that he had on his right and on his left two young ladies both of whom he had known and had loved throughout their entire lives, and now they were to be delivered over by their fathers, whom he delighted to welcome this Christmas-day at his modest board, each to the man who for the future was to be her lord and her husband. He did not know any occasion on which he, as a pastor of the church, could take greater delight, seeing that in both cases he had ample reason to be satisfied with the choice which the young ladies had made. The bridegrooms were in both instances of such a nature and had made for themselves such characters in the estimation of their friends and neighbours as to give all assurance of the happiness prepared for their wives. There was much more of it, but this was the gist of the Doctor's eloquence. And then he ended by saying that he would ask the two fathers to say a word in acknowledgment of the toast.

This he had done out of affection to Polly, whom he did not wish to distress by calling upon Jack Hollycombe to take a share in the speech-making of the evening. He felt that Jack would require a little practice before he could achieve comfort during such an operation; but the immediate effect was to plunge Mr. Greenmantle into a cold bath. What was he to say on such an opportunity? But he did blunder through, and gave occasion to none of that sorrow which Polly would have felt had Jack Hollycombe got upon his legs, and then been reduced to silence. Mr. Peppercorn in his turn made a better speech than could have been expected from him. He said that he was very proud of his position that day, which was due to his girl's manner and education. He was not entitled to be there by anything that he had done himself. Here the Doctor cried, "Yes, yes, yes, certainly." But Peppercorn shook his head. He wasn't specially proud of himself, he said, but he was awfully proud of his girl. And he thought that Jack Hollycombe was about the most fortunate young man of whom he had ever heard. Here Jack declared that he was quite aware of it.

After that the jollity of the evening commenced; and they were very jolly till the Doctor began to feel that it might be difficult to restrain the spirits which he had raised. But they were broken up before a very late hour by the necessity that Harry Gresham should return to Greshamsbury. Here we must bid farewell to the "two heroines of Plumplington," and to their young men, wishing them many joys in their new capacities. One little scene however must be described, which took place as the brides were putting on their hats in the Doctor's study. "Now I can call you Emily again," said Polly, "and now I can kiss you; though I know I ought to do neither the one nor the other."

"Yes, both, both, always do both," said Emily. Then Polly walked home with her father, who, however well satisfied he might have been in his heart, had not many words to say on that evening.

NOT IF I KNOW IT

"NOT IF I know it." It was an ill-natured answer to give, made in the tone that was used, by a brother-in-law to a brother-in-law, in the hearing of the sister of the one and wife of the other,—made, too, on Christmas Eve, when the married couple had come as visitors to the house of him who made it! There was no joke in the words, and the man who had uttered them had gone for the night. There was to be no other farewell spoken indicative of the brightness of the coming day. "Not if I know it!" and the door was slammed behind him. The words were very harsh in the ears even of a loving sister.

"He was always a cur," said the husband.

"No; not so. George has his ill-humours and his little periods of bad temper; but he was not always a cur. Don't say so of him, Wilfred."

"He always was to me. He wanted you to marry that fellow Cross because he had a lot of money."

"But I didn't," said the wife, who now had been three years married to Wilfred Horton.

"I cannot understand that you and he should have been children of the same parents. Just the use of his name, and there would be no risk."

"I suppose he thinks that there might have been risk," said the wife. "He cannot know you as I do."

"Had he asked me I would have given him mine without thinking of it. Though he knows that I am a busy man, I have never asked him to lend me a shilling. I never will."

"Wilfred!"

"All right, old girl—I am going to bed; and you will see that I shall treat him to-morrow just as though he had refused me nothing. But I shall think that he is a cur." And Wilfred Horton prepared to leave the room.

"Wilfred!"

"Well, Mary, out with it."

"Curs are curs—"

"Because other curs make them so; that is what you are going to say."

"No, dear, no; I will never call you a cur, because I know well that you are not one. There is nothing like a cur about you." Then she took him in her arms and kissed him. "But if there be any signs of ill-humour in a man, the way to increase it is to think much of it. Men are curs because other men think them so; women are angels sometimes, just because some loving husband like you tells them that they are. How can a woman not have something good about her when everything she does is taken to be good? I could be as cross as George is if only I were called cross. I don't suppose you want the use of his name so very badly."

"But I have condescended to ask for it. And then to be answered with that jeering pride! I wouldn't have his name to a paper now, though you and I were starving for the want of it. As it is, it doesn't much signify. I suppose you won't be long before you come." So saying, he took his departure.

She followed him, and went away through the house till she came to her brother's apartments. He was a bachelor, and was living all alone when he was in the country at Hallam Hall. It was a large, rambling house, in which there had been of custom many visitors at Christmas time. But Mrs. Wade, the widow, had died during the past year, and there was nobody there now but the owner of the house, and his sister, and his sister's husband. She followed him to his rooms, and found him sitting alone, with a pipe in his mouth, and as she entered she saw that preparations had been made for the comfort of more than one person. "If there be anything that I hate," said George Wage, "it is to be asked for the use of my name. I would sooner lend money to a fellow at once,—or give it to him."

"There is no question about money, George."

"Oh, isn't there? I never knew a man's name wanted when there was no question about money."

"I suppose there is a question—in some remote degree." Here George Wade shook his head. "In some remote degree," she went on repeating her words. "Surely you know him well enough not to be afraid of him."

"I know no man well enough not to be afraid of him where my name is concerned."

"You need not have refused him so crossly, just on Christmas Eve."

"I don't know much about Christmas where money is wanted."

"'Not if I know it!' you said."

"I simply meant that I did not wish to do it. Wilfred expects that everybody should answer him with such constrained courtesy! What I said was as good a way of answering him as any other; and if he didn't like it—he must lump it."

"Is that the message that you send him?" she asked.

"I don't send it as a message at all. If he wants a message you may tell him that I'm extremely sorry, but that it's against my principles. You are not going to quarrel with me as well as he?"

"Indeed, no" said she, as she prepared to leave him for the night. "I should be very unhappy to quarrel with either of you." Then she went.

"He is the most punctilious fellow living at this moment, I believe," said George Wade as he walked alone up and down the room. His brother-in-law had on the whole treated him well,—had been liberal to him in all those matters in which one brother comes in contact with another. He had never asked him for a shilling, or even for the use of his name. His sister was passionately devoted to her husband. In fact, he knew Wilfred Horton to be a fine fellow. He told himself that he had not meant to be especially uncourteous, but that he had been at the moment startled by the expression of Horton's wishes. But looking back over his conduct, he could remember, that in the course of their intimacy he himself had been occasionally rough to his brother-in-law, and he could remember that his brother-in-law had not liked it. "After all what does it mean, 'Not if I know it'? It is just a form of saying that I had rather not." Nevertheless, Wilfred Horton could not persuade himself to go to bed in a good humour with George Wade.

"I think I shall get back to London to-morrow," said Mr. Horton, speaking to his wife from beneath the bedclothes, as soon as she had entered the room.

"To-morrow?"

"It is not that I cannot bear his insolence, but that I should have to show by my face that I had made a request, and had been refused. You need not come."

"On Christmas Day?"

"Well, yes. You cannot understand the sort of flutter I am in. 'Not if I know it!' The insolence of the phrase in answering such a request! The suspicion that it showed! If he had told me that he had any feeling about it, I would have deposited the money in his hands. There is a train in the morning. You can stay here and go to church with him, while I run up to town."

"That you two should part like that on Christmas Day; you two dear ones! Wilfred, it will break my heart." Then he turned round and endeavoured to make himself comfortable among the bed-clothes. "Wilfred, say that you will not go out of this to-morrow."

"Oh, very well. You have only to speak and I obey. If you could only manage to make your brother more civil for the one day it would be an improvement."

"I think he will be civil. I have been speaking to him, and he seems to be sorry that he should have annoyed you."

"Well, yes; he did annoy me. 'Not if I know it!' in answer to such a request! As if I had asked him for five thousand pounds! I wouldn't have asked him or any man alive for five thousand pence. Coming down to his house at Christmastime, and to be suspected of such a thing!" Then he prepared himself steadily to sleep, and she, before she stretched herself by his side, prayed that God's mercy might obliterate the wrath between these men, whom she loved so well, before the morrow's sun should have come and gone.

The bells sounded merry from Hallam Church tower on the following morning, and told to each of the inhabitants of the old hall a tale that was varied according to the minds of the three inhabitants whom we know. With her it was all hope, but hope accompanied by that despondency which is apt to afflict the weak in the presence of those that are stronger. With her husband it was anger,—but mitigated anger. He seemed, as he came into his wife's room while dressing, to be aware that there was something which should be abandoned, but which still it did his heart some good to nourish. With George Wade there was more of Christian feeling, but of Christian feeling which it was disagreeable to entertain. "How on earth is a man to get on with his relatives, if he cannot speak a word above his breath?" But still he would have been very willing that those words had been left unsaid.

Any observer might have seen that the three persons as they sat down to breakfast were each under some little constraint. The lady was more than ordinarily courteous, or even affectionate, in her manner. This was natural on Christmas Day, but her too apparent anxiety was hardly natural. Her husband accosted his brother-in-law with almost loud good humour. "Well, George, a merry Christmas, and many of them. My word;—how hard it froze last night! You won't get any hunting for the next fortnight. I hope old Burnaby won't spin us a long yarn."

George Wade simply kissed his sister, and shook hands with his brother-in-law. But he shook hands with more apparent zeal than he would have done but for the quarrel, and when he pressed Wilfred Horton to eat some devilled turkey, he did it with more ardour than was usual with him. "Mrs. Jones is generally very successful with devilled turkey." Then, as he passed round the table behind his sister's back, she put out her hand to touch him, and as though to thank him for his goodness. But any one could see that it was not quite natural.

The two men as they left the house for church, were thinking of the request that had been made yesterday, and which had been refused. "Not if I know it!" said George Wade to himself. "There is nothing so unnatural in that, that a fellow should think so much of it. I didn't mean to do it. Of course, if he had said that he wanted it particularly I should have done it."

"Not if I know it!" said Wilfred Horton. "There was an insolence about it. I only came to him just because he was my brother-in-law. Jones, or Smith, or Walker would have done it without a word." Then the three walked into the church, and took their places in the front seat, just under Dr. Burnaby's reading-desk.

We will not attempt to describe the minds of the three as the Psalms were sung, and as the prayers were said. A twinge did cross the minds of the two men as the coming of the Prince of Peace was foretold to them; and a stronger hope did sink into the heart of her whose happiness depended so much on the manner in which they two stood with one another. And when Dr. Burnaby found time, in the fifteen minutes which he gave to his sermon, to tell his hearers why the Prophet had specially spoken of Christ as the Prince of Peace, and to describe what the blessings were, hitherto unknown, which had come upon the world since a desire for peace had filled the minds of men, a feeling did come on the hearts of both of them,—to one that the words had better not have been spoken, and to the other that they had better have been forgiven. Then came the Sacrament, more powerful with its thoughts than with its words, and the two men as they left the church were ready in truth to forgive each other—if they only knew how.

There was something a little sheep-faced about the two men as they walked up together across the grounds to the old hall,—something sheep-faced which Mrs. Horton fully understood, and which made her feel for the moment triumphant over them. It is always so with a woman when she knows that she has for the moment got the better of a man. How much more so when she has conquered two? She hovered about among them as though they were dear human beings subject to the power of some beneficent angel. The three sat down to lunch, and Dr. Burnaby could not but have been gratified had he heard the things that were said of him. "I tell you, you know," said George, "that Burnaby is a right good fellow, and awfully clever. There isn't a man or woman in the parish that he doesn't know how to get to the inside of."

"And he knows what to do when he gets there," said Mrs. Horton, who remembered with affection the gracious old parson as he had blessed her at her wedding.

"No; I couldn't let him do it for me." It was thus Horton spoke to his wife as they were walking together about the gardens. "Dear Wilfred, you ought to forgive him."

"I have forgiven him. There!" And he made a sign of blowing his anger away to the winds. "I do forgive him. I will think no more about it. It is as though the words had never been spoken,— though they were very unkind. 'Not if I know it!' All the same, they don't leave a sting behind."

"But they do."

"Nothing of the kind. I shall drink prosperity to the old house and a loving wife to the master just as cheerily by and by as though the words had never been spoken."

"But there will not be peace,—not the peace of which Dr. Burnaby told us. It must be as though it had really—really never been uttered. George has not spoken to me about it, not to-day, but if he asks, you will let him do it?"

"He will never ask—unless at your instigation."

"I will not speak to him," she answered,—"not without telling you. I would never go behind your back. But whether he does it or not, I feel that it is in his heart to do it." Then the brother came up and joined them in their walk, and told them of all the little plans he had in hand in reference to the garden. "You must wait till *she* comes, for that, George," said his sister.

"Oh, yes; there must always be a she when another she is talking. But what will you say if I tell you there is to be a she?"

"Oh, George!"

"Your nose is going to be put out of joint, as far as Hallam Hall is concerned." Then he told them all his love story, and so the afternoon was allowed to wear itself away till the dinner hour had nearly come.

"Just come in here, Wilfred," he said to his brother-in-law when his sister had gone up to dress. "I have something I want to say to you before dinner."

"All right," said Wilfred. As he got up to follow the master of the house, he told himself that after all his wife would prove herself too many for him.

"I don't know the least in the world what it was you were asking me to do yesterday."

"It was a matter of no consequence," said Wilfred, not able to avoid assuming an air of renewed injury.

"But I do know that I was cross," said George Wade.

"After that," said Wilfred, "everything is smooth between us. No man can expect anything more straightforward. I was a little hurt, but I know that I was a fool. Every man has a right to have his own ideas as to the use of his name."

"But that will not suffice," said George.

"Oh! yes it will."

"Not for me," repeated George. "I should have brought myself to ask your pardon for refusing, and you should bring yourself to accept my offer to do it."

"It was nothing. It was only because you were my brother-in-law, and therefore the nearest to me. The Turco-Egyptian New Waterworks Company simply requires somebody to assert that I am worth ten thousand pounds."

"Let me do it, Wilfred," said George Wade. "Nobody can know your circumstances better than I do. I have begged your pardon, and I think that you ought now in return to accept this at my hand."

"All right," said Wilfred Horton. "I will accept it at your hand." And then he went away to dress. What took place in the dressing-room need not here be told. But when Mrs. Horton came down to dinner the smile upon her face was a truer index of her heart than it had been in the morning.

"I have been very sorry for what took place last night," said George afterwards in the drawing-room, feeling himself obliged, as it were, to make full confession and restitution before the assembled multitude,—which consisted, however, of his brother-in-law and sister. "I have asked pardon, and have begged Wilfred to show his grace by accepting from me what I had before declined. I hope that he will not refuse me."

"Not if I know it," said Wilfred Horton.